A Time To Belong

Tricia Linden

Kingsburg Press
San Francisco, California

Kingsburg Press
P.O. Box 475146
San Francisco, California, 94147
www.KingsburgPress.com

A Time To Belong is a work of fiction. Names, characters, places,
and incidents are a product of the author's imagination. Locales
and public names are sometimes used for atmospheric purposes.
Any resemblance to actual people, living or dead, or to
businesses, companies, events, institutions, or locales is
completely coincidental.

Editor: Barbara Millman-Cole
Cover Design: Killion Group
A Time To Forgive / Tricia Linden – 2nd ed.
previously published as Somewhere To Belong

ISBN- 13:978-1-946177-04-9
ISBN- 10: 1-946177-04-0
eBook ISBN: 978-1-946177-05-6

Other Works by Tricia Linden

The MacNicol Clan Through Time
A Time To Begin – Book 1
A Time To Return – Book 2
A Time To Belong – Book 3
A Time To Forgive – Book 4

.

.

.

Dreaming In Moonlight

.

.

.

Jules Vanderzeit novels, set in the Gilded Age of New York
Until We Meet Again
Until Their Hearts Desire

.

Coming Soon: Until You Love Me

Dedication

For C.C., the best beau a woman could ask for,
Because I've always wanted one of those.

CHAPTER 1

San Francisco, California, Present Day

Daniel had heard all he wanted to hear, it was time to leave. Besides, he'd heard it all before in the rumor mill, this grandiose announcement only made it official. He just wished the damn meeting would end so he could get the hell out of there.

This made it final, a done deal. The votes were in; the docs were signed. They were dropping the mounted patrol from Golden Gate Park, another casualty of the city's budget cuts. The last team of horses would be pulled from the streets at the end of the month, and he'd be in a patrol car full-time. The way management spun it, he should be grateful he still had a job, even if it wasn't the job he wanted.

As soon as he and his colleagues were dismissed from the briefing room, he headed for the door to the parking garage. He didn't feel like hanging around at a local bar to commiserate with his fellow patrol officers. Right now, his only thought was to put some distance between him and police headquarters before he said or did something he might regret later. Maybe it was time to leave San Francisco behind for a while and rethink his life.

Sunlight from the exceptionally clear spring day was quickly giving way to streetlights and city glow as Daniel maneuvered his fire-engine-red Ford Mustang onto the Bay Bridge and headed out toward the Oakland hills. On the other side was Over Yonder, the place he called home, a large four-bedroom, semi-rural ranch house sitting on twelve acres tucked into the rolling hills of Diablo Valley. It was the house he'd grown up in along with his two elder brothers and younger sister. The years had slipped by, his siblings had moved away, his parents had passed on, and Daniel had become a thirty-one-year-old, single man living alone in a family home that no longer fit.

Rather than going straight home to the empty ranch, he decided to call his sister, Teressa, to see if she were up for a little company; he needed a dose of family right about now. After stopping to get gas, he hit his sister's number on the speed dial of his cell phone. Thankfully, it was still holding a charge.

"Hey, sis, what's up?" Daniel greeted Teressa when she answered.

"Hi, Daniel. Rory and I were just going to pick up Chinese and watch a movie. What are you up to?" Teressa was the only one who called her husband Rory instead of Robert. Daniel never asked why, and they didn't say.

"I just left work and was thinking I might stop by, if you don't mind. I'm near the Bay Bridge."

"You're close. Come on over and join us. No use spending Friday night alone."

"You sure? I don't want to rain on your parade," he hedged, hoping she would call his bluff. This was one night he didn't want to go home to an empty house, but he didn't exactly like the idea of being a third wheel either.

"Don't worry. Rory and I get plenty of alone time. Even newlyweds like to relax with family sometimes. Come on over."

He paused only for a moment. After all, it was what he wanted, to be with family. "Okay, you talked me into it. Is there anything I can bring?"

"You can pick up something to drink, unless you're happy with tea or water. Is Chinese okay with you?"

"Yeah, I'm good as long as you include some hot and sour soup. I'll pick up a six-pack, okay?"

"Rory will be glad to hear you're bringing the good beer. See you soon." Teressa clicked off her phone.

Looking forward to a hot meal and familiar company, Daniel smiled as he pulled onto the freeway and headed north toward Berkeley.

~*~

The remains of dinner covered the kitchen table, and the plan to watch a movie was forgotten. Once Daniel started talking about his problems at work, he couldn't stop until his frustrations were well vented. Teressa, being a certified relationship coach at San Francisco University, was eager to listen and lend her advice.

"When I signed up for the police academy, the only thing I wanted to do was mounted patrol. Maybe I had some romantic notion of being an urban cowboy, dispensing justice from the back of a horse, but the idea of being stuck in a patrol car doesn't exactly appeal to me."

"I know you, Daniel. I can't see you sitting in a car all day," Teressa agreed.

"Then there's the paperwork. With all these budget cuts, we have more paperwork than ever. The internal auditors are constantly breathing down our necks, making sure we dot our *i*'s and cross our *t*'s. It's eff'ing ridiculous, and I'm getting tired of it all."

"Why don't you take a break? Give yourself time to figure out what you want to do next," Teressa advised.

"That might be a good idea. I've got a ton of vacation stored up. I didn't want to take any time off until I knew what was going to happen to my unit. I figured as long as I could go to work and sit on a horse, I would."

"You know, Rory and I are going back to Scotland in June. Why don't you come with us? We're leaving right after they shut down your unit. It'll be a perfect time for you to get away."

"Scotland? That's a bit of a trip. I was thinking someplace close, like Yosemite."

"Oh, come on. You've been to Yosemite a dozen times. You need something bigger. This could be a life-changing decision. Besides, you've never even been out of the country. It's time for you to see the world."

"You and Robert are going to be gone for at least two weeks. I can't be gone from the ranch that long."

"Sure you can. I've got a plan."

Sure she did. His sister always had a plan.

"Rory's cousins, Jack and Jenny, are looking for a place to stay. They're moving here from Oregon. There's plenty of room at the ranch, and they can watch the place while you're gone. It wouldn't have to be forever, just until they find a place of their own."

Daniel looked over at his brother-in-law to confirm.

"Works for me," Robert said with a shrug. "You'd be doing us both a favor. I'd like to help them out, but our place is too small."

"You know I'd like to help, but I need to think about it." He hadn't considered taking on housemates, but it sounded like a good idea, especially if they were anything like Robert. In the short time he'd known Teressa's husband, they had become like brothers.

"Come on, what's not to like? Jenny and Jack need a place to stay, and you can use the extra help. It's a win-win situation," Teressa continued her campaign.

"I'm surprised you're already planning to go back to Skye," Daniel said. A year ago his sister had taken a trip to Scotland and had returned home with Robert as her new fiancé. At one o'clock in the afternoon on New Year's Day, Robert MacNicol and Teressa Ellers had become husband and wife. His sister had claimed there wasn't a better way to start the New Year.

"Rory still has a home and a business over there. He needs to check on his fishing boats. What if I told you there's a great horse ranch on the island not far from Rory's cottage?"

Daniel appreciated his sister's efforts to sell him on the idea of a Scottish vacation, but he wouldn't put deception beyond her as a means to get her way. He figured she was using his love of horses as leverage to get him to say yes, and he had to admit it was working. Or maybe he was just looking for a good excuse. Daniel looked to his brother-in-law for confirmation. "Would she lie to me just to get me to go?"

"Aye, she would, but no, she's not," Robert confirmed with a grin as he relaxed in his chair, his Scottish brogue as strong as ever. Apparently, he enjoyed watching his wife banter with her sibling.

Not missing a beat, Teressa continued on, "It won't cost you much, only the price of the plane ticket. You'll be able to stay at Rory's house."

"Our house," Robert interrupted.

She smiled brightly at her husband. "Our house," she corrected. "We'll show you around, or you can go off on your own as much as you want. What do you think?"

"That you're not going to let up until I say yes."

"See, I knew you were a smart man. I'll book you a ticket on our flight right now before you can change your mind. If I leave it up to you, it'll never get done." She jumped up and grabbed her laptop.

She was right. The Internet wasn't his thing, along with most other technologies of the twenty-first century. He had to admit, the ease and convenience of a cell phone was worth the venture into modern technology, but he couldn't see the appeal of video games, social-media, or the Internet. To him, they were just a time suck. And forget about e-mail, texting, IM, or all the other ways technology was trying to speed up people's lives. He was perfectly happy living life in the slow lane. Well, maybe not perfectly happy, but certainly better off. Heck, his car had windows that rolled down with a crank handle, not the push of an electric button.

Unfortunately, his lack of techno savvy was also a significant deterrent to any real success in the world of women and dating. More often than not, the women he met wanted the immediate gratification of being able to contact him electronically, but tech wasn't his style. Most of the time, he didn't even have his cell phone on unless he wanted to make a call, and it could be days before he listened to his voice messages. His cell phone battery had a tendency to die faster than he could remember to plug it in to be recharged. Though his family and closest friends had learned to accept his anti-technology quirk, the rest of the world seemed much less forgiving.

"Okay, all set." Teressa looked up from her laptop, satisfied with her effort. "We leave on the eighteenth of June. We'll be in Skye in time for the summer solstice."

"What's so special about the summer solstice?" Daniel asked.

"It's the anniversary of the day we met," she said, exchanging a sly glance with Robert. They were grinning like two kids sharing a secret, and Daniel knew well enough when to leave secrets alone.

~*~

A few weeks later, Daniel found himself on a plane sitting next to his sister and brother-in-law, questioning his choices as they headed toward the Atlantic coast on their way to Glasgow. It wasn't as though he didn't like to see new places. He had traveled up and down the West Coast with his dad visiting horse shows, and had been to Canada and Mexico, but this was the first time he'd be leaving the North American continent. Honestly, he found the prospect of a long transatlantic flight to be a bit unnerving. Knowing they would be spending the next few hours flying over miles of ocean before they reached land again was not in his comfort zone, he wondered how he had let his conniving little sister talk him into this adventure.

Dinner had been served, and the cabin lights were dimmed to encourage the passengers to sleep or rest quietly. Daniel figured it made the long hours of the flight a lot easier on the passengers and flight attendants, but it hardly helped to quell his anxiety. He was uncomfortably aware of his seatmates as he tried not to fidget, but hell, a body wasn't meant to sit still in one place for so long, and it was his bad luck to have ended up with the window seat.

Robert and Teressa were already sleeping, curled up under their airline-issued blankets. Apparently, they were okay with the long overnight trip, but Daniel was finding it much harder to settle in. The journey was long, and the large plane was nearly full for the nonstop flight. He was grateful Teressa and Robert had used their frequent-flyer miles to upgrade to roomier seats, but the space was still cramped for his six-foot-three-inch frame. And instead of being a soothing white noise, the hum of the engines created an annoying vibrating buzz in his ears.

He wanted to get up and stretch his legs, but he didn't want to disturb Teressa and Robert, so he sat and stared out the small oval window into the reflective blackness of the nighttime sky, regretting his misfortune of getting stuck with the inside seat. When they were boarding, he had agreed to let Robert take the aisle seat, always being the nice guy, and as he knew, nice guys always finished last. He glanced again at Teressa, his younger sister, happily married to the man of her dreams, and knew he was definitely finishing last. He was the last unmarried sibling and the last one still at home.

Daniel sat in the dim light cast by the overhead reading lamp, wondering what he could do to get some sleep, or at least relax enough to forget he was thirty thousand feet above endless ocean. Maybe not exactly endless ocean, but close enough.

He searched the seat back pocket in front of him and flipped through the airline's in-flight magazine. It was beyond boring and of no use for his insomnia. Looking over at the seat back pocket in front of Teressa, he noticed her travel journal poking halfway out. She'd been writing in it earlier. When he had asked her about the journal, she had explained she had started the travel journal during her first trip to the Isle of Skye. With each succeeding trip, she planned to add to the journal, creating a memoir of her travels to Scotland.

Daniel didn't usually go snooping into his sister's personal stuff, but since she hadn't seemed particularly secretive when she had told him about her journal, he figured she wouldn't mind. Hopefully, it would tell him about the places they planned to visit, and perhaps provide a little insight into his sister's opinions on their intended destination. With hardly a second thought, he reached for his sister's journal, flipped it open, and started reading.

A few hours later, and several disbelieving glances at the two people sleeping next to him, he wasn't sure if he had read a credible account of an incredible journey, or if his sister was a fantastic storyteller. She'd written about faeries, wizards, and time travel, and the kicker of it all was her belief that Robert, a.k.a. Rory, was the reincarnation of a thirteenth-century warrior and her soulmate. What the hell was she thinking? Although it had kept him enthralled for the past few hours, allowing him to completely forget his insomnia and discomfort with the overseas flight, it was darn near impossible to believe her fantastic tale. He wondered if Robert was aware of his wife's vivid imagination.

Daniel didn't know what to think of his sister's story except that it was simply unbelievable. Interesting, but unbelievable. He'd give her credit on one count: she and Robert seemed made for each other. Whether it was because they were soulmates across time or just lucky in love, he couldn't say, but they certainly seemed to belong together.

With a final shake of his head, Daniel tucked Teressa's journal back into the seat pocket in front of her and switched off his overhead light. It was time to close his eyes and rest even if he couldn't sleep. As he reached to close the shade of the little oval window next to him, he paused a moment and gazed out into the early morning sky.

The glow of the rising sun rushing to meet the eastward-flying plane was just beginning to leak above the horizon. A lone star still shone bright in his limited view of the vast endless sky. It occurred to him that this single star, shining alone in the vastness of space, had spent eons shining its light out into the cosmos, always existing exactly where it was meant to be. In a moment of honest confession, he softly whispered, "I wish I knew where I belong."

He dropped the shade, closed his eyes, and laid his head back to relax. A soft breeze danced across his forehead. Just before he unexpectedly fell into a deep and peaceful sleep, he heard a woman's voice softly whisper, "A wish expressed, a favor bestowed."

CHAPTER 2

Scorrybreac, September 1295

Kayla MacNicol sat at the outer edge of the family circle in a daze, cold as an icicle hanging from the eaves in the dead of winter. Shivering, she noted how her mother and brother seemed perfectly content to carry on with their conversation without her, discussing her life as though she weren't in the room. She was tempted to wave her arms and shout, "Hey, I'm here. Look at me. Listen to me." But she would never do that. It wasn't in her to cause a scene.

Her mother, Lady Lydia, was speaking to Duncan, Kayla's eldest brother and chief of the MacNicol clan. "'Tis past time for Kayla to be married."

"I haven't really given it much thought," Duncan replied.

Kayla believed her brother cared little one way or another if she were married. He'd rather train men for battle than arrange betrothals and weddings.

"She's seen twenty summers. A woman her age should be married by now, raising her own family, not tending to her brothers," her mother repeated her oft said words.

"Has she a suitor in mind?" Duncan asked. He glanced over at his wife, Janet, as if seeking her assistance. As usual, Janet remained quiet. She rarely spoke in matters that concerned the MacNicol clan except to support her husband. And she never questioned her mother-in-law, Lady Lydia.

Kayla finally opened her mouth to speak, but her mother spoke first.

"I have a suitor in mind," Lady Lydia said, as though *the suitor* were all that mattered, not Kayla. "I believe Arlin MacDonald would suit quite well."

Kayla's jaw dropped, and her eyes shot open. Arlin MacDonald was an insensitive brute. He had never been nice to her, nor had he shown her the least indication of affection. She had no desire to marry Arlin.

"My brother, Arlin?" Janet asked. She sounded as surprised as Kayla felt.

"Aye, yer brother. 'Tis only prudent for the MacNicols to pursue another marriage with the MacDonald clan. 'Twill strengthen family ties and seal our alliance," Lady Lydia said, without bothering to check Kayla's reaction.

"I wasn't aware our alliance needed strengthening," Duncan said.

"Alliances can never be too strong. We've nae had a bold leader since we lost our good king, Alexander. King John is nothing more than a puppet for Edward. I doona trust the English. The Scottish clans must unite if they wish to remain sovereign." Kayla wondered if her mother were voicing her opinion or sounding a call to arms, she sounded so alarmed.

"I've always favored our alliance with the MacLeods. Their fellowship has served us well," Duncan said.

"The MacLeods doona have any single sons available for marriage. We lost our only chance for a MacLeod marriage when Murdock   wed."

Kayla was appalled her mother would bring up Murdock MacLeod, knowing how she had once favored him as a suitor. He, however, did not return her sentiments and found Merrie Lewis more to his liking.

Kayla wished she had the strength to argue with her mother, but she knew it would do no good. Lady Lydia rarely listened to her youngest child and only daughter. Instead, Kayla sat stunned, quietly watching her family plan her life, her eyes moving from face to face, seeing their mouths move but no longer registering their words. They were plotting her life—her life—and yet the conversation seemed beyond her.

Even though she was sitting near the warmth of the hearth, she felt a chilly cloak surround her. She wanted to flee; she needed to be alone.

Dimly hearing the voices of her family as they carried on without her, Kayla slipped out the door of the great hall and made her way to the stone steps climbing the outer fortress wall. Treading her way along the battlement walkway, she sought a secluded place of private refuge beside a large circular stone tower standing guard near the main fortress gate. She rested her head against the cold, grey stones and gazed out at the familiar landscape. This was her home, the only land she had ever known. The thought of leaving her home and her family tore her heart.

Confusing thoughts swirled in her head. It didn't seem reasonable her mother wanted her to marry Arlin MacDonald. The MacNicols didn't need another marriage to secure an alliance. Duncan was already married to Janet MacDonald, and Duncan was the MacNicol chief. Surely that was good enough. It wasn't as if Arlin were in line to be the MacDonald chief. He had three elder brothers and at least a couple of nephews standing between him and Hugh MacDonald, the chief of their clan. Of course, she understood another marriage between the families would strengthen clan ties, and yes, she was aware there were limited—make that no other—matches available, but she didn't want to marry Arlin. In the end, regardless of what her mother or anyone else said, she simply did not want to marry Arlin MacDonald.

She hated the whining voice speaking in her head, and yet there was no use denying the always dutiful daughter of Lady Lydia and Chief Kennon MacNicol did not want to do her family's bidding. For all of her twenty years, she had always done everything expected, especially where her family was concerned—everything except get married.

Though she had always believed she would marry, it just hadn't happened yet. Being married brought security and social standing, but she also dreamed of someday finding her one true love and being allowed to marry the man of her choosing. A whimsical dream, of course, based on a silly childhood illusions she should have discarded long ago. It certainly wasn't grounded in the hard, cold reality of being the chief's only sister, but still, it was her dream. Her brothers, Michael and Duncan, had found love matches with their wives. Was she allowed to wish the same for herself?

Torchlight flickered in the great hall. Twilight was slipping away to darkness of night. She knew she should be down there, arguing with her family, refusing to accept decisions made on her behalf without her consent. Instead, she was standing alone on the fortress walkway, on the verge of tears.

Shifting her gaze skyward, she blinked several times to clear the moisture pooling in her eyes. A lone star appeared in the darkening sky. Her eyes locked upon the tiny pinpoint of twinkling light.

"Kind faeries," she spoke aloud. "Please help me find my own true love."

The radiant star twinkled, as if it had winked at her, and she heard a voice softly whisper in the wind. "A wish expressed, a favor bestowed."

"Who's there?" she wondered aloud. She turned around, looking anxiously about the walkway, but she was alone.

Too many of Mother's stories, she thought, trying to reason away what her senses so ardently told her. Lady Lydia often told her stories about the guardian faeries of Skye, and she wanted to believe they were true. There was even a legend that her great-grandmother Sophie was descended from the faeries, but it was only a story a mother told her child to ease her mind.

Turning her back on the lone twinkling star, she started to walk away, but her inner voice only spoke louder, refusing to dismiss what her senses were saying. This was not simply her imagination playing tricks on her; surely, there was a faerie was close by. She had heard her voice and felt her presence. For years, she'd felt the presence of an unseen faerie at her side, often at unexpected moments. Each time she had wished the faerie would appear, but each time she had been disappointed. Now, more than ever, Kayla fervently hoped, when the time was right, she would finally meet her guardian faerie.

CHAPTER 3

Scotland & the Isle of Skye, Present Day

Someone was poking him and he didn't like it. "Daniel, wake up. We've landed." Teressa's voice broke through the cushioned quiet of his slumber.

"What? Are we there yet?" Daniel jerked himself awake, aided by his sister's repeated jab to his shoulders.

"Yes, we're here. We've landed. I can't believe you slept through it all." Teressa was gathering her belongings, including her travel journal, as fellow passengers made their way single file down the aisles. "I didn't want to wake you. I know how hard jet lag can be for a novice traveler, but we've got to get off the plane."

"I'm surprised I was able to sleep at all," Daniel said, pulling himself out of his sleep-induced stupor. "I didn't think I'd ever fall asleep when, all of a sudden, I closed my eyes for a moment, and I was out like a light." He expected to feel travel weary, but in truth, he felt like he had just awakened from a long winter's nap, totally refreshed.

"Yeah, well you were sleeping like a bear in winter when it's the middle of June," Teressa said.

"A bear with a shit-eating grin," Robert smirked.

Daniel ignored their comments, but he didn't try to deny them. Based on the few lingering memories from his fleeting dream, he had reason to believe Robert's observation was quite accurate.

After they collected their luggage and made their way through customs, Teressa pulled out her travel itinerary and checked her notes. "We've got a little more than an hour before we have to catch the train to Inverness. Enough time for coffee and breakfast. Anyone interested?" She had assumed the role of travel guide, and Daniel had happily acquiesced. At this point, it wasn't as though he had much choice.

"Coffee sounds good to me, or maybe I should try some of that English breakfast tea. You know, when in London and all that rot. Do you have any Earl Grey?" Daniel joked, attempting to imitate an accent similar to the ones he was hearing around him.

"We're not in London, you goof. We're in Glasgow," Teressa corrected her brother.

"Earl Grey and some blueberry scones sound nice right about now," Robert said, lending his support to Daniel's suggestion in his deepest brogue.

Teressa rolled her eyes. "Boys," she mumbled. "Come on." She led the way to the taxi stand. "We'll eat at the train station. It's cheaper than the airport."

As they followed her lead, dragging their suitcases, Daniel exchanged a knowing look with Robert. They could tell she was enjoying her role as ringleader.

They barely had enough time to finish their breakfast before they were off and running to catch the train that would take them to Inverness. From there, they would travel to the Isle of Skye by car with Robert's mother.

Although reluctant to admit it to his little sister, Daniel found the farther they traveled into Scotland, the more at ease he felt. Stress from the long flight, work concerns, and big city hustle was slowly but unmistakably being replaced by an inner calm settling into his soul. He felt the weight and weariness of his life slipping away, leaving behind a feeling of well-being he hadn't experienced in years. Maybe it was a byproduct of all the soothing greenery provided by the passing countryside.

The youngest of three boys, he was the only one still at the family ranch, which had forced him to spend most of his time helping his parents manage the place. Being on the ranch was a life he loved; he'd been happy working side by side with his dad. But his dad had passed away nearly three years ago, followed by his mother earlier this year. Living all alone on the twelve-acre spread, he was beginning to wonder if Over-Yonder was where he belonged. The ranch had been his parents' dream, and they had done it justice, but it wasn't necessarily his. He wanted to make his own mark in the world; he just wasn't sure what or where that mark would be.

As he relaxed onto the gentle massaging vibrations of the train, he felt a soothing sensation and a return to innocence that had long been lacking in his life. The smile growing inside him pressed to break free, and he realized he needed to thank Teressa for forcing this leisure upon him. He couldn't remember the last time he had been able to sit back and relax without duties to tend to or schedules to meet as he simply watched the countryside pass by, lush and green, raw and rugged.

All in all, this vacation was looking much better than he had expected.

Robert's cousins, Jack and Jenny, had moved into the ranch before he left, and they had immediately made themselves useful, feeling right at home. Jack especially was looking forward to becoming a modern ranch hand, learning all he could about tending to horses. Daniel had two full weeks to leave the cares of tending the home fires behind, and he intended to make the most of it.

Though he didn't regret his guardianship of the ranch, he felt a need to let it go and find a place where *he* belonged. Losing his job with the mounted police had him questioning what he should do next. He still had the ranch, but it was no longer as self-supporting as it used to be when his dad was alive. It would take considerable changes and an infusion of cash to bring it back to full production. Maybe it was time to consider other options.

He had proved he was capable of earning a living; now he wondered if he were capable of creating a life, one that included his own home and family. The ranch was a great place to raise a family, but it was too big for a single man, and he had no prospects for a family anytime soon.

As Daniel watched the Scottish countryside roll by, an idea began to crystallize. He'd been playing with the thought for quite some time. Now seemed like a perfect time to present his plan to Teressa and Robert.

Pulling his gaze from the window's view, he turned to catch his sister making another entry into her travel journal. What might she have to write about this time? Daniel figured that was one question better left unspoken. He had no intention of divulging his covert knowledge of her unbelievable journal.

"Hey sis . . ." Breaking the silence, he moved quickly into his topic. "I wanted to let you know, I've been thinking of cleaning up the ranch to put it on the market. Since it's the family home, I want to give you a heads up in case you're interested in keeping the place. It's just gotten too big for me, being by myself and all."

Teressa and Robert looked at Daniel with undisguised surprise.

"You're thinking of selling the ranch?" Teressa questioned. "It's been in the family since Brett was a baby."

"I know; it was a great place to grow up, but I'm the last one living there, and I'm ready to move on. I'm thinking someplace smaller and closer to work would be more practical."

"Have you mentioned this to Brett and Connor? Are you sure they're not interested in taking over the place?" Teressa set down her journal and gave Daniel her full attention.

"Of course I'll tell them I'm ready to sell, but Brett and Connor have been down in L.A. for years. I can't see them wanting to come back to run the ranch. We haven't had a good stock of horses for a few years now, and the cost of rebuilding the stables is more than I can afford. It's just not the same without Dad." Daniel shrugged. He didn't see his older brothers wanting to preserve the family home. Brett and Connor were married with families of their own. They'd both moved to Southern California to work in the aerospace industry, leaving the ranch life far behind.

He was also pretty sure, once he put the ranch up for sale, it would be scooped up by one of the big land developers. They'd been knocking on his dad's door for years, anxious to get their hands on the prime real estate nestled in Diablo Valley. Allen Ellers had always refused, preferring to hold onto his land. He said the space was worth more than the money. After their father's passing, there'd been a whole new wave of interest, but Daniel had remained committed to letting his mother live out the last years of her life on the land she loved only second to her family.

"Since we're all equal partners in the place, they'll have to sign off on the deal," Teressa reminded him.

"Yeah, or you could just buy me out, but I don't see that happening." Daniel had made up his mind. Now that his parents were gone, it was time to move on.

Teressa turned to her husband. "What do you think Rory? Would you be interested in running the ranch?" She wore a playful grin, and Daniel was pretty sure her question was more for show than anything else.

Robert studied his wife. "Honey, I'm a fisherman. What do I know about running a ranch? No, this is your family affair. I'll leave it up to you."

"I didn't think so, darling, but I had to ask." Directing her comments back to Daniel, she continued, "I guess we should arrange a conference call when we get back home to get everyone on the same page. Are you in a big hurry to sell?"

"No, not really. I just think it's time for me to move on. Maybe find a place that feels right, a place where I belong. I don't really want to live in the city, even though I enjoy working there. But I don't want to continue living alone on the ranch, either. I'm probably better suited to a house than an apartment. Can't see myself boxed into such a small space. I want a yard, and a garage, and my own driveway, although I haven't begun looking yet. I figure I still have plenty of time."

In the Ellers family, Daniel was known for taking his time and moving a tad slower than the rest of the world. It was one of the reasons he preferred being with the mounted police rather than in a patrol car all day.

"I'll help you any way I can. I'm sure there's a ton of family history stored at the place. We'll need to go through it all. Do you know if Brett and Connor still have any stuff stored there?"

"Some, but not much. They cleared out most of their stuff after dad passed. Almost all of Dad and Mom's stuff is still there. I'm thinking we'll all have to go through it as a family to see what everyone wants to keep." Daniel's mind turned to the practical aspects of dealing with almost forty years of accumulated family history. It wouldn't be an easy task. Their parents had led good hard lives on the ranch. They both had passed while still in their seventies, relatively young by Daniel's standards.

Almost as though reading his thoughts, Teressa spoke, "Dad always said he didn't want to grow old and feeble, and Mom said she didn't want to grow old without him. I guess they got what they wanted."

"Yeah, I guess so." Daniel resumed his leisurely observation of the Scottish countryside, relieved he'd been able to get the idea of selling the farm off his chest. Saying it out loud had been the hardest part. Now it was real; no longer just a thought in his head.

~*~

It was his second day on Skye, and already he was back in the saddle, riding free as the wind in the wide-open spaces. After an exhilarating all-out run that had taken man and beast to the brink of exhaustion, Daniel slowed his horse to a gentle walking pace. Leaning forward, he ran his hand along the stallion's neck, soothing the heated animal. The path they were on ran along a swift running river, and he directed the horse down to the water.

"Hey, Wilbur, I think we've earned a rest and a good long drink." Daniel spoke to the animal in a cheery tone. He dismounted near the water's edge and led Wilbur to drink his fill from the cool, clear stream flowing freely through the shallow valley. He'd been pleased with the selection of horseflesh available at the Skyeland Stables, and Garrett Riggs, the stable manager, had picked a perfect mount for him. Once they had started swapping stories of life on a horse ranch, Garrett had quickly chosen the steed as exactly the right horse for Daniel.

"Wilber's as loyal as a dog, and as spirited as the day is long. He'll give you a good ride," Garrett had assured him.

The stable manager also provided him with a map of the established horse paths around the island and Daniel had plenty of snacks and bottled water. It was shaping up to be a very good day.

Daniel knelt down and dipped his bandana into the running stream then swiped the wet fabric across his face and over the back of his neck, feeling refreshed by the brisk slap of the cold cloth. Reaching into one of the saddlebags, he pulled out the water bottle and took a long cool drink. Once he was rested and rehydrated, he checked Garrett's map, examining the various horse trails to decide which one he would take. He chose a route that followed the riverbed a ways more before linking up to a path leading back to Portree and the Skyeland Stables. The loop trail would give him a nice long ride and still get him back early enough to get ready for the summer solstice party Teressa was planning.

After stowing the map and canteen in the saddlebag, Daniel got back on his horse and spurred Wilbur along the flowing stream, heading for the next trail marker. His gaze swept the horizon as he took in the view of the landscape. He was impressed by its rugged beauty. Lush green growth clashed with the abundance of volcanic hills and rocks, each claiming their foothold in the rough rolling countryside. It wasn't a soft or easy land like the rolling pastures and fields he'd seen in the lowlands of Scotland. Skye presented its own unique challenges. He could see how the island continued to draw Robert back to his family's roots.

More so than he had expected, Daniel was grateful his sister had talked him into taking this trip. Robert and Teressa had gone out of their way to ensure he didn't feel like a third wheel, tagging along behind a newly married couple. Robert treated him like a brother, and Daniel easily returned the sentiment. It was easy to see how well Robert and Teressa fit together, almost as if made for each other, and he envied their relationship.

It must be nice to have someone to share your life.

For himself, he figured she'd have to be someone pretty special and a little out of the ordinary in this day and age. He was looking for a kind of old-fashioned, stay-at-home kind of woman who'd be committed to raising a family, rather like his mom. He wasn't interested in settling for less. So far, his relationships with women left something to be desired. It seemed there were plenty of women who were willing to speed-date their way into a relationship and then use text messaging as their primary form of communication. That type of courtship wasn't for him; he'd rather take his time. He'd never experienced love at first sight and wasn't sure he believed in the phenomenon.

Lost in his thoughts, Daniel was enjoying the warmth of the sun when suddenly, the mild summer breeze turned violent. The drastic change in weather spooked Wilbur. The horse whinnied and pranced, turning away from the rising storm, but it was unavoidable. Horse and rider were hit hard by the hot fierce wind as it sprang up from nowhere, engulfing them in its furor.

The gale-force wind kicked up loose dirt, and twigs flew through the air like bits of straw. It scattered leaves and sent debris flying around Daniel's body. He raised his arms to protect his face from the stinging pricks of the flying rubble. His instinctive reaction caused him to lose his grip on the reins. Panic welled up inside him as he fought against the unnatural phenomenon. Rational thought eluded him.

Daniel felt the air being sucked from his lungs. He fought to catch his breath while struggling to regain the reins and maintain control over Wilbur. It was a losing battle. The combined force of the vicious wind and the bucking of the frightened animal threw Daniel off balance. He felt himself being ripped from the saddle. Knowing it was going to hurt like the dickens, he twisted his body as he fell toward the hard-packed ground. With a painful thud, he landed on his backside. A second before he blacked out, he swore he saw Wilbur suddenly disappear. Then everything went black.

CHAPTER 4

Isle of Skye, September, 1295

By the next morning, Kayla had formulated a plan. It wasn't a very good plan, and it was full of risks, but her emotions were such that she knew she had to give it a try. While she wasn't comfortable confronting her mother about her marriage prospects, she believed it was perfectly acceptable to send a message to Arlin, asking him to oppose the betrothal. Even if he was the youngest son of the MacDonald chief, he was a man, and her mother was much more likely to accept his choice in the matter. Maybe her own family wouldn't listen to her, but surely they would listen to Arlin.

There was the risk Arlin was in favor of their betrothal, but she was fairly certain he wasn't interested in an arranged marriage, at least not with her. They had known each other since childhood, and he had never showed an interest in her. Most often he treated her with a sense of superior disdain, as if being a MacDonald made him better than her. She was counting on the likelihood his lack of interest in a betrothal was equal to hers.

She didn't consider him truly ugly or anything like that; he was fairly attractive, with a strong muscular body. Although she believed his nose was a tad too big for his face, she doubted many of her friends would kick him out of a marriage bed. Unfortunately, she didn't share their sentiment.

Her only real concern was Arlin might have developed a fondness for her she didn't return. It was unlikely, but she supposed it was possible. Choosing not to dwell on such a disparaging prospect, she clung to her hopeful expectations he would agree to oppose a betrothal.

After a restless night with not nearly enough sleep, Kayla knew she had to take action. She had wasted enough time while her family plotted her future. While she was intent on sending a message to Arlin MacDonald, she didn't feel right asking anyone at Scorrybreac keep for help. Kayla needed a true friend who would listen to her and support her without any questions. Fern McLarkin was that type of friend. Certainly, Fern would agree to help her get a message to Arlin. And hopefully, Arlin would agree to oppose the betrothal. With any luck, her plan would work.

Fern had married a few years earlier and lived with her husband and little boy in a cottage outside the village where they tended their sheep. It was a long ride, and Kayla wanted to get an early start. When the sun began making its appearance above the horizon, she went down to the stables to prepare Sallie, her brown mare, for the ride. Gavin, the oldest of the boys who tended the stables, greeted her.

"Good morn, milady. Ye be here early. Do ye need any help with Sallie?" Gavin asked.

"Nay, Gavin. I can manage by myself." Kayla gave another tug on the cinch belt holding the saddle in place.

"Is anyone going with ye?" Gavin asked, taking a look down the row of stalls.

"I'm going to see my friend, Fern McLarkin. We're riding up to the hills to enjoy the first day of summer. I expect to be gone all day."

"Do yer brothers ken?" Gavin looked skeptical, and he had good reason. It wasn't like her to leave Scorrybreac on her own.

"I doona need my brothers' permission to visit my friend. I can take care of myself." She spoke with greater confidence than she felt. "If any of them asks, ye can tell my brothers what I told ye. Do ye understand?"

"Aye, I think I do," Gavin answered, scratching his head. "I just hope they doona come asking."

As soon as Kayla was out of sight from the watchtowers, she spurred her horse into a spirited gallop, heading quickly across the rough countryside. She knew Sallie couldn't maintain this pace for long, but she was anxious to see Fern. Once she had ridden a good distance, and all was going well, she allowed Sallie to slow to a walking pace. Kayla felt invigorated with renewed confidence.

Soon after she crested the rise above the banks of the Glenmore River, her plan was thrown off course.

Her first reaction was gut-gripping fear. Lying at the river's edged was a man she'd never seen before. She wasn't sure if he were alive or dead, but either way, it wasn't good. His mere presence and obvious need for assistance created a problem she couldn't ignore.

She paused before approaching him, scanning the countryside while she listened for signs of anyone else in the area. For a brief moment, her fears almost got the better of her and she considered riding on without investigating the stranger's condition. In the end, her growing curiosity, along with her natural tendency to offer healing whenever it was needed, finally won out. Convinced he was indeed alone and probably injured, she dismounted and cautiously approached the figure sprawled on the shore of the shallow running river. Her visit with Fern would have to wait.

Though she was certain she had never seen him before, something about him looked vaguely familiar. His unusual style of clothing marked him as an outlander, probably English, or maybe from the continent. He wore sturdy boots and a short leather jacket that looked expensive and well-made. Something about his boots looked familiar, but for the moment, she couldn't remember why. Perhaps she was too busy noticing his unusual indigo-blue breeches and how extraordinarily well they fit the shape of his body. They looked good on him.

Kneeling beside him, she paused for a moment to study her find. The stranger was alive, of that she was certain. Kayla could detect his breathing by the shallow rise and fall of his chest. He was also disarmingly handsome. His dark brown hair, cut short and neat, was brushed back from his forehead, highlighting the strength of his well-formed chin and sharply defined cheekbones. She focused a second longer on his mouth, taking in the fullness of his lips, slightly parted as he breathed. Tentatively, she reached out her hand to touch his face, laying her palm across his forehead to check for fever.

"Whatever shall I do with ye?" she whispered.

~*~

Daniel woke to the face of an angel. Backlit by the sun, her features were framed by a halo of radiant red hair. Her pale white skin had an iridescent glow, and her innocent green eyes peered back at him. He smiled, thinking he'd gone to heaven.

Startled, the woman pulled back. "Ye are alive!"

His smile deepened. "Alive? You mean I'm not in heaven?"

29

The angelic vision shook her head. "Nay."

Of course, there was still the possibility he was dreaming. He felt dazed and lightheaded. If this were a dream, he figured he could do whatever he wanted, and right now he wanted very much to kiss his angel. He attempted to lift his head toward the delicate face bending over him, but the painful protest of his muscles as he started to move confirmed he was both awake and alive.

"Oww, what happened to me?" His hand came up to rub the back of his head.

"I doona know. I just found ye." She sat back on her heels, giving him room to move.

Daniel rolled gingerly to his side, and with the young woman's help, he sat upright. Looking around, he took stock of his situation. Apparently, he'd been knocked out when he fell from his horse. He didn't know how long he'd been unconscious, but he figured it couldn't have been too long. The sun was still climbing high in the sky.

He slowly moved his head from side to side, cautiously checking the extent of his injuries, softly groaning as his muscles rebelled. His back and neck were sore, but not too bad considering his fall. Other than suffering some aches and pains, nothing felt broken or out of place.

"You didn't happen to see my horse, did you?" Daniel looked at the young woman sitting on the ground next to him. She had curious large eyes. They were really quite unique.

She shook her head. "Nay."

Struggling to stand with her assistance, Daniel looked around and confirmed her statement. There was a little brown mare standing nearby that the woman must have been riding, but his horse was nowhere in sight. Noticing the landscape, he was struck by an uncanny feeling something wasn't right.

Everything looked pretty much the same, and yet somehow everything was different. Some trees seemed taller while others looked shorter, and the scrubby undergrowth appeared thicker than he remembered. It didn't make sense to think the river, rocks, and trees could look different from one moment to the next, but they did. He blinked and shook his head, but the sensation remained.

Choosing to ignore the anomaly for the moment, he directed his focus back to the woman by his side. Standing no taller than his shoulder, she looked up at him with those beautifully expressive green eyes. She was dressed in a long grey wool skirt and a white linen tunic belted at her waist with a thick leather cord. Unruly curls of red hair escaped the long braid hanging down to the middle of her back. The young woman looked like someone he might see in the Haight-Ashby district of San Francisco, or maybe around Berkeley. Her style seemed like a throwback to the hippy era, but on her, it looked good, better than good.

"I suppose introductions are in order. My name's Daniel." He flashed a friendly smile.

"I'm Kayla." Timidly, she returned his smile.

"It's a pleasure to meet you, Kayla. Do you live around here?" He hoped she could give him a ride back to the stables or at least into town. He was pretty sure Wilbur had run off after being spooked by the windstorm and figured the horse had hightailed it back to the stables. That left him with the option of walking back or catching a ride with his angel of mercy. Given his choices, he was hoping he could hitch a ride with the angel.

"I'm from Scorrybreac." She seemed reluctant to say more.

He remembered Scorrybreac marked as a point of interest on his trail map and hoped maybe he'd find a phone there. "I know it's a bit much to ask, but do you think I could get a ride back to your village?"

She looked back over the hill and then down the river path, as if deciding which way to go. Finally, a timid smile reached her lips. "I suppose it wouldn't be right to simply leave ye stranded here."

"There are many who would. I'm glad you're not one of them. Thanks."

Kayla scurried to retrieve her horse and led it over to a boulder. Daniel immediately understood her intentions. The horse was large, and she was small, making it difficult to mount up without assistance. A step-up would make it easier.

He halted her movement. Lacing his fingers together, he leaned forward to offer his assistance. "Here, allow me."

"Oh nay, I couldn't." She resisted, stepping back from his gallant gesture.

"Please, allow me. I insist," he repeated his offer, maintaining his position.

Wide-eyed, she hesitated a moment before she timidly accepted his assistance. Gently placing her left foot in his cupped hands, she pushed off to swing her right leg over her horse. As soon as she was securely settled, Daniel braced his hands on the saddle, and in one powerful lunge he mounted up behind her.

Daniel was tempted to cuddle up close to Kayla's backside and embrace her in his arms, but that seemed too forward for this shy little lady. Instead, he opted for the more gentlemanly and prudent choice of leaving a precious inch of space between them. Gently placing his hands at her waist, he indicated he was ready to go. He felt her flinch at his touch before she gave a firm kick to the horse's side.

"You handle your horse well. Have you been riding long?"

"Since I was a wee lass."

It was obvious she wasn't much of a talker. He was going to have to work harder. "Where did you learn to ride?"

She hesitated a moment and then said, "My brothers. They took me riding afore I learned to walk. I've had Sallie for several years now." As she spoke, she seemed to relax a little. He was encouraged.

"I've been around horses my whole life. I grew up on a ranch. My dad raised horses for the rodeo. Do you ride often?" Maybe they could go riding together on another day, preferably a day when he had his own horse and wasn't in need of a favor. Although riding with her did have its advantages.

"My duties often keep me close to home." She hesitated a moment before asking, "May I ask where ye are from?"

"I guess my accent gives me away. I'm from America—California. I've traveled for days to get here." He was about to say he was traveling with his sister, Teressa, and her husband, Robert MacNicol, but the thought slipped from his mind, replaced by a heightened awareness of his arousal as he detected the gap between them inching smaller and smaller as the rhythm of the horse slid them closer and closer together.

"America, California?" she repeated slowly, looking puzzled. "That sounds interesting."

He couldn't blame her. She probably didn't encounter many American tourists on this remote Isle of Skye. "Yeah, well, it wasn't my idea, but now that I'm here, I'm liking it."

"Will ye be staying long on Skye?"

"I just arrived yesterday. I'll be here for another couple of weeks before I head back home."

"Oh, I see," was all she said.

Daniel felt her sink into silence. He understood. There was an aura of innocence about her. She probably wasn't interested in a vacation fling with an American tourist and saw no reason to encourage his attentions. Unfortunately for him, his attentions were already encouraged by her mere presence. Itching to run his hands along her slender arms and massage her delicate shoulders, he was strongly aware of his desire to touch her. His whole being yearned to know the feel of her body against his. He didn't know how far it was to her village, but surely this would seem like one of the longest rides of his life.

He was beginning to understand the appeal this island held for his sister.

Searching for something to say to break the awkward silence descending upon them, he opted for the safest topic he could think of. He asked about her family. "You said your brothers taught you to ride. Tell me about them." Most people felt more comfortable talking about their family than about themselves.

"I have three older brothers, Duncan, Michael, and Roderick. I'm the youngest, and they rarely let me forget. They're very protective of me. They all ride well, but 'twas Michael who taught me to ride. Of my brothers, he has the greatest patience."

"Your family sounds a lot like mine. I'm the youngest of three boys, and then there's my little sister. My older brothers have moved away, with families of their own, but I'm still close to my sister. Do you get to see your brothers often?"

"Of course, every day. We all live at Scorrybreac with our mother. My older brothers, Duncan and Michael, are married, but Rory and I are still unmatched."

Her family started to sound vaguely familiar to Daniel, and he was trying to remember why. Again, the thought was lost as he became distracted once more by the nearness of his riding companion. He hoped she wasn't offended when his hands slipped from her waist. They were now resting lightly on her hips. She had such a lovely curve to her hips.

"Wait, did you say you have a brother named Rory?" he asked as his mind stepped back from the gutter it was about to visit.

"Aye, Roderick. We all call him Rory."

"And your brother Duncan is married?"

"Aye, to Janet MacDonald. They have a wee daughter, Amy. My brother Michael is married to Shannon. They have two young boys, Tanner and Torrin, and are expecting another bairn soon."

Interestingly, the description of her family sounded all too familiar in a bizarre sort of way. These were the names of the people in Teressa's travel journal, a journal that described traveling over seven hundred years into the past. Had his sister had drawn on this local family to create her fantastic tale, or was it possible . . . ? No. He stopped his thoughts. It was far too unbelievable, and he certainly wasn't going to ask what year it was, like some dim-witted numbskull.

Daniel wanted to proceed with caution. It was probably just one big coincidence. Rather than rushing to rash conclusions, he preferred to take it slow while he gathered more information.

"Your family sounds interesting. Do you think I'll be able to meet them?" If Teressa had met these people, it might be interesting to swap stories with them. Perhaps he could find out why she had written a tale of faeries and time travel. He wondered if she had used some of their local legends in her travel journal to add some spice.

"Ye will meet them when we reach the keep. I'm sure Duncan will help ye return home. He always takes care of everything. We're almost there."

"That's great. I'd like to use your phone . . ." His words faltered abruptly. They had come to the crest of a ridge overlooking a low rolling plain and on the far side of the shallow valley, sitting high on the cliffs overlooking the sea, stood a large medieval fortress in all its glory.

"What did ye say?" She twisted in the saddle to look at Daniel.

He didn't answer. He only stared at the castle off in the distance.

"What's wrong?" she asked.

Daniel felt his blood drain from his face, and his mouth hung open. Spread out before him was a village of humble ancient cottages. Curls of smoke rose from thatched roofs supported by walls of mud plaster. Some of them were painted in whitewash, most were dull grey. Farther up, on the opposite bluff, sat what he could only describe as a medieval fortress surrounding a castle.

His mind struggled to understand what his eyes were seeing.

He figured it was either a perfectly well-preserved ancient castle or a recently built replica, and a darn convincing one at that. The village and castle looked like ancient Scottish dwellings, and everyone in sight looked dressed for the part. This had to be a living museum, rather like colonial Williamsburg in Virginia. That explained it. No wonder Teressa had written about being in the thirteenth century. As he looked at the scene before them, it was easy to imagine such a far-fetched adventure.

Finally, he grabbed hold of his wits, setting aside his initial shock. He needed to get a grip.

"Wow, this place looks like a real medieval village. You say you live near here?"

"Aye. I live in Scorrybreac keep." She pointed off toward the castle.

"In the castle? They let you live in the castle?"

"Of course, we live there. 'Tis the home of the MacNicol clan."

As Daniel continued to study his surroundings, an uneasy feeling churned in his gut.

"Are ye nay well?" Kayla asked, sounding concerned.

"Yeah, yeah, I'm fine. I'm just taking this all in," he answered. "This isn't quite what I expected."

Taking another look at the woman seated in front of him, he realized she was dressed like the others. He wondered if she were a history buff, or one of those reenactment nuts who couldn't leave the past behind. His blunt reaction must have alerted her to his state of confusion, and he concentrated on regaining his composure. He didn't want to sound like some idiot tourist, rambling on about reenactment sites, living museums, or how bizarre the place looked, he said nothing, keeping his thoughts to himself. Kayla followed his lead, and they rode the rest of the way in silence.

As they rode through the village, Daniel noticed how the crude and ancient dwellings were sturdy but simply built. For the most part, they appeared to be in good repair. Each little cottage showed signs of active habitation with a collection of men tending to chores, women washing clothes, and children playing with wooden swords. With unconcealed curiosity, several of them stopped what they were doing to watch him pass.

Word of the approaching riders must have traveled quickly through the compound. When Kayla and Daniel emerged through the fortress gates, two large men in ancient costumes were already standing at the center of the courtyard, ready to receive them. They wore long woolen tunics belted at the waist over knitted leggings and handmade leather boots held in place with straps.

Daniel slid off the back of the horse and reached up to help Kayla dismount. He left his hand resting possessively at her waist as he stood his ground beside her.

"Who do we have here?" the larger man asked. He stood with his arms folded across his chest, legs firmly planted. His face bore a dark expression. Daniel guessed him to be the man in charge.

Shooting a quick silencing glance at Daniel, Kayla rushed to explain, "This man is Daniel. I found him injured and alone near the river. He was thrown from his horse. It must have run off. He needed help, so I brought him here. I believe ye would ken what to do."

Turning to Daniel, she continued the introductions, "This is my brother, Duncan, chief of the MacNicols."

An uneasy silence consumed the small group as the two men openly assessed each other. Duncan fixed his steadfast gaze on Daniel, his rigid features clearly expressing his concern at encountering an unexpected visitor.

Daniel broke the standoff with a friendly half smile. "Duncan, chief of the MacNicols, is it? I believe it's my honor to meet you. I'm Daniel Ellers." A hint of macho arrogance leached into Daniel's voice as he addressed the clan leader. He stretched out his right hand in greeting.

Kayla stepped away from his side. "Daniel Ellers! Do ye ken Teressa Ellers?"

Daniel broke his focus from Duncan, dropped his hand, and turned to look at Kayla. "Of course. She's my sister."

Kayla's eyes grew wide with amazement. "Yer sister?"

Duncan stepped forward, taking control of the situation. "Kayla, go find Rory. Send him to my study. Say nothing of this."

Kayla looked at Duncan in disbelief, as if ready to voice her dissent.

"Go. Now," he barked. The stern look on his face let her know there was no room for argument.

She hesitated a moment longer, casting a sideways glance at Daniel before she turned and stomped off toward the large stone structure dominating the fortress courtyard.

Duncan turned back to the stranger before him. "Come with me." Not waiting for a response, he turned and headed back toward the keep.

The exchange between Kayla and her brother indicated something big was going on, and Daniel was definitely the outsider. Believing Duncan held the answers he needed, Daniel willingly followed the MacNicol chief into the castle. As they crossed the courtyard, he kept an eye on Kayla. She was greeted by another woman, who turned to gape at him with a look of trepidation, before they hurried off together toward the far side of the building.

The authenticity of his surroundings continued to amaze him as he followed Duncan toward the main entrance of the large stone castle. He noticed the battlement wall of the fortress was guarded by realistic Scottish warriors, carrying authentic swords and longbows with quivers of arrows slung on their backs. Kayla's horse was being led to a nearby stable by a mop-haired young boy costumed in a rough woolen tunic and ill-fitting tights. As he walked through the courtyard, many of the workers stopped their actions to turn and stare at him, as though he were an alien and not just another lost tourist.

Daniel thought back to Teressa's travel journal. He recalled how she had reported it was the lack of modern technology that led her to believe she had actually traveled through time. Taking a close look around, he realized he was having much the same experience. When he had first regained consciousness next to the stream, he had instinctively felt a change in his surroundings, but hadn't been able to figure out what it was. Thinking about it now, he took into consideration the missing trail markers, the lack of paved roads or electrical wires, and the complete absence of mechanical or motorized sounds. It was getting harder and harder to believe this was a staged historical village. It seemed as if everything modern had completely disappeared.

He continued to question his initial theory this was simply a working replica of an ancient Scottish fortress. As disconcerting as the alternative might be, he was gradually, although reluctantly, considering the reality of the hard evidence presented before him. As a policeman, he heavily relied on both gut feelings and hard evidence. From all appearances, this wasn't a working museum, and these people weren't historical actors. He'd seen places like that, and there were always traces of the modern world: phone and electrical lines, modern signage pointing out exits and bathrooms, or even wrist watches and jewelry, but there were none here. This was the real deal. That uneasy thought left him with a whole new set of questions regarding how and why.

Duncan led Daniel through the great hall to a smaller room tucked in the far corner of the keep. Its furnishings were sparse. There was a table that served as a desk, two chairs, a stool, and a storage chest sitting next to a cupboard set against the thick stone wall. Motioning to one of the chairs near the small stone hearth, Duncan invited Daniel to take a seat.

"So, Daniel Ellers, tell me how ye got here."

If Duncan's expression was meant to intimidate him, he was doing a good job; however, Daniel detected an undertone of curiosity leaking through.

"I was out on a ride this morning when I suddenly got caught in a freak summer storm and was thrown from my horse. I must have passed out. When I woke up, I was looking at your sister, and my horse was gone. She was kind enough to bring me here for assistance. Like she said, it seemed like the best course of action at the time. I was hoping I could use your phone to call for a ride back to Skyeland Stables."

"That may be a problem. I doona ken what a *phone* is, and I've never heard of Skyeland Stables," Duncan said.

Daniel sized up the man across from him. He wondered if Duncan were being honest or if he were so immersed in his historical role, he refused to step out of character. Judging by the look on Duncan's face, Daniel opted for honest and figured this guy was his best shot at getting some valuable information.

"Okay then, if you don't mind me asking—and I know this might sound a bit strange; chalk it up to jet lag and the blow to my head—but can you tell me what day this is? More precisely, what year?" The very idea he was even asking such a question made Daniel uneasy, and he wondered if the blow to his head had caused more damage than he wanted to believe.

Unfortunately, it seemed Duncan understood the question all too well. "'Tis the twenty-first day of September, twelve ninety-five. Shall I guess, ye are from the future?"

Daniel stared at the man. "Are you pulling my leg?" His mind was racing, seeking answers before the questions could even be formed.

"Do I look like I'm pulling yer leg?" Duncan eyed him with a mixture of wariness and disbelief as he returned Daniel's stare.

"You're telling me the truth? It's really the thirteenth century?" Daniel raised his brow in disbelief.

"Aye," Duncan confirmed.

"You mean this isn't some kind of historical reenactment, you know, where you guys are all actors performing a living history or something?"

"Why would anyone do that?" Duncan looked at him as though he were a stark raving idiot, which was pretty much how he felt.

Daniel pressed the palm of his hand against his forehead. His head was starting to ache. It occurred to him Duncan was looking pretty calm for a man speaking to someone from the future. "Does this type of thing happen often around here?"

"Nay, not often. Ye are only the second such *visitor*. I thought even once was highly unusual. Yer sister visited us about three years ago. Did she nae tell ye?"

"Well, not directly. She never actually told me what happened to her, but she kept a journal. Recently, I had an opportunity to read it, so yes, you could say I'm aware of the story, which up until now I didn't believe. I'm still not sure what to think about all this." He was struck by how amazingly prepared he was to deal with the situation, and all because he had inadvertently read Teressa's journal. As unbelievable as he had thought her story to be, without her validation this was even possible, he might very well have gone stark raving mad from the unfathomable situation he was now facing. His logical mind, the one that placed such high value on hard evidence, might have deserted him when faced with such an improbable—no, make that impossible—situation, and yet here he was, talking to the chief of the MacNicol clan in the thirteenth century.

"How is it that Ellers keep showing up at my keep? Are ye cursed, or am I?"

"Honestly, I don't know. According to Teressa's story, it has something to do with faeries, but I haven't encountered any faeries." Daniel found it hard to believe he was having this conversation, but he was certain he was awake, and preferable as it might be, he was fairly certain this wasn't a hallucination.

There was a sharp knock on the door, followed by a man entering the study.

"Holy shit!" Daniel leaped to his feet. It seemed he was the victim of an elaborate hoax. The man standing before him was Robert, Teressa's husband. "Robert, are you in on this? Is this some kind of weird joke? 'Cause if it is, I don't think it's funny."

"My name is Roderick and I ken nothing about a weird joke." The man's stoic expression held no hint of a smile.

"You expect me to believe you're not Robert and this isn't a joke?" Daniel scoffed.

"I doona care what ye believe. My name is nae Robert." Robert's double turned to Duncan. "What's this about? Why have you sent for me?"

"Rory, this man claims he's Daniel Ellers." Duncan stood, pausing for only a second before adding, "Teressa's brother."

"Teressa's brother?" Rory repeated, his voice heavy with amazement.

"Aye, so he says, and I believe he speaks the truth," Duncan confirmed.

Rory stared at Daniel for a long moment, looking him over. "I've many unanswered questions, but there's only one that truly matters. Did Teressa return home safe?"

For a brief moment, Daniel remained silent. He needed time to digest what he was seeing. At first glance, he'd been certain Rory was his brother-in-law, Robert, but on closer inspection, he could see the differences. This man wore his hair longer, and while he had nearly the same height and build as Robert, Rory was bulkier, more like a bodybuilder. He looked a lot like Robert, but his face was thinner and carried a weary sadness that made him appear older. Daniel could see this man wasn't his brother-in-law, and yet he felt an immediate connection to him, a sort of kinship.

One step at a time, Daniel told himself, *I can get through this if I just take it one step at a time.* Finally, gaining control of his thoughts, he answered Rory's question, "Teressa is well. She returned home safely."

"Does she speak of me?" Rory asked.

Daniel registered a flash of longing racing through Rory's eyes, and he instantly understood the man's concerns. He grappled with the idea Teressa believed this man had reincarnated as Robert in the twenty-first century to be with her. Figuring time travel by itself was strange enough to deal with, he didn't need to add reincarnation into the mix. A clear and resounding voice in his head screamed. *Do not tell.* His gut instincts told him this was one can of worms he didn't want to open. Knowing some things were better left unsaid, he resolved not to say anything about Rory becoming Robert sometime in the future, regardless of whether it was true or not.

"Not a day goes by that I'm not aware of how much she loves you," Daniel answered. He felt it was a small act of kindness to give such reassurance to the man whom Teressa believed to be her future husband.

"What happened to her after she left here? Why has she nae returned?"

"I'm sure you've got a lot of questions, but I'm sorry to say I don't have a lot of answers. I can tell you she came home a changed woman. And I can tell you she's still very much in love with you. Right now, that's about all I've got." Daniel wished he had more to offer the guy, but until a few days ago he'd been completely unaware of Teressa's deep dark secret.

Rory nodded, accepting Daniel's reply. "Thank you, brother."

"Brother?" Daniel was taken aback by Rory's fitting use of the term.

"If Teressa were here, I would have made her my wife. As far as I am concerned, that makes ye my brother."

Yeah, well, maybe someday you'll get your wish, Daniel thought, awestruck by Rory's declaration.

"So what happens now?" Daniel questioned his hosts. He looked from Rory to Duncan.

"First we have a drink." The MacNicol chief motioned for Daniel and Rory to sit down and went to the wooden cupboard to retrieve a bottle of amber liquid. He poured them each a drink. Judging by the fumes, Daniel guessed it to be old-fashioned Scottish whisky.

Speaking to Daniel, Duncan asked, "Ye say ye haven't encountered any faeries?"

If he hadn't read Teressa's journal, he might have thought the man was wacked to be talking about faeries. As things were, it seemed fairly reasonable. Daniel settled back into the armchair he had abruptly vacated and accepted the much needed libation. "Nope, no faeries," he said. *Just an angel,* he thought, thinking of Kayla.

"Other than to bring news of Teressa back to Rory, do ye have any idea of why ye're here?" Duncan asked, taking a serious swallow of whisky.

"Nope, none at all. I only recently discovered everything that happened to Teressa while she was here. I'm still finding this all pretty hard to accept. I've no clue as to why, much less how this is even possible. One minute I'm riding along on my horse, and the next I wake up in the past." Daniel shook his head, perplexed. Taking a sip of the strong liquor, he nearly coughed, but held it back, his throat burning. He was determined not to look weak in front of these guys.

"From what Duncan and I were able to piece together, a powerful faerie named Moezell brought yer sister here to secure a match between Duncan and Janet MacDonald. When her task was finished, she was sent back home, to her time," Rory told Daniel.

"Yeah, that's pretty much the same information I have," Daniel confirmed. "But I have no idea why I'm here."

"Since Moezell did it afore, 'tis my guess she did it again. We'll have to wait and see if she lets us in on her plans." Duncan shrugged.

"Isn't there anything else we can do? No other way to send me back?" Daniel asked. While it was pretty much in keeping with what Teressa had written in her journal, he found it hard to believe he was at the mercy of an unseen faerie.

"'Tis nae in our hands. 'Tis up to Moezell. We have to trust she kens what she's doing." Rory said sounding hopeful.

"You want me to believe, much less trust, in a faerie I've never even seen?" Daniel was still finding it hard to believe they were talking about faeries, as if they were an everyday occurrence.

"My previous encounter with Moezell gives me a wee measure of reassurance."

"Wait! You've met this faerie?"

"Aye, 'twas when she sent Teressa home. She appeared to me briefly after yer sister disappeared from the beach, which was fair shocking enough. Ye can imagine how I felt meeting a faerie. She told me Teressa had to return to her own time. I've nae seen any sign of her since," Rory explained.

"So, it's been what, a year since you've seen her?" Daniel asked.

"Nay, 'twas over three years ago," Rory said.

"*Three years!* In my time, Teressa's visit to Skye happened only a year ago." Daniel was becoming confused; or to be honest, more confused, since confusion seemed to be the rule of the day.

"Three years and three months have passed since I last saw Teressa," Rory said.

Only a year ago, Tesessa had returned home to California from Scotland with her new finance, Robert, but these guys hadn't seen her in over three years. "I wonder why she waited so long," Daniel mused, referring to the faerie.

"Moezell has her reasons, I'm sure. There's nae much we can do 'til she makes herself known," Duncan said.

"Ye've been sent here by magic," Rory added, as if it were no big deal. "And ye needs magic to send ye home."

"Magic! You believe in magic?"

"Aye. What else would ye call it?" Rory asked.

"Honestly, I don't know what I believe, but I can tell you, I've never believed in magic." Daniel shook his head. Of course, before today, he hadn't believed time travel was possible either.

"I would think now is a good time to start," Rory said, flashing a mocking grin.

CHAPTER 5

From what Daniel had read in Teressa's journal, he was pretty certain his sister claimed she had returned from the past to the same time and place as when she left. That part of her story had led him to believe it was just something she had made up, like a little fantasy trip into ancient history for her own amusement. If Moezell really were behind all this, hopefully she would do the same for him. Granted, it wasn't much to hold onto, but if he really were at the mercy of some mysterious unseen faerie, he felt a lot better thinking sooner or later she would return him to where he had been when this whole fiasco began.

Until then, as Teressa had written in her journal, he planned to make the most of his unusual experience. He figured it wasn't often a man got to travel back in time, much less be met by such understanding and welcoming people. Most folks would probably think him crazy and lock him up. All things considered, these MacNicol brothers were being extraordinarily accommodating. Thankfully, Duncan's fine Scottish whisky was helping to take the edge off an experience that could only be described as mind-boggling.

"Magic may be all well and good," Daniel said, "and hopefully, it'll provide some answers sooner or later. But until then, if you don't mind, I'd like to return to the scene of my, um, accident to have a look around. I don't know what I expect to find, but I'll feel better if I can go take a look."

He had almost said the scene of the crime, but it was hard to say what type of crime had been committed. Would being sucked back in time by a meddlesome faerie be considered kidnapping? This certainly was a new one for the books, and he had no other place to start than back at the beginning. Either way, whether he found something or nothing, he knew he'd feel better if he could take another look around.

"That seems reasonable. Afore ye go, ye'll need to change out of those clothes. They look out of place, and ye've already caused enough of a disturbance showing up as ye have. We doona want more problems or people asking too many questions," Duncan said.

"What about Kayla? Doesn't she know I'm from the future?"

"Nay. We never told her about Teressa. We agreed to limit the number of people who knew. And we'd like to keep it that way." Duncan looked pointedly at Daniel, making his meaning clear.

As unbelievable and bizarre as it was, Daniel realized he'd been thrust into an elite league of gentlemen. Their membership was based on the shared and very secret knowledge of his and Teressa's origins, which included time travel and a powerful faerie. It ranked right up there as being one of the strangest set of circumstances he could ever imagine, and yet it created an unspoken bond of loyalty that united them in fraternal brotherhood. The feeling of belonging to this elite brotherhood provided a measure of security for Daniel. He felt he could trust these men with his life, and like his fellow police officers, he knew they had his back.

"Rory, ye should go with him," Duncan continued. "Help him find the place, and make sure he makes it back. We wouldn't want him to get lost now, would we?" Duncan shot Daniel an ominous grin then took another drink, finishing off the last of his whisky.

"Thanks. You know, I've got a lot to learn about how things are done around here, being from a different time and all. I'm hoping you'll help me out. What do you say?" Daniel addressed Rory. Of the two brothers, he felt he had better odds with Rory.

"Certainly. What are brothers for?" Rory grinned, swallowing the last of his drink.

"Great. Let's start with the toilet." Becoming uncomfortable, Daniel fought the nervous release of his bowels.

Rory scowled, indicating a lack of understanding.

"The head. The john. The shit house?" Daniel kept trying until amused recognition lit Rory's face.

"Aye, the shit house; we call it the garderobe. There's one outside. Come, I'll get you a change of clothes while you take a crap." Rory laughed out loud at Daniel's discomfort.

As Rory led him to his much needed relief at the garderobe, Daniel took in every detail of his surroundings. They exited the great hall through a thick arched doorway and crossed to a small alcove built into the thick stone wall of the fortress. Along with the rather unavoidable dirt and grime, there was the strong scent of humans and animals and the distant sound of swords clanging as men trained in the nearby field. Seeing the ancient weapons and crude clothing along with the badass fortress finally cemented the idea he had stepped back in time. *Yep, amazing,* he thought. *This is just freaking amazing. And it looks like I'm in for one hell of a ride.*

After Daniel's encounter with the ancient equivalent of an outhouse, Rory met him with a change of clothes. All he'd been able to find on such short notice was a fresh linen shirt and a pair of funny-looking leggings. They looked rather funny, and didn't exactly fit, but they would have to do for now. At least he looked more like everyone else, even if he felt like an alien from Mars.

Following Daniel's description of where Kayla had found him, Rory and Daniel rode out to find the site of Daniel's strange appearance along the river road. When the area he recognized as his landing site came into view, Daniel asked that they dismount and proceed on foot to prevent their horses from disrupting the original tracks. Retracing the hoof prints of Kayla's horse, both Rory and Daniel could clearly see where she had ridden in. Then, marked by the deeper indentations of the horse's hoofs, they could see where the two of them had ridden out together on Sallie. They found the crushed section of grass showing where Daniel had landed when he was thrown off Wilbur, but there weren't any fresh horse tracks leading up to the site from the opposite direction. From observable appearances, it looked as though he had simply dropped from the sky to land in this time and place.

Standing over the section of crushed grass, Rory shook his head, running a rough hand across his chin. "The only other time I've seen anything like this was when Teressa disappeared. She was running along the beach, trying to reach me. I saw her footsteps in the sand leading up to where she disappeared, and then they simply ended. If I hadn't seen her disappear right afore my very eyes, I wouldn't have believed it. If nothing else, Moezell's warning confirms her disappearance was indeed magic."

"Moezell's warning?" Daniel asked, standing. He'd been crouched near his landing site to examine any clues left in the area. Other than the tracks leading away from the site, there was nothing to be found.

"Teressa left the Isle Faire with my mother and sister, riding back to the keep with Duncan and his men. I was with the supply wagons. We were delayed getting back to the keep due to a fierce summer storm. That night, I had a vivid dream of Teressa slipping from my fingers, being pulled from my grasp. Early the next morning, I knew something was wrong. I headed back to the keep as fast as Blazer could take me. When I reached the bluffs overlooking the beach, I saw Teressa. We were running down the beach towards each other, but afore I reached her, she disappeared."

"Just like that?" Daniel snapped his fingers. "She disappeared?"

"Just like that." Rory did the same. "All that was left were her footprints in the sand. If I hadn't seen it myself, I'd find it mighty hard to believe. That's when I saw Moezell."

"What about Moezell? What did she do?"

"Looking back, I think she was trying to comfort me. I was mighty upset. She told me someday we'd be reunited, Teressa and I, if my soul desired. I've wanted nothing else since." Rory gave Daniel an appraising look. "The last time I saw your sister, she was wearing strange clothes, like yours. Duncan told me they were the clothes she'd been wearing when he found her, when she first arrived. Apparently, women in the future choose to dress like men."

Daniel laughed at Rory's comment. "Yeah, I guess to your way of thinking, modern women do dress like men, but their clothes fit so much nicer on their bodies."

The two men headed back up the slight incline to where they left their horses. "Has it really been over three years since you last saw Teressa?" Daniel asked.

"Aye. Every year on the summer solstice, I've gone down to the beach to wait and watch for her return. Every year, for three summers, there's been nay sign. Now ye show up. 'Tis encouraging to meet her brother, but I canna deny, I'd rather see Teressa."

"No doubt," Daniel murmured as he mounted up beside Rory. "Three summers and you still keep watch?"

"Think of all the women who have passed through yer life. Has any of them ever stirred feelings in ye beyond mere male lust?"

"I've had a few nice girlfriends." Daniel shrugged, defending his dating history. "None that stuck, but we've had some good times."

"I'm certain many a lass has turned yer head with her bonnie appearance, but has any stirred yer heart?" Rory tapped his chest. "'Tis easy to fall for the sway of a young woman's hips and just as easy to seek another once the lass has satisfied yer needs." Rory cast him a long hard look. "I know, I was once like that."

That last bit of confession surprised Daniel. "Really? What changed?" They had reached the horses, but Daniel paused before mounting up.

"I met your sister. I wanted to claim her in a way I've nae felt for another. Since her departure, nay other woman has stirred my interest. Believe me, I've thought long and hard on this. It seems I'm fated to love only her. What keeps my hope alive is Moezell's promise we shall be reunited if my soul desires."

"Moezell told you you'd be reunited with Teressa?" Daniel realized he was staring. He blinked and shook his head.

Rory nodded. "Aye," he said and mounted his horse.

"Did she tell you how that would happen?" With practiced grace, Daniel swung his long legs astride his horse.

"Nay. Her only clue was I would someday return to her. She also said 'twas important I live my life well. I doona know what it all means, but I can tell ye, I intend to live a good life and stay true to Teressa if it means we have a chance to be together again."

Impressed, Daniel sat back on the saddle and gave a low, slow whistle. To know a love that transcended time was beyond anything he could imagine in his life.

~*~

Kayla rushed from the courtyard to find Rory filled with a mixture of anger, anxiety, and curiosity. To know Daniel Ellers, Teressa's brother, was in their keep, speaking to her brother, set her mind racing. She stopped along the way to ask Bonnie about Rory's whereabouts, and she pointed out Duncan speaking with their latest visitor. The chamber maid had a number of questions, but Kayla had few answers. Her first priority was to find Rory, and then her mother.

Luckily, she found them both together. Rory was helping their mother, Lady Lydia, tend to her garden. Lydia was busy amending the soil in preparation for next spring's planting, and Rory was supervising the workers moving stones to section off a new herb garden. He worked right along with his men, making sure the planting beds were exactly as his mother requested. Being the youngest of the MacNicol brothers, Rory was known for his relaxed attitude toward life in general, but Kayla knew he took immense pride in a job well done.

She had delivered Duncan's request for Rory to meet him in his solar, telling him it was important, and as instructed by Duncan, she didn't tell him why. However, that didn't stop her from telling her mother as soon as Rory left the garden. She was bursting at the seams with the news and needed to tell someone.

"Mother, you'll never guess what happened to me." She knelt down next to her mother, agitated and excited by the morning's events.

"Nay, but I expect you're going to tell me," Lydia said, barely looking up from her garden bed. She was absorbed in turning over the soil, adding in handfuls of chopped-up vegetation that would enrich the soil as it decayed in the ground.

"I found a man injured along the road near the Glenmore River and brought him back to the keep."

"Were ye out riding alone?"

"Aye, but that's nae important. The man I found is Daniel Ellers, Teressa's brother."

Lydia stopped what she was doing, still holding a handful of ground greens, and gave her daughter her full attention. "Ye canna be serious."

"Aye, Mother, very serious. He's with Duncan in his study right now. That's why Duncan sent for Rory."

Lady Lydia stared at her daughter in disbelief. "Are ye sure he's Teressa's brother? Could ye be mistaken?"

"Nay, Mother. I'm sure. He told us so himself."

Lydia dropped the mulch she was holding and stared off into the distance.

Kayla took advantage of her mother's silence and began to vent. "I canna believe he has the gall to show up here after all these years. Especially after his sister disappeared so suddenly without even so much as a farewell to Rory. He acted like he knows nothing about his sister's visit here, like he hadn't even heard of Scorrybreac 'til today. Why would he make the effort to travel so far unless his sister had sent him? Or would they have us believe 'tis some strange family coincidence that they keep showing up at Scorrybreac?" She was angry over the exposed identity of their wayward stranger and was more focused on venting her rage than on questioning her mother's reaction.

"Aye, it does seem strange." Lydia patted Kayla's hand, somewhat distracted. Finally, she looked over at Kayla. "Excuse me. I need to go to my chamber now. There's something I must do."

Without waiting for Kayla's response, Lydia rose to her feet and headed toward the keep.

"But, Mother, aren't ye even curious as to why Daniel Ellers is here? Aren't ye going to talk to Duncan?" Kayla called after her, taken aback by her mother's apparent lack of interest.

"Of course. Mayhap later." Lady Lydia waved off her daughter's concerns. She was already halfway to the garden gate.

Kayla sat back on her heels, stumped. What was happening to everyone? First, Duncan, and now her mother. Why weren't they more upset about Teressa's brother showing up unexpectedly? Regrettably, she acknowledged with a frown he hadn't exactly shown up from nowhere. She was the one who had found him and brought him to their home.

When she found him lying alone on the side of the road, she had immediately assessed her predicament, running through her options one by one. Even after she was assured he was uninjured and fit enough to walk, she knew she couldn't simply leave him on his own. She had dismissed that option as being too unkind. Also, she knew she couldn't take him with her to see Fern. That would have raised far too many questions, putting her in the awkward position of having to explain his presence. In her mind, that had left her with only one option. Take him back home to Scorrybreac, and let Duncan deal with him as he always did with everything else.

A small corner of her mind was aware this last option had granted her more time with the attractive man, but now she dismissed such thoughts as unimportant. She reassured herself it was only due to the MacNicols' customary rule of hospitality that she had assisted the mysterious stranger, not because of her own personal interest.

Everything had changed when she learned he was Teressa Ellers' brother. She wondered why he acted as though he had never heard of Scorrybreac. Surely, his sister must have told him about her visit here. She had been lost and stranded at their keep for several days. Kayla recalled with disdain how Teressa had called it an unexpected detour, as if that somehow made it acceptable for a woman to be traveling alone and unafraid.

Kayla had been exceptionally angry when Teressa had simply disappeared one day, leaving Rory brokenhearted. As far as she knew, Teressa hadn't bothered to offer an excuse for her hasty departure, nor had she given her brother a proper farewell. She had simply left to return home, wherever that was. And poor Rory was so in love with her. Right from the start, when Teressa had first appeared at their keep, Kayla had worried Rory's affections for Teressa were inappropriate. Unfortunately, she had been right.

In the three years since Teressa's unexpected visit and abrupt departure, they had received no word from her or any of her family. At least not until now. She had left without a trace, and Rory had been left brokenhearted. Kayla, with her protective nature, had taken Rory's loss to heart, holding deep-seated resentment toward the woman who had hurt her brother.

Now she had a tangible object at which to direct her resentment—Teressa's brother, Daniel Ellers.

~*~

Lady Lydia had no doubt about *how* Daniel Ellers had suddenly appeared at their keep. She knew of only one person who could have arranged his appearance. What bothered her most was she had no knowledge as to *why* he had been brought back in time. She needed to speak with her cousin—now. She hoped her distant relative would come when she called. Lately, her cousin was becoming more and more independent, making decisions without consulting Lydia. Now it appeared her cousin, the little faerie Moezell, might have gone too far.

Lydia hastened to the door of Duncan's study. She could hear the muffled voices of men speaking on the other side, at least two and possibly three. The thickness of the door prevented her from clearly hearing what was being said, but even if she could understand their words, she doubted it would yield the information she needed.

After a moment of unproductive listening, she quickly proceeded to her chamber. Once securely behind the equally thick and private door of her bedchamber, she worked to calm herself, resting quietly in her favorite armchair and taking deep, relaxing breaths. It would work against her if she allowed herself to be upset. When she felt her mind was sufficiently calm and under control, she closed her eyes and mentally reached out to her cousin, calling her name, requesting Moezell to show herself.

Nothing.

Lady Lydia called out again and waited.

In Lydia's irritated state, it seemed Moezell was taking far too long to make an appearance. She began to wonder what could possibly be delaying her little cousin. Was Moezell busy at the fae queen's court? Distracted by some inconsequential suitor? Or merely being difficult? Lydia's lack of control over the situation ate at her gut, and she was reaching the end of her patience. She was about to call out for a third time when a brilliant blue light filled the room.

"Ah, cousin Lydia. I thought I heard your call. What a delight. Are you in need of my assistance?" The light dimmed, and a lovely young woman appeared in the chamber. She had long silver-blond hair, which hung freely to her waist, and ice-blue eyes. A long, flowing, iridescent silver-blue gown draped softly over her delicate body. There was a soft glow surrounding her, adding brightness to the room. As she moved to stand before Lydia, an impish smile lit her lovely oval face.

Lydia did not return the faerie's smile. "I'm hoping ye can tell me. What has been occupying yer attention lately? Are ye working on anything of interest? Mayhap something I should know about, little cousin?"

Moezell's pixy face scrunched with a look of grave concern, as though she were in deep thought. "Nothing out of the ordinary. Just your usual wish fulfillment." The smile returned to her face with the brightness of several candles. "You know how I love to indulge in wish fulfillment."

"Really . . . wish fulfillment?" Lady Lydia's expression remained calm, but she wasn't falling for her cousin's innocence. Her eyes narrowed. "Please, tell me more."

"Oh no, cousin, you know that wouldn't be right. I can't discuss the wishes of humans. That would interfere with the outcome," Moezell stated innocently.

"Interfere with the outcome?" Lady Lydia raised her brows, tamping down her irritation. "Moezell, if this has something to do with my family, I have a right to interfere."

"No, I don't think so." Moezell held her smile. "I am responsible for granting these wishes. And besides, who said they involve your family?"

Lady Lydia glared at her cousin for a long moment. It seemed the young faerie was growing some new wings. "All right. Wishes are private, as ye say. Let's approach this from another direction." Lady Lydia resisted raising her voice. Although she was only half fae, such a lack of composure would be unseemly. She still held the ancient bloodline of the fae from her grandmother, Sophie, a full-blooded fae who had married a human and bore him a family. The fae bloodline, passed from mother to daughter, was strong and carried dominance over her human heritage. In a controlled, yet firm tone, she continued, "Tell me what Daniel Ellers is doing in my keep."

"Daniel Ellers?" Moezell asked, tapping a finger to her chin. "Could he be the brother of Teressa Ellers, the woman you brought here three years ago to do your bidding and fulfill *your* wishes?" Moezell seemed to be testing her recently enhanced strength, and it appeared she was enjoying the moment.

"Ye know very well she was brought here to secure the marriage between Janet MacDonald and my son. Do ye call that fulfilling *my* wishes?"

"If not yours, then whose wishes could they be?" Moezell looked unreasonably calm in the midst of her cousin's ire.

"I did it for my family, to preserve our peaceful relations with the MacDonald clan."

"Admittedly, you had good intentions from the start. But was it also your intention to deny Roderick his one true love, his soulmate?"

"She was nae brought here to become Rory's soulmate. And besides, I've already made arrangements for them to be together again, if they truly are soulmates as ye seem to think." Lady

Lydia grew incredulous that her actions were being questioned. It seemed her greater experience no longer held sway over the younger faerie, and she didn't like it.

"What you arranged was for your son to give up his chance at happiness in this lifetime so you could keep him close." Moezell was no longer smiling.

"How dare ye. I love my son."

"Apparently, not enough to set him free, to allow him to make his own choices. For years, I have heard Roderick's wish to be reunited with the woman he loves, but for now, that wish cannot be granted because of the solution you have so wisely chosen for him."

"You question my choices?"

"Yes, when I see the pain it inflects on another person's soul."

Lydia stewed. Of course, she was aware of her youngest son's discontent. She had hoped, over time, his sadness would fade, and he would once again regain his love of life. It had always been such a large part of his character, but in recent years, it had grown small. His body and mind had remained true and loyal to his family, but Lady Lydia was aware he'd given his whole heart and a piece of his soul to Teressa.

"What is done is done. It canna be changed. Ye still have nae explained why Daniel Ellers is here at my keep," Lydia said, hoping to gain control of the conversation.

"Didn't I tell you? I am granting wishes." There was more than a hint of mischief in Moezell's ice-blue eyes.

"Are ye telling me Daniel Ellers wished to be sent back over seven hundred years in time?" Lydia was highly doubtful of that idea.

"Actually, I am not telling you anything about anyone's wishes, as I've already mentioned, but perhaps you weren't listening. That seems to happen a lot with you."

"I heard ye just fine," Lydia snapped.

"It is one thing to hear what is said. It's entirely another to listen. Now please excuse me. I have humans to watch over." With her final comment, Moezell vanished from the room.

"I'm nae done with ye." Lydia struggled not to shout. Any louder and her voice would surely have been heard through her thick chamber door.

Lady Lydia quickly reviewed what Moezell had said, which, to the younger faerie's credit, had been very little. It seemed Lydia had taught her cousin too well in the fine art of purposeful evasion. All Lydia had learned from the faerie was that she was working on wishes, and she implied the wishes involved more than one human. She still didn't know how these wishes concerned her family, but she was certain they did. Unfortunately, she had no way of knowing whom it involved, at least not yet. Was it for Rory? Had Moezell brought Daniel back to act as a messenger between Teressa and Rory, since she couldn't bring Teressa by herself? It was possible, and as good a guess as any.

Lydia had also learned Moezell was still in a snit over the way she handled their previous encounter with Teressa Ellers. What had seemed like a good solution at the time was now proving to be packed with problems. Rory would be united with Teressa someday, if she proved to be his soulmate. He merely had to wait seven hundred years and another lifetime for that to happen. Maybe it had been asking too much, but what was done was done. There was no turning back her decision. Once circumstances were set in motion, results had to play themselves out. It made her wonder what circumstances Moezell had set into motion.

CHAPTER 6

The smile plastered on Kayla's face was a poor disguise for the rage brewing beneath the surface. It was one thing for Duncan to offer Daniel Ellers lodging in one of the chambers of the high tower where the druid Souyer lived, but to invite him to dine at their evening table was simply offensive. If it had been up to her, she would have handed him a crust of bread with some goat cheese and sent him on his way.

Instead, here he was, sitting across the table from her in all his frustratingly handsome glory. That was part of the problem, she reluctantly acknowledged. He was too good-looking, scary good, all sharp, neat, and very foreign. Not at all like the men from around Skye. It only complicated her problem that she was drawn to his unique presence.

Kayla's intention to simply ignore the man was proving to be more difficult than she had anticipated. For most of the meal, she managed to focus her attention on her sister-in-law, Shannon, even though the conversation repeatedly centered on the joys of motherhood and the new bairn Shannon was

64

carrying. That didn't mean she wasn't aware of what was being discussed with Daniel, only that she chose not to participate.

When Lady Janet politely asked why they had not received any word from Teressa for the past three years, Kayla's ears perked up. She was interested to hear Daniel's answer. Lady Janet thought of Teressa as a friend after all she had done to secure her match with Duncan, and Kayla knew she missed her.

"I believe Teressa would send her best wishes personally, if it were possible. Shortly after she returned home, our mother became seriously ill. Earlier this year, she passed away," Daniel said, honest regret darkening his gaze.

"I'm so sorry to hear of yer loss. Please know ye and Teressa have our deepest sympathies. I hope ye'll pass them on to yer sister when ye see her again," Lady Janet offered her condolences.

"I certainly will. She spoke highly of you and Duncan. I'm sure your kind words will mean a great deal to her." Daniel gave Lady Janet a kind look in return.

Kayla felt small, realizing she'd been harshly judging Teressa's absence only to discover Daniel and Teressa had suffered the loss of their mother. She turned to look at Lady Lydia sitting next to her. The thought of losing her mother saddened her. Granted, in recent years, they weren't always close, and it seemed as if their previously strong bond were growing thin, but she knew it would strike a blow to her heart if she lost her mother.

Interestingly, Kayla noticed her mother was unusually quiet during their evening meal. Lydia was known for being somewhat overbearing and dominating. Although she usually held herself with perfect decorum, as matriarch of the clan, Lady Lydia had a way of letting her family know exactly how she felt on any given subject. Even though she was keeping her thoughts to herself, Kayla noticed her mother was studying Daniel like a hawk stalking its prey. It made Kayla wonder if Daniel's presence also caused her mother distress.

Maybe, like her, Lydia was also unable to completely forgive Teressa for her sudden disappearance and the pain it had caused Rory. The passing of Teressa's mother went a long way toward explaining why she hadn't returned, but it didn't excuse her untimely departure. Undeserving as it might be, Kayla felt a lingering need to hang on to her resentment. It had lived too long to die a quick death.

Kayla recalled how everyone had wanted to ignore Teressa's sudden departure from Scorrybreac, as though it were of little importance. Although Teressa had always clearly stated she expected to return home, to leave so suddenly seemed downright rude, especially since Kayla knew Rory had hoped to accompany Teressa back to her homeland. At the time, her brother had avoided discussing the matter with her, and since then Kayla had stopped asking, but she could clearly see the pain it still caused him.

Duncan had been more concerned with ensuring his new wife, Lady Janet, was happy and comfortable in her new home than worrying over Teressa's sudden disappearance. Even their mother had shown no interest in pursuing the subject of her son's lost love. Now, whatever thoughts Lady Lydia had regarding Daniel's unexpected appearance, she was keeping them to herself. Once again, Kayla felt distanced from her family.

Perhaps she was misguided by the poisonous logic anger often provokes, which a small part of her acknowledged, but Kayla strongly believed holding onto her resentment of Teressa Ellers was a show of support for Rory. It was only natural her logic, ill-conceived as it may be, extended to Teressa's brother, as well. Unfortunately, this new target of her resentment was proving to be unfailingly charming as well as disarmingly attractive.

The sun-bronzed skin of his finely formed face was starting to show a shadow of stubble, and she liked the reddish hue of his thick brown hair. It was hard not to notice how his hazel eyes, with their swirls of dark green specks, created a hypnotic kaleidoscope effect when she stared into them, which she tried to avoid doing. Unfair as it seemed, there was an uncontrollable nervous tingling in her belly whenever he looked her way, and her heart seemed to beat faster. She loathed these wild, overwhelming feelings, and resented her body conspiring against her.

When she brought her thoughts back to the conversation, she realized her brother Michael was showing an interest in Daniel. Of her three brothers, Michael tended to be the quiet one. Being stuck in the middle between Duncan, the firstborn heir apparent and now chief of their clan, and Rory, his vivacious younger brother, Michael usually went about his business unnoticed, which Kayla suspected worked perfectly well for him. It had allowed him to build a pleasant and quiet life with his wife, Shannon, with little interference from his family, particularly their mother. Instead, Lady Lydia had a tendency to direct her attentions at Duncan or Rory, which suited Michael just fine. That didn't mean he wasn't aware of the happenings at Scorrybreac keep, only that he picked his encounters well. Apparently, Kayla wasn't the only one concerned with the appearance of another Ellers at their keep. Unlike her, Michael was letting it be known Daniel had succeeded in catching his interest. Daniel, she noticed, seemed quite capable of holding his own against Michael's frontal assault.

~*~

"I wonder what has brought ye so far from your home." Michael asked Daniel. "Have ye business in these parts?"

Judging by the suspicious look in his eyes, it seemed the middle brother had not been brought up to speed on where Daniel came from. In respect to Duncan and Rory, Daniel wasn't going to be the one to let the cat out of the bag. He figured it was best to play it safe and let the MacNicol brothers handle their own.

"Actually, I traveled to the Isle of Skye at the request of my sister. She still speaks fondly of the time she spent here. Teressa felt the adventure would be good for me after so much heartache at home," Daniel said. The jury was still out on how well his adventure was going, but the idea that world travel provided opportunities for unexpected adventures was most certainly accurate.

"What is it ye do for yer people at home?" Michael asked.

"I'm a police officer, mounted patrol," Daniel answered. When Michael gave him a puzzled look he went on to explain, "I patrol the streets of my city to ensure the safety of our citizens, to serve and protect."

"Ye are a guard," Michael clarified. He tore off a generous hunk of crusty bread and used it to sop up the gravy of his stew before biting off an oversized mouthful.

"Yeah, something like that," Daniel agreed. He followed Michael's example, enjoying the thick mutton stew.

"Would ye be interested in training with my men in the lists tomorrow?"

"Sure, that sounds great," Daniel replied. Michael's offer seemed friendly enough, and he had been wondering what to do with his time while he was trapped in the past. The idea of sitting around twiddling his thumbs while he waited for some unseen faerie to direct his fate didn't exactly appeal to him. He needed to stay busy, and learning their ancient methods of self-defense would indeed be interesting. All of the MacNicol men were built like trees—tall, sturdy, and muscular—and he wondered what training routine they used to produce such results.

"Good. We start right after the morning meal." A snide smile slithered from Michael's lips.

Daniel quickly understood Michael's underlying intentions. The ancient warrior wanted to test the new kid on the block. That was fine with him. Bring it on. He figured his police training and extensive knowledge of martial arts would provide the basic skills he needed to hold his own, even in ancient combat training.

"How well can ye wield a sword?" Michael asked. He took a long swallow of ale, keeping an eye on Daniel as he drank.

"A sword?" Daniel questioned, stalling for time. Maybe he hadn't given this enough thought.

"Aye, swords, or do ye have another weapon of choice?" Michael swiped the back of his hand across his mouth. His smirk grew deeper.

A gun would be nice, Daniel thought. During his police training, he had qualified as an expert rifle and pistol marksman, but he doubted those skills would be of much use to him here.

"Most of my training has been in hand-to-hand combat," he said, thinking of his martial arts experience, "but I'm also familiar with the baton, you know, a fighting staff." Although he hadn't considered fighting with a sword, he wasn't about to back down from the challenge.

"So be it. I'm sure we can find a suitable method to test yer skills." Michael's smile bordered on devious.

Oh great, Daniel thought, *he's looking for a smack down.* Eyeing the three MacNicol brothers sitting around the large plank table, he considered the odds. They were definitely stacked against him, and it didn't look good. He hoped he hadn't just set himself up for a brutal beating. He looked at Rory, wondering if he could get some backup from him. "What's your weapon of choice?" he asked.

"I'm good at them all," Rory said with a laughing grin. "We all are."

Yep, he was definitely in for a smack down.

"Ye needn't worry, we'll go easy on ye, at first," Duncan interjected, laughing along with his brothers.

"Don't worry about me. I can hold my own," Daniel shot back with more bravado than he felt. With two older brothers back home, this wouldn't be the first time he took a beating; he just hoped he would live through this one. He would hate to travel seven hundred years into the past only to meet his demise. But heaven forbid, if he did, God, or that faerie Moezell, had some explaining to do.

Long after the meal had ended, and the womenfolk had left the table, the four men lingered to drink their ale and exchange war stories. Daniel was fascinated to hear tales of the local feuds and battles the MacNicol brothers had encountered. These were tough times for the country of Scotland. After the death of their king, Alexander III, followed by his daughter, Margaret, Edward I of England had declared himself as feudal overlord of Scotland. All hell had been released, and the country was immersed in a political turmoil that threatened the lives of Scottish supporters. These days, Daniel was quickly learning, it was hard to know your friends from your foes.

Duncan's first priority was the safety of his clan, and he hoped the worst of the fighting would not reach Skye. Michael's first priority was to keep his men well trained and ready to do battle. Obviously, life in the thirteenth century wasn't for the faint of heart. And Rory's first priority was to do right by his family.

Daniel did his best to monitor the effects of the unfamiliar alcohol, trying to limit his intake of the heavy brew. In the company of the MacNicol brothers, it was a daunting task. Given the choice of matching their ale intake, becoming drunk, and acting like a fool, or taking his time to nurse his drinks, he opted to nurse his drink with shallow sips instead of deep gulps. Too many times, he'd seen firsthand the ugly side of inebriation and what it did to a man.

As the evening wore on, it became obvious even his best wasn't a fair match against the MacNicol brothers. It was later than he expected, and Daniel was more intoxicated than he liked to admit when he finally made his way back to his assigned bedchamber. As he walked away from the dining hall, he wasn't exactly bouncing off the walls, but he was staggering. At least he was still standing. The circular stone staircase of the high tower where he would sleep was a greater challenge, but he managed to make it to the top and into his chamber before he lost his cookies in the chamber pot conveniently provided.

He quickly stripped, and fell soundly into the large feather bed, mentally and physically exhausted. While he was fairly certain this wasn't all a dream, he wouldn't be at all surprised if he woke up and found himself back at Robert's cottage, as though none of this had happened. Crazy as the day had been, he realized he had no way of knowing what to expect next.

~*~

Kayla retired to her bedchamber, feeling more agitated than relieved. She was pleased to think she had made it through the evening meal without displaying undue interest in Daniel. It had helped that Michael and her brothers had dominated the conversation. This was as it should be, she told herself, for in truth, she had no interest in the man. He could disappear tomorrow, and she wouldn't suffer at all for his absence.

Besides, she still had a bigger problem to deal with—her possible betrothal to Arlin MacDonald. Unfortunately, thanks to the strange and unexpected appearance of Daniel Ellers, she was no closer to solving that dilemma than she'd been when she awoke that morning. She wondered why no one else found his presence disturbing. The calm reactions of her mother and brothers rattled her nerves.

"Why are my brothers so intent on welcoming this stranger to our keep?" she wondered aloud as she paced her bedchamber. "Do they nae see the threat of danger? He says he's from America, wherever that is, but for all we know, he could be an English spy."

Suddenly, flash of a bright blue light filled the room, and Kayla raised her hands to shield her eyes. When the light had dimmed, Kayla needed to blink several times to clear her vision before she could see the beautiful, young woman standing afore her.

"Is he really such a stranger?" the woman said, speaking softly. "After all, he is Teressa's brother."

Startled, Kayla took two quick steps back before she bumped up against her bed. If she hadn't felt the presence of the fae for so many years, she might have jumped right out of her skin. As it was, she only needed a moment to control the fright-induced pounding of her heart.

"Who are ye?" she asked slowly, feeling somewhat in awe.

"I am Moezell. Perhaps you have heard of me."

"Ye are a faerie, are ye nae? Tell me ye are fae."

"Of course, I'm fae. I'm also your cousin. I thought it was time we met." Moezell smiled, and the room grew brighter.

"My cousin! Ye are fae, and ye are my cousin?" Kayla's brows lifted in amazement.

"You are descended from the royal family of the fae, on your mother's side, of course. Fae blood is always passed from mother to daughter, not that a few drops haven't mingled in with your brothers', but the lineage is most strongly passed from mother to daughter. Surely, you know your great-grandmother Sophie was full-blooded fae, born as a fae in the fae realm."

"My great-grandmother Sophie! I thought she was a legend. I mean, I know Mother told me stories, but I dinna think they were real," Kayla sputtered her words.

"Oh they are real, and true enough to be sure. In her own way, perhaps a bit more slowly than necessary, I believe cousin Lydia has been preparing you for your initiation to your heritage."

"My heritage?" Kayla asked, momentarily flustered. "Does that mean, since great-grandmother Sophie was fae, that I'm also descended from the fae?"

"Quite the disappointment to know cousin Lydia has failed to mention this, but yes, you're also fae. Not only are you fae, you are a direct relation to Queen Danu. Your great-grandmother Sophie was the faerie queen's youngest sister. Sophie, being a rather passionate faerie, had a fling with a human."

Seeing the look on Moezell's face, Kayla wondered whether the faerie approved of her ancestor's actions, or if she were envious.

"After the affair, Queen Danu gave Sophie the choice of living with the faeries or crossing over to the material world to live her life as a human. Sophie chose to live in the world of the humans. Not necessarily a bad choice. Less powers, but 'tis a far grander adventure. When she had first crossed over, she met your great-grandfather Herrick, and well, I believe you know the rest."

Kayla nodded. She knew the story. And Moezell was definitely envious.

"Fae blood is always passed pure from mother to daughter and now runs through your veins. Have you not felt it through all these years, your connection to the fae?"

"Aye, I have." Kayla was awed, remembering all the times she had felt their presence. "I believed someday, when the time was right, the faeries would show themselves to me."

"Well, here I am." Moezell spread her arms briefly, reconfirming her presence.

"But why now? Why nae when I've asked for yer help?" Such as the time she was on the battlements, seeking comfort while her family was in the great hall of the keep plotting her future.

"Such as when ye wished to find yer own true love?"

It were as though Moezell could read her thoughts. "Ye know about that?"

"Of course, I was there. It was me you felt. Me you heard. You could not see me, but I was there. Often, I'm by your side to watch over you," Moezell said with fond affection.

"Is that why ye're here, because of my wish?"

"When it comes to finding love, true love, there is little the fae can do. The fae have no power to compel humans to fall in love. Humans have free will. 'Tis their greatest gift. All I can do is provide opportunities, assistance, and resources. Falling in love is always the choice of the individual."

"Mother is trying to arrange my betrothal to Arlin MacDonald."

Moezell nodded. "A mother wants what she thinks is best for her daughter. The daughter must learn what is best for herself."

"Arlin is a fine man, but I feel nay love for him." A spark of suspicion suddenly flickered through Kayla's mind. "Are ye trying to tell me I should simply *choose* to love Arlin?"

"In matters of love, you should always follow your heart. I would suggest nothing less. But first, you must open your heart to find that which you seek. You claim you wish to find true love, but to find, you must seek with an open heart."

Kayla felt a soft glow of loving affection radiate from Moezell. She sat on the edge of her bed and stared at her hands clasped in her lap as she contemplated Moezell's words. It wasn't a pleasant thought, but in a flash of self-honesty, she acknowledged how often she endeavored to keep her heart closed, hoping to keep herself safe from hurt.

While still a young girl, she had seen her eldest brother suffer dearly after he sent Janet MacDonald back to her family, and she had begun to build a defensive wall around her heart. Duncan had feared Janet would not be loyal to the MacNicol clan and had broken their betrothal. It was years later before they were brought together again, in large part due to Teressa Ellers' matchmaking skills.

Then Kayla had watched as Rory gave his heart to Teressa, and she had seen how Teressa had deserted her brother, leaving him with a broken heart. So she built her wall a little higher, a little thicker, believing it made her strong.

Kayla claimed she wanted to find her own true love, and yet she had done nothing to allow it to happen. Perhaps in some strange way, like the legend of her great-grandmother Sophie, she believed her true love would simply appear to her out of the morning mists.

Now, after asking the faeries to help her find her own true love, she was being told she must seek him with an open heart. While she understood the rightness of Moezell's words, the leap of faith was too great. Kayla needed time to consider the consequences of such a possibility. She had reached the age of twenty summers without finding love largely because she had worked so hard to avoid seeking it.

Moezell's advice was a bitter broth to swallow.

"I have nay idea how an open heart feels. It seems rather scary, as though I'm leaving myself open to a whole world of hurt that I doona want and have nay way to control." Kayla's chest tightened with fear.

"Ah-ha," said the faerie, "there's the rub. To lose yourself in love, you must let go of the fear that is holding you back. The greatest risk is to take no risk at all. You believe you can avoid pain if you avoid love, and yet I clearly see your pain. What you fail to see is the pleasure, the joy, yes, even the ecstasies only love can provide. Rory understands the love he has known with Teressa is worth any pain. And yet his pain is borne, even healed, by that same heartfelt love."

"The love of a woman who deserted him?" Kayla embraced the anger such a thought provoked.

"You judge that which you do not understand. Teressa did not desert Rory. She was required to return home. The choice was not hers."

"Without even saying goodbye."

"How would you know? You weren't there."

Kayla turned her gaze from Moezell. She held such ill will toward the woman she believed had hurt her brother, she was unwilling to believe it was unjustified. "If that is true, why dinna he ever tell me?"

"Why did you not ask?" Mozell asked without malice.

Kayla said nothing; she had no answer.

"Your anger at Teressa and your compassion for Rory's pain drove you to see only what you wanted to see."

Kayla remained silent, feeling a heavy dose of remorse and a touch of self-pity as her misjudgments were brought to bear. She returned her gaze to her entwined fingers. "He looked so sad, so lost after she left. I blamed it all on her." Her voice was small and wounded.

"He is sad over the loss of Teressa, but not for the love they shared. That is something he carries with him still. Have you not thought to ask Rory how he feels?"

"It seemed too personal, too painful to discuss," Kayla admitted.

"So, instead, you came to your own conclusions. How very human of you. Human imaginations seem to know no limits. It's fascinating, but oftentimes frustrating to observe."

Kayla didn't know what to say. How could she defend such actions? After an uncomfortable moment of quiet reflection, she asked, "I am still nae sure what I should do. How can ye help me?"

"I am here to be of assistance, to provide opportunities and resources to help you seek your own true love. Have my words of wisdom been of no assistance to you?" Moezell asked, looking hopeful.

"Aye, yer wise words help me greatly." Kayla brightened, encouraged by something Moezell had said. Perhaps the faerie could help her solve her dilemma. "I want to ask Arlin to oppose the betrothal. Can ye tell me if that is the right thing to do?"

"That choice is yours to make. I suggest you sleep on it, and see where your heart leads you in the morn," Moezell offered.

"That doesn't seem like much help." Kayla pouted, retreating once again into self-induced melancholy.

Moezell stepped forward and stroked Kayla's long red hair. "Always so quick to judge." She shook her head, frustrated. "Surely, you can wait to see what the morrow will bring."

"I hope 'twill nae bring another stranger such as Daniel Ellers. He ruined my whole day." Kayla spoke her mind without censor. She immediately felt the faerie's displeasure wash over her, but she'd been unable to stop her judgmental words.

Moezell walked back to the center of the room, her gentle glow not nearly as bright as when she had arrived. "Tsk, tsk, little one, be careful what ye wish for. Faeries are listening." Moezell blew her cousin a kiss and stepped through the veil, returning to the unseen realm.

Kayla blinked and found herself staring at the empty space where Moezell had just stood. *Amazing,* she thought. The faerie's visit was an amazing ending to an already exceedingly strange day.

Although Kayla considered everything Moezell had told her as she prepared for bed, she felt as if she were no closer to knowing what to do about Arlin and her pending betrothal than when the day had started. The faerie had told her to sleep on it, but she didn't know how she would sleep with all these thoughts whirling about in her head.

CHAPTER 7

The day had been long, the night short. Daniel woke the next morning with wisps of a dream lingering at the edge of his mind. He was a knight, on a white steed, pursuing a quest. Surrounded by mists and dense green forests, he felt lost, as if unsure of what he were searching for. A woman wearing a long, pale blue robe with silver-blond hair and stunning ice-blue eyes appeared. She had a surreal presence, much like an angel. Her ethereal movements mesmerized him as she approached then handed him something. It looked like a map, but he couldn't read it. In a faraway voice, she gave him instructions, saying, "Seek and ye shall find, and when ye find, ye shall know her name." Then the angel disappeared, and he was thrown from his horse, unable to proceed, still surrounded by mists.

Breaking through the veil of slumber, he blinked several times, rubbing the sleep from his eyes. *Darn dreams*, he thought. *They never make any sense.*

He stretched and lingered a moment longer in bed, appreciating how well he had slept. Of course, he had been dog-tired when he fell into bed, and somewhat less than sober. Thankfully, the mattress he slept on was surprisingly comfortable, better than he had expected.

With the morning light filtering in through the window, he was able to get a better look at the chamber in which he slept. The bed was wide but barely long enough to hold his six-foot-three-inch body. Large wooden posts rose from each corner, supporting rods holding heavy wool drapes pushed back toward the posts. He wished he had noticed them the night before. They would have kept out the morning sun and kept in some warmth. Feeling the cold draft seeping in through the one window located in the chamber's thick stone walls, he shivered. It held no glass, only a wooden shutter, which he had also failed to close. Obviously, he was still in the thirteenth century.

Daniel's first thoughts were of Kayla, the angel of mercy who had found him and brought him to Scorrybreac. Just the thought of her heavenly face made his cock hard. He imagined her greeting him with the dawn, as she had the previous day down by the river. It made for a most pleasant daydream while he rubbed his swollen boner.

A single vigorous knock on the door announced Rory's entrance only a second before the MacNicol brother entered the chamber.

"Do ye plan to laze the day away? Michael is expecting ye in the lists for training, or have ye forgotten?" He tossed a bundle of clothing down on the chest at the foot of the bed. "These are for ye."

"I haven't forgotten. He said it was after breakfast." Daniel hastened to sit up, resting his back against the headboard, grateful for the cover the wool blankets provided while his daydream quickly deflated.

"The morning meal is already being served in the great hall. Ye best hurry. Soon the servants will be eating, and I can assure ye, when they are done, there will be nothing left," Rory informed him with a mocking grin.

Daniel picked through the clothes Rory had deposited at the foot of the bed. He found a serviceable pair of drawstring pants made of rough linen and pulled them on. Fumbling around, he found his socks and riding boots. Lacing up his boots, he noticed Rory eyeing them with a curious look. "What?" Daniel asked.

"Nothing." Rory shrugged. "'Tis that Teressa had boots similar to yours. She was quite fond of them."

"That sounds like my sister. She has a thing for comfortable shoes." Daniel stood, ready to head out to breakfast, wishing he had a toothbrush.

On their way to the great hall, Daniel spied Kayla heading out of the keep on her way to the stables. "Hey, give me a minute, will ya? I'll be right back." Daniel clapped Rory on his shoulder.

"Ye're going to miss breakfast," Rory warned.

"Don't worry about me. I'll find something," Daniel yelled back. He was already halfway across the courtyard.

Rory shook his head at Daniel's impulsive actions and headed off to the lists, leaving Daniel to fend for himself.

"Hey, Kayla," Daniel called out as he jogged over to catch up with her. "Can I speak to you for a minute?"

Kayla glanced over her shoulder but continued walking toward the stables.

"Kayla," Daniel called her name again, coming up beside her, "I wanted to thank you."

She finally stopped and turned to face him, but she wasn't smiling. In fact, judging by her frown, she looked a little annoyed.

"Thank me for what?" she asked, curtly.

Daniel maintained his friendly smile, hoping to win her over. "For everything. For being the one who found me. For bringing me to Scorrybreac. But mostly, for being my angel of mercy." His eyes feasted on the beauty of her face. Her unruly mass of autumn-red curls was once again pulled back into its thick braid. Golden specks of color sprinkled throughout her dusty-green eyes sparkled in the early morning sunlight. She was dessert for his hungry gaze.

"Yer angel of mercy?" she asked, clearly curious.

"Yesterday, when I opened my eyes and saw your face, I thought I was in heaven seeing an angel."

For a moment, an unguarded smile lit her face. She was flattered, he could tell. In another instant, the smile faded, and she struck a pose of grim determination, lifting her chin and drawing her back a bit straighter. "Ye have nae need to thank me. Anyone passing by would have offered ye help."

"Maybe so," he shrugged. "But it wasn't anyone else." He lowered his voice to a husky whisper as he spoke, causing her to lean forward to hear. "It was you. And I'm grateful."

Pulling back, she anxiously looked away, searching the training field across the way. "Are ye nae expected to train with Michael this morn?"

"I'll get there." He shrugged. Being a guest, he hoped the MacNicol brothers would cut him some slack. He figured Michael wouldn't be happy, but maybe his delay wouldn't be too harshly criticized. Even if it were, worse things could happen, like missing this chance to speak with Kayla, alone.

"Are you going riding again today?" He motioned toward the stables.

"Why do ye ask?"

"I was hoping I could join you, sometime, I mean, if that's all right with you." He hoped he didn't sound like a complete idiot. He had no idea how to go about asking a woman in the thirteenth century out for a date.

"Mayhap later, but nae now. I'm busy." Looking delightfully flustered, she paused then added, "Ye best go. My brothers will be waiting." She waved her hand off toward the lists.

"Okay, later then." He wanted to kiss her, to take a long, slow taste of her. She looked so cute standing there trying hard to present a face of cold indifference, but he detected more than a hint of interest from her. Yes, a full-blown kiss would be nice right about now, with her sweet pink lips looking so ripe for the picking. He would take her breath away; of that, he was sure. From the look in her eyes, he figured such a move would be too much, and certainly too soon. Instead, he leaned in and gave her a brief brush of his lips upon her cheek, no more than a peck. Then, he turned to head off toward the keep.

His casual kiss must have taken her by surprise. He watched over his shoulder as she stood there a long moment, her mouth gaping, before calling out, "Where are ye going?"

"To the dining hall. I haven't had any breakfast." He stopped and turned to look at her.

"The cooks have stopped serving. There will be nothing left." She took a deep breath, shaking her head in disgust. "My word, I canna let ye starve," she mumbled under her breath. "Are ye always this helpless?" she grumbled louder.

She started after him and grabbed his hand, as if he were a wayward child. "Come with me. We'll find Bonnie. She will find something for ye, but doona expect much."

Daniel smiled a silly grin as he allowed himself to be led away by Kayla.

~~~

Kayla had planned to ride out to the hills to speak with Fern. Her restless night had failed to produce a solution to her dilemma, and she was hoping to gain some much needed advice from her married friend. For the second day in a row, Kayla had failed to reach her intended destination, and once again, she had Daniel Ellers to thank for her futile attempt.

He had delayed her departure before she had even reached the stables, stopping her so he could thank her for her valiant rescue. As if that wasn't enough, he had been so bold as to call her his angel of mercy. Reluctantly, she had to admit, she appreciated the acknowledgement.

When she realized he was going to miss his morning meal, after his declaration of gratitude for her assistance, the least she could do was to escort him to the kitchens. She was certain he would go hungry without her help, especially if he approached the kitchens alone. Milly did not take kindly to strangers showing up at her door asking to be served after a meal had ended. As head cook of the keep, Milly was already hard at work preparing for the midday meal, and morning leftovers were rare.

With Bonnie's help, Kayla grabbed a hunk of bread and some oatcakes just before the stable hands were set to finish them off. Those young boys were like bottomless pits and would lick the serving bowls dry if Milly let them. Thankfully, she did not.

"Here." Kayla directed Daniel to take a seat at the kitchen table where she placed the half full platter of food. "Sit at this table, and stay out of Milly's way, or she'll skin ye alive and serve ye for the evening meal."

Daniel complied, smiling at her display of frustration, which only served to irritate her more, though she tried to remain in control.

"I'm mighty grateful, and I'm sorry to take you away from your duties. I hope you know, you don't have to go to any trouble," Daniel said. That was an unlikely story. His seductive grin only served to contradict his polite words.

"Yea, I must, unless ye wish to be sent away hungry," Kayla disagreed with him.

"If it's not too much trouble, can I get a cup of coffee?" he asked.

"What is *coffee*?"

"It's a hot drink made from roasted ground coffee beans. I like it strong and dark. Plus, it's a great way to kick-start your morning, or relieve the effects of a hangover. Don't you have anything like that?" he asked, still maintaining his silly grin and innocent puppy-dog eyes.

My word, how that man can grin, she thought.

She eyed him with bewilderment, trying to think of a suitable substitute. Why he persisted in frustrating her, and why she was trying to please him, she wasn't sure. More disgusted with herself than with him, she shook her head.

"I can brew a hot drink made from a mixture of dried herbs. Mayhap it will suffice. 'Tis used to relieve nervous stomachs and ale-induced headaches," she offered, her voice sounding much kinder than she felt.

"Sounds good to me. Certainly worth a try."

Rummaging loudly through her selection of jars stored in a cool corner of the pantry, she finally found the selected blend of herbs she had in mind. She mixed the herbs into a pot of hot water, and a comforting fragrance filled the room. The mere scent of it helped settle her nerves. After the herbs had steeped long enough, she poured the brew into a mug and set it in front of Daniel.

"Thank you kindly, ma'am," he said before taking a tentative sip of the hot drink. "Ah, now that's good." He gave her a blissful smile. His short dark brown hair looked as though he had done no more than run his fingers through it to get it off his face, and the dark shadow of stubble gracing his jaw was handsomely appealing. She didn't like it one bit.

Though Kayla tried to bear in mind her feelings of resentment toward Daniel, a nervous fluttering ran rampant through her body. The sooner she was rid of him, the sooner she could regain control of her senses. It was unusual for her to feel this flustered, and she didn't like it. Turning, she started to walk away.

"Won't you join me?" he asked. "It's not right for a man to eat alone." He looked up at her, all sweet-faced and innocent.

She didn't buy it for a moment, but that darn smile of his was so charming, and he had an interesting way of speaking. Alarm bells sounded in her brain, and the nervous flutter she'd been feeling suddenly condensed, taking up residence in her belly. Determined to overcome the uneasy sensation, she poured another mug of the steaming hot brew and sat down across from him. Hopefully, the soothing drink would help calm her stomach.

When he lingered over the meal, Kayla was a wee bit surprised. Instead of gulping down the food, as she expected, he ate slowly, displaying unusually nice table manners, like chewing with his mouth closed. Not at all barbaric. He didn't appear to be in much of a hurry to reach the lists for his scheduled training with Michael, either. Instead, he took time to politely engage her in a pleasant conversation, asking one question after another as he ate the oatcakes and bread, washing them down with the hot herbal brew.

"If you don't mind my asking, where did you learn the recipe for this tea?" he asked.

"Tea?" she repeated, unfamiliar with the term.

"This brew," he said, lifting the mug. "I don't know what you call it, but I'd call it herbal tea."

"From my mother. Since I was a child, she has schooled me in the healing arts. 'Tis a legacy all MacNicol women share."

"I'm impressed. It hits the spot. When I stopped you, you were on your way to the stables. Were you planning to take a ride?"

"Aye, I was planning to visit my friend Fern. She's married, with a wee bairn. I thought the visit would do me good." She didn't know why she was explaining this all to him. She glanced over at Bonnie, who was cutting up chunks of vegetables for the midday meal. The serving woman seemed to be thoroughly enjoying Kayla's discomfort.

"Do you usually like to ride in the morning?" He seemed genuinely interested.

"Aye. I've always enjoyed the morning and watching the sunrise."

"Ah, a morning person. It suits you." Again he flashed her that darn smile, as though he knew something he wasn't saying.

"I've always liked sunrises better than sunsets. Sunsets are beautiful to behold, if ye have the time to sit for a spell, but there's nothing grander than the breaking dawn of each new

day. Sunrises are more cheerful, more hopeful than sunsets."
She wondered why she was babbling on like a foolish girl.

"I never thought of it that way, but now that you mention
it, yeah, I'd have to agree." He looked at her as if she had just
said the most amazing thing he had ever heard. She felt the color
rise in her cheeks.

This foreigner had a talent for gathering information, she
noted, pouring on his charm and getting her to drop her well-
developed defenses. Something in his manner made it all too
easy to relax around him. She found herself telling him far more
about herself than she had expected. He merely needed to ask
her something, in his well-mannered and charming way, and
she would answer, as if she had nothing better to do, which
simply wasn't true.

Seeing that he was almost finished with his meal, she
rushed him along. "Ye best be heading out to the lists. Michael
will be waiting."

"You're right. But you can't blame a fellow for wanting to
enjoy the company of a charming woman." He chugged down
the last of his brew, then glanced over at Bonnie and gave her a
wink. Bonnie nodded in return. Kayla felt a tinge of jealousy, as
if they were sharing a silent communication to which she wasn't
privy. The feeling churned in her stomach.

After Daniel finished his meager meal, he bid her farewell
and headed out to the lists, and Kayla breathed a sigh of relief.

"He's a right fine young man, is he nae?" Bonnie offered her
unsolicited opinion.

"He's a visitor to our keep and deserving of our hospitality.
Nothing more," Kayla replied in a huff. She was in no mood to
explain herself to her serving woman.

"I'm just saying . . ." Bonnie began.

"There's no need for ye to say anything," Kayla interrupted her. She refused to engage in such talk with Bonnie, even though she was her oldest and dearest servant. It wasn't right, and she was too flustered to discuss the matter further.

Bonnie held her thoughts, but the smile on her face was spread a mile long. Kayla ignored her, turning her focus on cleaning up after Daniel before she headed back to the stables.

~*~

"I see ye have decided to grace us with yer presence after all," Michael chided Daniel as he approached the training field. "I was beginning to think ye had decided to back out on the training."

"No, not at all. I just got a little delayed. I'm new here, remember? I'm still learning my way around." Daniel had willingly indulged in the opportunity to enjoy Kayla's hospitality before he finally managed to keep his appointment with Michael. Besides the benefit of being pampered by Kayla, his delay had provided the additional advantage of being able to observe the training already in progress as he made his way to the lists.

The men training under Michael's direction were engaged in swordplay, wielding heavy-ass swords as though they were mere extensions of their arms, which for a true Scottish warrior was probably a fairly accurate description. Daniel knew his lack of experience would make him no match for these men. They'd easily have him cut to ribbons and tied in a bow before he could get his game on.

Eyeing the layout of the lists, he saw the stockpile of weapons located at the outer edge of the training field. A bundle of fighting staffs stood among the various blades and bows ready for the warriors' use. He ambled over and picked up one of the long rods, checking its feel and balance. It felt good in his hand, he noted, and was well balanced at its center. Daniel estimated the poles to be nearly seven feet in length, much longer than the practice batons he was familiar with, but he figured he could easily compensate for the difference. These practice poles were blunt at both ends, whereas a real fighting weapon would be outfitted with a blade. Testing the pole, Daniel nodded his approval. The hand-hewn fighting staffs were well made.

Michael walked over and picked up one the staffs then swung it through the air with a whoosh of speed, barely concealing his snarky grin. His steel-blue eyes glared at Daniel. "Ready?" he asked.

Daniel rotated his arms a few times, stretched, and loosened the muscles in his neck with a few twists and turns of his head. He would have preferred time to warm up, but it seemed he had missed that opportunity unless he wanted to appear wimpy in front of these men, and that wasn't going to happen. "Yeah, I'm ready," he replied with confidence.

Michael led the way to a clear space in the lists. Duncan and Rory left their groups to watch the sparring match.

"Where's yer coin?" Rory asked his eldest brother.

Duncan raised a quizzical brow, grinning. "Daniel's unproven. I'll place my coin on Michael."

"I'll take yer bet, just to make it interesting." Rory returned his brother's grin.

Daniel knew he was in for trouble.

Michael and Daniel entered the training circle and faced off, each assuming a fighting stance. Their eyes burned with awareness of the other's slightest moves. Michael gave a sharp nod of his head, and they were off.

Thrusting and swinging their staffs, they each tested the other's defenses. Daniel held his skills in check, looking for the right opening to put them to use. For a while, he made a point of mimicking Michael's moves, testing his opponent's skills. Michael's brute force was greater than his talent, not that the warrior's stance or footwork was clumsy, just lacking skillful finesse. However, there was still much to be said for brute force. The two men circled and jabbed. With each thrust and counterthrust, their staffs clapped hard against the other. Daniel felt the vibrations of the forceful blows surge through the wooden pole, into his hands, and up his arms.

After a few minutes of well-matched effort, Michael faked a left swing, then charged forward, knocking Daniel backward. Daniel stumbled, struggling to hold his balance. He stepped back but lost his footing. Then, Michael swung the staff hard right, taking advantage of the stumble and sending Daniel reeling toward the hard-packed ground.

Duncan elbowed Rory in his ribs.

Drawing on the momentum of the fall, Daniel rolled on his back as he hit the ground and somersaulted away from Michael. At the end of the roll, he threw his legs up and quickly back down, springing to his feet. Michael didn't even have time to enjoy his momentary victory before Daniel recovered his footing. Using the staff for leverage, Daniel spiked the long rod into the ground, and twisted sideways to bring his feet up and out, delivering a staggering blow to Michael's chest. The quick action caught his opponent off guard and sent Michael stumbling backward, his arms flailing. Daniel swiftly brought the staff around to knock Michael's feet out from under him. Too quick for Michael to react, Daniel twirled the staff twirled in his hands and pointed it at Michael's chest as the man lay splayed upon the ground. The pressure he levied against Michael's chest was just enough to let him know Daniel had him well pinned.

Michael instinctively grabbed for the weapon to yank it aside, but Daniel forced the blunt end of the rod under his opponent's chin, allowing Michael to consider the possibility of a crushed esophagus before he released the pressure.

Anger, fueled by a bruised ego, flared in Michael's eyes as he let go of the staff.

Daniel smiled. Not a gloating smile of victory, but one of friendly admiration. He backed it up with a genuine tribute. "It was a good fight. You gave me quite a run for my money. Almost had me."

Michael raised his hands in surrender, accepting defeat.

Rory got the last elbow jab at his eldest brother.

Pulling the staff away, Daniel offered his hand to Michael. The fallen warrior reluctantly accepted Daniel's assistance, overcoming his deflated ego. Knowing it was in his best interest to keep the peace, Daniel pulled Michael into a friendly man hug, clapping him firmly on the back.

"It's good to see ye can hold yer own." Michael brushed the dust from his breeches. His comment fell shy of being an outright compliment.

"Beginner's luck, I'm sure." Daniel modestly accepted the conservative accolade.

"Would ye like to try yer luck again?"

"What I'd really like is for you to give me some training with those big-ass swords your men are using." Daniel's gaze was drawn in the direction of clanging swords coming from warriors training across the field.

"Claymores. Have ye nay experience with them? Ye claim to be a guard for yer people." Michael sounded surprised.

Mesmerized by the swordplay he was watching, Daniel answered without thinking, "Nope, can't say I do. We don't have much use for them where I come from." As soon as he spoke the words, he realized his error.

"Where exactly do ye come from?" Michael's interest was piqued.

Daniel pulled his focus back to the men surrounding him. Duncan and Rory looked at him with blank expressions. He was on his own with this one. "A land far, far away across the sea called America. Have you ever heard of it?" The best defense was usually a good offense, and turning the question back on Michael gave him time to recover from his fumble.

Michael looked stumped. "I have nay knowledge of such a place." He turned to his brothers. "Do ye know of this America?"

Duncan and Rory shook their heads.

"Canna say that I do," Duncan replied.

"Must be a wee small place," said Michael.

Daniel jumped in to retrieve the ball. "Let's just say we do things differently there. So, are you going to give me training with your claymores or not?" He shot Michael a look of defiance.

Michael took up the challenge. "Aye, let's see what ye've got."

Daniel grinned with relief and anticipation. He felt he had handled the situation well enough. There had been a moment when he thought Michael was going to get the best of him in the sparring match. Luckily, he had pulled off the final blow that landed the aggressive warrior on his back. It was shaping up to be a good day. Being misplaced in time, it seemed, presented all sorts of unexpected challenges, and for the moment, he was finding the experience much to his liking.

~*~

As Kayla made her way across the courtyard, she found herself slowing to watch the sparring match between Daniel and Michael. She told herself she was only going to watch for a moment. It would be interesting to see his fighting technique, especially since he came from someplace strange and far away. Then she absolutely, positively had to be on her way. She needed to speak with Fern.

But as she watched him spar with Michael, she got caught up in the moment; the man had powerful skills. She gasped when Michael got the upper hand and knocked Daniel off his feet, and she had very nearly cheered when Daniel quickly recovered to end the match with Michael pinned to the ground by the end of his staff.

Silently, she berated herself for her reaction. A wave of embarrassment washed over her as she realized she was standing in the middle of the courtyard gaping at the men as they trained. Hurrying along to the shadow of the stables, she tried to collect her wits, hoping she hadn't been noticed.

Such a show of emotion made Kayla question her loyalties. Why would she cheer the victory of a man she hardly knew over her dear brother? She'd been determined not to like the man, and yet she found it hard to focus on her resentment.

Just as she was about to leave her hiding space and head into the stables, she was distracted by the sight of Daniel taking his claymore training from Michael. From the way he held the weapon, she could tell he was a novice, and yet he took to the training with impressive zeal, quickly gaining skill under Michael's expert tutorage.

It took a call from Bonnie to finally pull her away from watching him. She came to inform her Lady Lydia wanted Kayla to accompany her on a trip to the village to tend a sick child. Apparently, Kayla's plan to visit Fern would have to wait yet another day. It were as if the fates were conspiring against her.

~*~

Training with Michael was grueling. The man was your typical fair-but-tough taskmaster, and Daniel couldn't remember the last time he had worked so hard or enjoyed himself more. By the time they reached a break in the training, the only thing demanding more attention than his hunger were the aching muscles developing in his arms and shoulders. A few hours of swinging a five-pound claymore added up to weary bones for an out-of-place citified cop like him.

He joined the MacNicol brothers and their warriors in the great hall for a hearty meal of mutton stew sopped up with crusty bread. After their break, Michael and Rory were called away to deal with a broken door in the barracks. According to Rory, one of the guards had gotten a wee bit too drunk the night before and had used his foot to open the door to his room instead of the latch. Michael needed to take disciplinary action in the matter, and Rory went along for support, leaving Daniel to wander on his own.

Having some time on his hands, he was hoping to find Kayla and convince her to act as a tour guide to show him around the castle. The idea was vastly appealing and full of merit. Besides providing an opportunity to explore the ancient compound, it held the possibility of having time alone with his little angel.

Standing outside the large stone keep, considering where to start his search, he spied Bonnie, the woman in charge of the serving staff. She was heading toward the building that housed the kitchens. He figured she would know where Kayla could be found.

Bonnie struck him as a woman who knew her way around the castle and the people who lived there. Maybe, if he got her talking, she would tell him more about Lady Lydia. From what he had read in Teressa's journal, he figured Lady Lydia knew a whole lot more about his time travel adventure than she was saying.

Rushing after her, he hoped to catch up with Bonnie before she disappeared into the confines of the kitchens. His experience with people who worked on the streets of San Francisco had taught him acknowledgement of a person's services went a long way toward opening doors of goodwill. Unintentionally, but to his great fortune, it had been his gratitude expressed to Kayla earlier that morning that had secured him the meager leftovers from breakfast.

"Bonnie," he called out. "I wanted to thank you for getting me breakfast this morning. I don't know what I would have done without your help." He greeted her with his usual friendly smile.

"Oh goodness, sir, nay thanks are needed. I was only doing my job, as Kayla asked. I could nae disappoint my mistress. 'Tis Kayla ye must thank. Ye should be glad she has made ye a friend. She's a good one to have on yer side," Bonnie gushed, returning his friendly smile with one of her own.

"Speaking of Kayla, do you happen to know where she is? I haven't seen her since breakfast." That wasn't completely truthful. He had caught a glimpse of her as she stood near the stables watching the field training. Since it was apparent she was trying to conceal her observation, he kept that particular piece of information to himself. Not letting people know you knew something they didn't want you to know was usually a good idea. He was flattered when he noticed her watching his training session, apparently forgoing her morning ride.

"The young mistress and her mother were called away to the village to see a wee bairn down with a cough. Poor little lad. They took some of Lady Lydia's herbs over to his mother and will do a healing for his chest. With their help, he'll be right as the sunrise by the morrow. 'Tis a blessing they are to provide such healing to our village folk."

Daniel noted the head servant of the keep was not one to hold back her thoughts. She was well on her way to middle age and had a well-rounded motherly look about her. She seemed the type who would have served the MacNicol boys milk and cookies when they were younger and encouraged them to laugh away their hurts. Chestnut brown hair streaked with grey haloed a cheerful face blessed with merry chocolate brown eyes and a constant warm smile.

"You speak well of Lady Lydia and Kayla. Have you known them long?" He fell in step beside Bonnie as she continued to the kitchens, not wanting to hold her back from her work while he attempted to pick her brain.

"Only all my life. I was born here in this keep. Raised to work for the clan chief and his family like my dear mother afore me, I am proud to say. I also have an elder sister, Anna, who lives in the village. She takes on the sewing, mending, and such; she's real fine with a needle and thread. Nae something I ever took a liking to. I'd rather wash a floor or clean a chamber than sit still with needle and thread, but my sister has a real talent for the work. It may nae be as fine as the needlework Lady Lydia does, but few can match our mistress. If ye were to see her fancy work, I believe ye would be mighty impressed, even if ye are a man. I believe ye appreciate the finer things in life, if I am nae mistaken, and I rarely am."

Nodding obligingly, Daniel tried to keep up with Bonnie's running commentary; she was a powerhouse of opinions.

The head servant's attention was momentarily diverted to one of the many young boys working in the kitchens. "Make sure ye scrub them pots clean. Milly will throw a fit if ye give her a dirty pot for her soup." She bent to pick up a large basket of vegetables set just inside the kitchen door.

"Here, let me help you with that." Daniel reached out to help carry the large basket and move it over to the large plank table where food was prepared.

Bonnie nearly blushed at his offered assistance. "There's nay need for ye to be here working in the kitchens. This is women's work, and we've plenty of young lads to help. Shouldn't ye be off training with the MacNicol brothers?" Even as she spoke, she accepted his assistance, letting him move the heavy basket for her.

"Michael and Rory are busy dealing with a drunken guard, and I've no idea where Duncan has gone. Besides, where I come from, it's not unusual for men to work in the kitchens. Some of our best-known chefs are men. I'm just trying to help where I can, earn my keep, so to speak. I don't see this as women's work, just something that needs to get done, so we can all eat. And Lord knows how I like to eat." He flashed her a winning smile. "I've spent all morning with the MacNicol brothers. I'm finding the pleasure of your company to be far more enjoyable."

Bonnie cast a skeptical eye at him. Though she might appear simple, Daniel knew she was no fool. Quite aware she knew better than to believe a young guy like him was hanging at her skirts because he found her attractive, he figured she'd have no reservations about putting him to work, since he was offering his services.

"Well, ye are here, so mayhap ye can help me get these vegetables cleaned and sorted for Milly. And while we're at it, ye can tell me about yer travels. What brings ye to Scorrybreac." Bonnie's perpetual smile never left her face as she engaged in the friendly exchanging of gossip.

Daniel's appreciation of her company only deepened. Story swapping with Bonnie would definitely be a pleasant diversion. He began dunking and washing the fresh-picked vegetables. A basin of water had already been set up on the sturdy prep table that dominated the large well-kept kitchens. Racks holding an array of pots and pans lined the walls. The large open-face fireplace and built-in brick ovens had been fired up since before sunrise and would burn until well into the evening hours doing service for the cook and her staff. Baskets of food had been brought up from the cold storage cellar, waiting for Milly's cooking talents to turn it all into tasty dishes for the MacNicol clan's evening meal.

"You could say I'm here at my sister's request. She was so impressed with Skye after her visit here, she wanted me to see Scorrybreac for myself. She spoke highly of you. Said you were a big help to her during her visit."

Bonnie shined under the unexpected compliment. "Yer sister made a big impression here, as well. 'Twas her matchmaking skills that brought Duncan and Janet together again after their broken betrothal. Cut right through all the bluster and pride of those two young folks like a hot knife in fresh churned butter, she did. But her leaving left Rory with a broken heart. Is she nae expected to return? We've heard nothing from her since her sudden disappearance some years ago."

Daniel did his best to answer truthfully as he evaded Bonnie's search for answers he couldn't provide. "I'm fairly certain Rory will see Teressa again someday. It's just hard to say when." Especially considering, according to Teressa's journal, their reunion wouldn't happen for another seven hundred years. "But I'm certain Teressa shares Rory's feelings."

"Och, 'tis glad I am to be hearing such news. I want nothing but the best for my lad, Rory, and if he thinks Teressa is what's best, then so be it."

Now it was his turn to dig for some dirt. "Didn't Lady Lydia have something to do with Duncan and Janet's reunion? I understand she was rather keen on them getting back together."

"Aye, Lady Lydia always hoped Duncan would fulfill his duty as chief by joining the two clans through marriage. Those two young folks had been expected to marry since they were wee bairns. When Duncan sent Janet away, it was a great disappointment for Lady Lydia. For certain, she knew she could nae challenge Duncan's choice. She could nae go against her own son and the chief of the clan. I believe she was waiting for the right opportunity to present itself." Bonnie moved the washed vegetables onto a clean basket lined with a drying cloth, ready for the kitchen lads to slice and dice under Milly's direction.

"And the right opportunity included Teressa?" Daniel wiped his hands on the drying towel Bonnie offered to him.

"'Twould seem so. 'Twas mighty convenient for a skilled matchmaker to show up just afore the Gathering at the Isle Faire, especially since 'twas the first time in years Lady Janet had been there. I believe Lady Lydia was right pleased to get those two together in such a quick fashion."

Yes, very convenient, Daniel thought, since he knew Lady Lydia, with the help of Moezell, had been instrumental in bringing Teressa to Skye at exactly the right time. Hoping to gain further insight into some other information that might be useful, Daniel gently guided the conversation along a different path. "Teressa mentioned something about legends of faeries and a great-grandmother of the MacNicol clan. Do you know anything about that?"

"Aye, 'tis true. The legend tells of the beautiful Sophie appearing from the morning mists to find Herrick, of the MacNicol clan. He was weary and wounded from battle, making his way back home. Sophie tended his wounds and restored him to health with loving care. 'Tis said her healing powers came directly from the faeries." Bonnie gazed off to some distant point, as though playing out the vision in her mind's eye.

"You mean her healing power? Didn't Kayla say they were passed from mother to daughter?"

"Aye, 'tis the same. Lady Lydia learned from her mother, who learned from her mother, who learned from her mother all the way back to Sophie. Now she passes the knowledge on to Kayla. 'Tis a gift they have, these daughters of Sophie."

"I wonder what other powers the faeries have passed along." Daniel watched Bonnie, evaluating her reaction, hoping she'd be caught off guard by his nonchalant question.

"The MacNicol women are blessed by the fae, 'tis true. Why, they only need ask, and the faeries . . ." Bonnie halted her words in midsentence and directed her focus back to Daniel with narrowed eyes. She must have sensed his desire for confidential information and realized she needed to be more cautious around him. "Och, ye only need look at the bounty of the MacNicol keep to know the fates have smiled well upon this clan."

Milly walked in on the tail end of Bonnie's comment. She was followed by a boy carrying a basket of preserved meats they had retrieved from the smokehouse. "Aye, the fates have smiled upon these MacNicols, but if we doona have the evening meal prepared on time, I doubt anyone will be smiling. Now off with ye, lad. I have nay place for ye in my kitchen." She waved a weathered old hand at Daniel, shooing him from the prep table, where she deposited the heavy load. "A busy kitchen is nay place for a lazy warrior." Without missing a beat, she reached

101

for her large meat cleaver, wielding the knife with well-honed precision. She cut into the raw meat with an amazing show of force for a woman of her age. Her hands, though aged from the daily chores of cooking, still held the strength of a younger maid.

Quickly stepping away from the prep table, and safely beyond the reach of Milly's blade, Daniel acknowledged it was time for him to go. He took his leave, wishing the kitchen servants well as they prepared the evening meal. Stepping out into the sunlit courtyard, he whistled a happy tune and headed back to the lists to finish out the day of training.

CHAPTER 8

Kayla and her mother approached a simple cottage at the far end of the lane where a sick boy awaited their care. The cottage was one of the smaller ones in the village, and yet it housed a rather large family with seven children, last time she counted. One of the younger boys was down with a deep cough in his chest. Their biggest fear was the ailment would spread to the rest of the family in the tightly cramped quarters and rob them of the many hands needed to work their land.

Lady Lydia knocked on the battered wood door. For a moment, it looked as though the door were swinging open on its own accord until Kayla saw a wee lass peeking through the opening. Her face and hands were clean, but her hair was uncombed, and her grey tunic was patched and dirty. The lass bid them enter.

Kayla fought the urge to draw back from the odor escaping through the open cottage door. Smoke from the peat fire mixed with the smell of cooking and human sweat to create an unpleasant result. It was hard to evade the concentrated stench produced by so many bodies living so close together. The effect gave her pause to appreciate the airiness of her home in the large keep. A glance at her mother showed she was less inclined to hide her reaction, as Lady Lydia drew her headscarf across her nose and mouth.

Following her mother, Kayla ducked through the entrance and stepped into the main room of the cottage. It was dark and musty with all the shutters of the windows closed up tight. The young girl was about to shut the door behind them when Lady Lydia stopped her.

"Leave it open, child. We need the air and light."

The mistress of the cottage stepped forward. "My lady, thank ye for coming to me humble home. My lad is ill. Is it nae better to keep the chill in the air from reaching him?" she asked. She was respectful, but Kayla could see her first priority was her son.

"Nay. This stale air is far harder on him than a fresh cool breeze. Open the doors and windows. Let the air flow through," Lydia ordered.

The mother complied, doing as Lady Lydia instructed. As her eyes became accustomed to the dimness of the room, Kayla could see the young boy huddled on a thin straw pallet near the rear of the room, his body clenched against another hacking cough. She glanced at her mother, who was still standing near the open door. Lydia motioned her forward. Kneeling next to the boy, Kayla took to her task.

His one wool blanket was thin and barely covered his little body. Kayla pulled her wool cloak off her shoulders and draped it over the boy. He looked up at her in gratitude with eyes too large and fearful for one so young.

Kayla placed the palm of her one hand across his forehead. With the other, she reached beneath his covers and lightly pressed his chest. She could feel the rattle as he struggled to breathe. With an encouraging smile, she assured him, "Ye will be well, lad. Ye must believe."

He nodded, indicating his trust.

She turned to address the boy's mother. "I need a bowl of fresh water, and a clean washcloth."

"I can manage the fresh water; we've a rain barrel out back, but I will be hard-pressed to produce a clean scrap o'cloth."

"The water will do fine." Kayla pulled off her headscarf, bit at the edge, and tore the linen fabric in two.

The mother placed a bowl of water next to her.

Kayla dipped a piece of the linen into the water and began washing the young boy's face and hands, cleaning off the spittle left behind by his coughing. After rinsing out the scrap of fabric, she folded it and placed it on his forehead, allowing it to cover his eyes. She felt him relax as he closed his eyes under the cool weight of the cloth.

Seeing she had calmed the boy, she brought her hands near her face, blew on her palms, and then rubbed her hands together, reinforcing the energy held within. Then she placed both hands on the boy's chest, one near his throat and the other over his heart. She closed her eyes and let the healing warmth seep through her fingers.

At first, his breathing remained shallow and raspy, but as she continued to send her healing energy to his weakened body, she began to feel the results. His breathing became deeper, more relaxed, and the fluid-filled rattle abated.

She sat with him for nearly half an hour before she felt the treatment was complete. During the course of the treatment, her energy had drained as she felt his return.

Sitting back on her haunches, she brought her awareness back to the room. Kayla looked up and saw the boy's mother standing over her. Apparently, she had stood watch over her son the whole time. The open windows and door had helped clear out the stale air, blowing out the sour scents and replacing them with a fresh ocean breeze. The temperature of the cottage was invigorating, but not cold enough to cause her to worry.

"Ye may close the shutters in the eve afore the sun sets, but allow them to remain open throughout the sunny time of day. He will still need a day or two of rest, but soon yer bairn will be well," Kayla addressed the mother.

"Have him drink this brew several times a day 'til he regains his strength," Lydia said, indicating a kettle of herbal brew she had prepared while Kayla had tended the child.

"I canna thank you enough," the mother said.

"Yer healthy lad will be thanks enough," Lydia assured her. She turned toward the door, looking relieved to be leaving the cottage.

Feeling drained, Kayla walked beside her mother in silence as they returned from their work in the village. She had spent a good deal of energy tending to the sick lad, and the effort had worn her out. It was always this way, giving her gift took a toll on her strength, but it would not last. Besides, her weariness was a small price to pay to provide healing to a young lad who otherwise may not have survived.

Weary as she was, her mind churned with thoughts from her late-night conversation with Moezell. Why hadn't her mother told her about her connection to the fae? What was she trying to hide? Had she hoped Kayla was unaware of her fae blood?

Possibly due to her fatigue, or maybe it was her distracting thoughts, she stepped into a deep rut as she walked along the rocky pathway and twisted her ankle. Her mother reached out to grab her before she fell, but the damage was done. Soon her injured foot began to throb, but she shoved her irritation at her misstep aside and focused once more on her mother's incomprehensible and vexing decision to keep her true lineage from her.

Unable to stand the nagging disappointment a moment longer, and too exhausted to care what Lydia might think, she gathered her courage and confronted her mother.

"I had a rather unexpected visitor in my chamber last night," Kayla began.

"Ye did?" From the look of shock on her mother's face, Kayla wondered if she had someone particular in mind.

"Aye, my cousin, Moezell. I believe ye know her."

Lady Lydia's expression changed from shock to one of apprehension. Apparently, Kayla's revelation was not what her mother had expected.

"Why have ye nae told me about our connection to the fae?" Kayla asked.

"'Tis nae a simple thing," Lydia said, sounding defensive. "I have been preparing ye, awaiting the right time to reveal such knowledge. For years, I have been training ye in the healing arts. They are a significant gift of our heritage."

"And I'm grateful, but that's nae what I mean." Kayla was limping and wished she could reach out to her mother for support, but she chose to ignore the pain as best she could.

"Have I nae told you the stories of the fae and our great-grandmother Sophie?"

"Mother, I am twenty. When were ye thinking ye should tell me *I'm* part fae? Did ye plan to wait 'til I'm married and have children of my own? Moezell told me this is something I should have been told years ago."

"Aye, well, Moezell. Apparently, she has started doing things on her own now. She did not consult me on this matter," Lydia huffed.

"Why should she consult ye?"

Lydia looked away before answering. "She should respect my position as her elder cousin and the matriarch of this clan."

"What about yer respect for me, yer daughter? Have ye nay consideration for my feelings in this matter? Why must my fae cousin be the one to tell me what ye have always known?" Disappointment over her mother's lack of respect for her feelings surged through Kayla.

"I have been preparing ye for the right time. Obviously, Moezell and I disagree on when that time should be." Haughty as always, Lady Lydia continued to defend her position.

"In this matter, I believe Moezell is right."

"So now ye ken. Does it make ye feel better to challenge yer mother? Is this what yer fae cousin has taught ye?"

Kayla felt the sting of her mother's words. "Ye could have told me sooner."

"What would it have changed? I have been teaching ye the healing arts. Look at how well ye preformed today. Knowing ye're half fey wouldna matter."

"Ye doona know that. Mayhap knowing I'm half fae would strengthen my gift. Make me a better healer." Kayla stiffened her lip as she swallowed her pain.

"Aye, and mayhap such power would have helped ye find a husband." Lydia focused on the path before them, refusing to look at her daughter.

Kayla bit her lip, holding back her tears. Her mother could have slapped her in the face and it wouldn't have hurt any more. Pain and anger swept through her, but she held her tongue. Her deeply ingrained respect for her mother kept her from voicing her discontent further.

It willna always be this way. Someday, hopefully someday soon, when she was stronger, she would stand up for herself. She knew the day was coming.

Limping slightly from the increasing pain in her ankle, Kayla walked beside her mother in stiff, stony silence.

~*~

Daniel had spent hours testing out some of the fiercest weaponry available for ancient Scottish warfare. He rejected the battle-ax. It was too coarse and unmanageable for his taste. Though he was impressed by the quality of the smaller blades possessed by the MacNicol brothers, the dirks and daggers had limited uses. At the end of the day, it was the claymore that gave him the greatest satisfaction. There was something about the immense feeling of power that only the long broadsword could deliver.

Unfortunately, he was reluctant to admit a hard day of training with the strange weaponry had taken a toll on his body. Even though he considered himself in good physical condition, hours of wielding the heavy swords and sundry weapons had utilized a whole new set of muscles, and his taxed limbs were strongly voicing their dissent.

After being dismissed by Michael, a ruthless but admirable taskmaster, Daniel stopped at the nearest rain barrel he could find to wash the sweat and grime of training from his body. He headed back toward the keep, intent on climbing to his chamber for what he considered was a well-deserved rest before dinner. Though he could already feel the stiffness setting in, he took the extra effort to ensure nothing about his gait or posture revealed the tentacles of pain snaking their way through his body.

Nagging discomfort started at his shoulder blades and was now working its way toward his lower back.

As he approached the front of the courtyard, he spied Kayla and Lady Lydia returning to the keep. Choosing to ignore the rebellious cries of his muscles, he jogged to catch up with them. When he came closer, he noticed Kayla was limping slightly, favoring her right foot.

"Hey there," he called out to Kayla. "Are you alright?" To Lady Lydia he added, "Did your day in the village go well?"

"Good day, Daniel Ellers," Lady Lydia returned his greeting with formal politeness. "I believe our healing work will provide great comfort to the child and his mother."

Directing his gaze at Kayla, he noticed the pain reflected in her eyes. "Did you hurt your foot? I saw you limping."

"'Tis nothing. I stepped in a rut and turned my ankle. Some soothing salve and rest is all I need." Regardless of her words, Daniel heard the pain in her voice.

"Can I do anything to help?" he asked. Not waiting for her to respond, he reached out for her, wrapping his arm around her waist to help support her weight.

Lady Lydia took note of the bold gesture with a fair measure of disapproval. It was obvious she wasn't comfortable with Daniel's relaxed familiarity toward her daughter.

"Ye need nae bother over me. Some of Mother's salve and a bit of rest before the evening meal is all I need. I'm sure all will be well." Her steps were tentative as she continued walking, but at least she accepted his assistance.

Daniel didn't believe her. Her face bore the effect of her aches, belying her words. He tightened his grip, letting her know he wasn't about to let go. The look in Kayla's eyes went from shy reluctance to watchful curiosity. Finally, as if she had assured herself he wasn't going to bite, she shifted her weight and braced her arm against his shoulder.

"I have experience with muscle injuries; I've had plenty of my own. I'd be happy to massage your ankle for you," Daniel offered as they made their way toward the steps of the keep. He welcomed the opportunity to massage her feet or any other sensitive body part that needed tending and could already imagine starting at her ankles then working his way up from there.

"I'm perfectly capable of assisting my daughter." Lady Lydia stepped forward.

"No offense. I was merely offering to help." He quickly took stock of Lady Lydia's possessive disapproval. Pausing for only a moment, he looked for a way to turn the confrontation back to a cordial interaction in his favor. "You know, I have a bit of soreness developing in my shoulders. Not used to training with a claymore, I guess. Do you think I could get some of that salve for my back?" He rolled his shoulders as a sign of the discomfort he felt, hoping to gain some sympathy votes from Kayla's mother.

Lady Lydia's gaze darted between him and Kayla. "You may have a small portion of the salve, if need be, but that is all." Her curt answer left him with little doubt regarding her lack of sympathy for his alleged injury.

Daniel refused to be discouraged. He might be pushing the boundaries of Lady Lydia's tolerance, but he wouldn't back down. Ignoring the older woman, he turned to Kayla. "You said you're a student of the healing arts. Perhaps if I rub your ankle, you could massage my back." He held her gaze.

Kayla appeared stunned by his bold suggestion. She didn't speak. Her expressive eyes widened in dismay, but she didn't look away. A slight gasp escaped her lips before an appreciative smile settled in.

Lady Lydia was quicker to respond. "I am quite capable of assisting my daughter. She is not a servant girl to be waiting on you and your aches."

"Hey, don't misunderstand me." Daniel held up a hand in a gesture of peace. "It's not my intention to offend you, or your daughter. I just thought she'd be the best person for the job, being a healer and all."

Apparently, this was one battle he was going to lose. At best, he hoped to minimize his loss. It wouldn't do him any good to really piss off Kayla's mother, she seemed mad enough already. He could feel her animosity, and he had no intention of creating an outright enemy, especially since his sister had recorded she was part fae and able to communicate with this mysterious Moezell person. Daniel figured she was well aware he came from the future. Not only that, her demeanor suggested she hadn't been involved in summoning him back in time. She obviously wasn't pleased by his presence.

~~~

Kayla finally found her tongue, which for a moment had been lodged firmly between her teeth. "Mother, Daniel is right. I am quite able to see to his injuries." She lifted her chin a bit higher in a show of defiant determination.

"Ye are?" Lady Lydia looked amazed, obviously taken aback by her daughter's outspoken manner.

"I am!" Daniel's wide eyes focused on Kayla. No doubt, he was as surprised as her mother that she had taken his side.

"Aye. And I know Janet is expecting ye to visit with Amy. I'm confident Daniel's knowledge of muscle injuries will be sufficient to deal with my minor strain. If his skills are lacking, I am quite capable of directing his efforts."

Daniel and Lady Lydia took a moment to stare at Kayla, each displaying their individual response to her unexpected declaration. The anger in her mother's eyes showed her blatant displeasure over Kayla's sudden assertiveness, while Daniel struggled to conceal his obvious delight with his silly grin.

Acting quickly to take advantage of her mother's shocked silence, Kayla continued her instructions, "Daniel, if ye could assist me to my chamber, we can begin the healing treatments at once. I believe I have enough of the salve to serve both our needs."

"Ye will do nay such thing," Lady Lydia said.

"Why? 'Tis a reasonable solution. I'm tired and injured. Daniel has offered to ease my pain. As the clan healer, 'tis my duty to treat him." This time, Kayla was not backing down. Bolstered by the strength of Daniel's support, for the first time in her life, she was standing up to her mother, and it felt good. Scary, but good.

"Ye would have him treat you, alone, in your chamber?" Lady Lydia nearly screeched her protest. "That canna be allowed. 'Tis highly inappropriate."

"It seems far more appropriate than his chamber in the high tower. Or would ye rather we tend to our pains in the middle of the great hall for all to see?"

"I doona approve." Lady Lydia glared at Kayla.

"I doona ask for yer approval." Kayla returned her mother's stare.

Her mother's reaction didn't surprise her. She was well aware of the shocking implications of her suggested actions. At any other time, her mother's reaction would have been considered reasonable, even proper, but not this time. Not after all her mother had said, and hadn't told her regarding her fae heritage. This time, the tethering cord of compliance had been

113

stretched to its breaking point. Something snapped inside her. In a burst of confidence, boosted by Daniel's supportive presence, she willfully challenged her mother's controlling ways.

This was the first time someone outside of her family had offered to tend her pains, see to her needs, or show a real interest in her welfare. It was simply unacceptable for her mother to deny her that satisfaction. After all, it was only a healing. She did them all the time.

This is why she dinna tell me I'm part fae, Kayla thought, *and why she believes I will marry Arlin. It never occurs to her to ask what I want. 'Tis always what she thinks is best, always her way. Even the reunion of Duncan and Janet was as she wished. 'Twas merely good fortune Teressa was there to help them rekindle their love for each other.*

Never before had she questioned her family's requests, much less her mother's demands. She had taken comfort, even refuge in being their dutiful daughter and sister, shying away from confrontations with her family. Rather than face them alone in her struggle for independence, she had even thought to seek out her best friend Fern to request her assistance against the demands of the family. That was all about to change.

Kayla's sudden surge of defiance spurred a newfound appreciation for the strong and independent ways of Teressa Ellers, a woman she had once judged so harshly for those very traits. For the first time in her life, she tasted the sweet joy of self-determination. It made her hunger for more.

"I certainly hope ye know what ye're doing—and what ye are risking." Lady Lydia's glaring eyes threatened to burn holes into Kayla's newly developed confidence.

"I believe I do." Kayla stood firm, returning her mother's glare. Nervous as she was, she felt her spirit soar while the implications of her choices settled in. Not only was she being openly defiant of her mother, but if word got out about her being alone with Daniel—and she was sure it would—it would put a huge damper on her mother's plans to arrange the intended betrothal. It was one thing to *think* of disagreeing with her family, and even more precarious to *voice* her disagreement, but this open display of independence was a whole new level of risk. The spontaneously chosen course of action gave her a measure of discomfort, yet she was equally emboldened by her newfound courage. If she had any hope of securing her future happiness, she needed to prove she could stand for herself. 'Twas no longer necessary to seek Fern's assistance, or anyone else, for her to thwart her mother's control.

Kayla knew her mother was furious. Thankfully, she refused to make a scene in front of Daniel. Delivering one final glare to each of them, Lady Lydia stomped off into the keep, doing her best to maintain her dignity.

A surge of excitement swept through Kayla. Her argument had worked. Going against her mother's wishes was scary, but it had worked. She had defied her; she knew her mother would be mad as hornets, but still, for the first time in her life, she had stood up to the great and powerful Lady Lydia. Kayla trembled with excitement over her minor victory, but there was also fear—fear she was stepping into uncharted waters, and she had no clue how to proceed.

Turning her gaze back to Daniel, she felt the strength of his arm supporting her around her waist. His hypnotic green eyes conveyed a sense of pride, even appreciation. She took a deep breath and gestured toward the keep. Kayla felt stronger than she could ever remember.

~~~

Daniel watched in amazement as Kayla stood up to her controlling mother, then watched with greater amazement as

Lady Lydia retreated into the depths of the great hall. As soon as her mother was out of sight, Kayla slumped against Daniel.

"Come. 'Tis yer turn to be my angel of mercy," she said. "Help me to my room. My ankle has begun to swell. If I doona rest soon, I shall pay dearly tomorrow." She completely gave in to Daniel's support, dropping the pretense of strength she had been maintaining for Lady Lydia's benefit.

He reached an arm beneath her knees and scooped her off her feet. She gave a little squeak of protest, looking duly impressed, but offered no resistance.

"Why didn't you say something earlier?" He relished the excuse to hold her near, regretting it was due to her injury, but not regretting the opportunity her injury provided. Moving up the narrow staircase leading into the keep, he could already picture massaging her aching feet in the privacy of her bedchamber.

"I dinna want Mother to know. She would fuss over me. I am nay longer a child, and I wish she would stop treating me as one," Kayla said with conviction. "Ye need nay fuss either. There is nay need for ye to carry me. I can walk with yer aid."

She claimed she didn't need his help, but the way she reached her arms around his neck and held on contradicted her words.

"Believe me, fussing over you is my pleasure."

He walked through the great hall toward the narrow circular stairwell, holding her easily in his arms. She was strong and yet so fragile. It were as though she had no understanding of her own true value. It seemed nothing short of amazing how the mere act of carrying her, instead of adding to his aches, relieved the stress and strain in his shoulders and back. He felt better than ever as comforting warmth pulsed through his body, delivering painkilling relief to his aching bones. *Endorphins,* he thought, linking the pleasurable sensation to the well-known runner's high.

Kayla directed Daniel to her room, where he set her down on a chair near the hearth. He intentionally left the door to her chamber propped open, hoping to avoid the appearance of improper intimacy for her sake. Though, he would have preferred to close the door and create a private getaway, his better judgment respected the precarious predicament they were creating. Even if she didn't, he understood the risk she was taking.

Daniel had to laugh. *Good God, I'm actually in her bed chamber. What would Teressa say about that?*

For him, the open door helped to lessen the opportunity, if not the temptation, to take advantage of the situation. It was something he thought best to avoid. He appreciated the trust and respect she had placed upon him, and he had no intention of letting her down. This way, they would be in plain view of anyone walking along the hallway, seeking to spy on their activities. As a police officer, he had seen firsthand how the mere act of closing a door could produce devastating results. Acting in plain sight made it much harder to spawn false accusations. It would also help him control any inappropriate impulses.

He had flagged down Bonnie on the way to Kayla's room and asked her to bring him a basin of water and a towel. Once he had Kayla settled in her chair, he pulled a wool blanket from her bed and placed it on her lap. A sweet half smile lit her face as he tended to her needs. Taking a look around her bed chamber, he found the footstool she kept near her bed and set it down in front of her chair.

When this was all done, he asked, "Okay, tell me where this special ointment of yours is stashed."

"'Tis kept there in the baskets near the window. The one on the far right." She pointed to the row of baskets. "That one, with the brown leather pouch."

When Bonnie arrived with the washbasin and towel, he asked her to set them on the floor in front of Kayla.

"Is there anything else ye may need from me?" Bonnie asked, looking noticeably uncomfortable.

"No, thanks, nothing else. You're welcome to sit and watch if you'd like," Daniel said, grinning. He silently prayed she would decline.

Bonnie seemed hesitant to answer. Out of the corner of his eye, he saw Kayla shake her head no.

"Mayhap I best be going and leave ye to yer task," Bonnie stepped over to the doorway. "Do ye want me to leave this open?"

"Yes, please. If we need anything, I'll give you a call," Daniel replied.

With one last look of consternation, Bonnie gave a nod and disappeared into the hallway.

Daniel breathed a sigh of relief.

After collecting the salve, he settled his large frame on the diminutive footstool in front of Kayla. When he reached out to remove her short leather boots, first the right and then the left, Kayla began to protest.

"Only my right ankle is injured. Ye doona need to remove both boots."

"Trust me. I, uh, need to evaluate both ankles to determine the extent of your injury," he said, improvising. Daniel gave her a look of confidence, hoping his explanation sounded reasonable. He had every intention of taking full advantage of the opportunity to not only soothe her aches and pains but also pamper her in a manner exceeding anything she had experienced before. As far as he was concerned, such indulgence required nothing less than massaging both her feet.

She hesitated, pouted for a second, and then nodded, accepting his actions.

He gently bathed her feet in the refreshingly cool water with all the care one might apply to a newborn babe, washing away the dust and dirt. All the while, he was careful to avoid creating any further discomfort to her swollen ankle. Daniel wanted her to feel cherished.

It seemed to be working. She watched his every move, enthralled by his actions.

After laying the drying cloth across his thighs, he set the water aside and placed her feet on his lap to dry them before he began his massage. Her feet were small and well formed, but not dainty. They'd been toughened by years of hard work and the freedom of going barefoot.

Daniel began with her left foot and ankle, running his hands over her skin to test the muscles that lay beneath the surface. Tightness had built up in her left ankle and calf as they took on the burden of compensating for her injured foot.

Looking into her eyes, he saw her apprehension. Her bravado was beginning to fade. "You're holding a lot of tension. You have to relax for this to work."

~~~

Kayla nodded her acceptance, not trusting herself to speak. She was unaccustomed to the sensation created by the feel of a man's hands on her skin, and it was having a greater effect than she had anticipated. And he was only touching her feet and ankles.

"Tell me if this hurts," he said. He reached for her right ankle, and with gentle pressure, he walked his fingertips along the sole of her foot, beginning with her toes, which tickled at his touch. He pressed his fingers over the ball of her foot and across her arch. Moving slowly and methodically, he gradually inched his fingers toward the site of the injury. Her ankle was already showing signs of stress, becoming red and swollen. When his fingers reached the edge of the tender tissue, she winced ever so slightly, indicating he had reached his target, but she said nothing, waiting for him to explore further.

He stilled his hands. "Does this hurt?"

"Only a wee bit," she admitted. "Please proceed." She nibbled nervously on the inside of her bottom lip. Her rigid resolve seemed to melt away under the tender mercies of his touch.

Daniel dipped his fingers into the salve and rubbed his hands together for a moment to warm the lotion. With great care, he began to massage her foot, running his fingers over every inch of her now intensely sensitive skin. He began with her toes, and slowly, so very slowly, he moved along the muscles of her foot, constantly checking her reactions to the amount of pressure he applied, noting when she responded with pleasure or distress.

She was acutely aware of the effect his massage was having on her. At first she tried to fight it, but each time he reminded her to relax. Soon she stopped fighting and gave into the care of his compassionate touch. By the time he reached the site of the injury, she had relaxed enough to allow him to continue the soothing massage and healing manipulations, releasing the stress and soreness from her overworked muscles. She was grateful when he continued to massage her calves, pulling the tension and stress from her legs. Nothing before had ever felt so good.

Kayla felt herself drift into a state of dreamy relaxation. In her mind, she slipped into the role of a well-tended woman. Had her mother ever felt care, she wondered, or Fern, or Janet? It was a new experience for her, having a man fuss over her, as if she were a person of value. Reluctantly at first, but then with increased self-assurance, she gave herself permission to enjoy the new sensation.

"I have never imagined such—" she paused, censoring her words, "—such relief from the touch of another." Each word was weighed and measured as she endeavored to avoid the appearance of impropriety.

"But you're a healer. Haven't you ever received healing in return?" His broad strong hands continued to rub soothing circles over her legs.

"None such as this. 'Tis my task to provide comfort, nae receive."

"You need to be more generous with yourself. If you aren't, who will be?"

She sat in silence, digesting the thought.

"Is my massage helping to relieve your pain?" he asked.

"Aye, very much so. Where did ye learn such a fine technique?" Her eyes were half-closed as she savored the pleasurable relief his hands were providing. There were times when the pressure of the massage reached the edge of pain, but it hurt so good as he dug deep into the muscles of her feet, ankles, and calves, relieving the deposits of stress built up through the long hard day.

"I've never had any formal training, but I've experienced these types of treatments for myself."

"Ye must have been badly injured."

"No, not really. Massage therapy is usually more of a perk to fend off stiff muscles than to fix real injuries."

"I canna picture my brothers seeking out such relief from a healer, at least nay for something as minor as an ankle sprain.

They would rather disavow the pain than surrender to such pampering."

"This type of treatment is pretty common where I come. We're probably a bit soft by your standards."

"I believe I would have nay problem embracing such healing arts. It must be grand. Tell me more about yer home, the place where ye are from."

His hands drew lazy circles on her feet. It felt so good, she didn't want him to stop.

He stared off for a moment, as though remembering. "Well, I had a great childhood; I can't complain. I was born on a horse ranch where my dad bred and trained rodeo horses. He was damn good, and we worked hard.

"I've got two older brothers, and you already know Teressa, my little sister. My dad's name was Allen, and he named his three sons in alphabetical order: Brett, Conner, and me, Daniel. When Teressa was born, my mom, Francine, decided to stop with the alphabet game and chose to name her only daughter after our two grandmothers, Terrie Ellers and Ressa Withers."

Kayla cocked her head. "I doona understand."

"Terrie and Ressa. Teressa," he explained.

"How sweet. What a lovely way to honor both grandmothers. I must keep that in mind. Was Teressa close to yer mother?"

"Mom loved us all, with all her heart, but we all knew she loved Teressa best. They respected each other. I think you could say they were best friends. I'm told that's kinda rare between mother and daughter."

Kayla was envious. In recent years, her relationship with her mother had become strained, losing much of the comforting warmth she had known in her youth. She tried to tell herself it was to be expected. It was simply a part of growing up. But she was no longer Mother's little girl.

"What about ye, Daniel? Were ye close to yer parents?"

"Yeah, I was. Dad liked having boys. Being the youngest, I got more than my share of teasing, but I was able to hold my own. I'll have to admit, I think Mom had a tendency to favor me over my brothers, being the youngest boy and all. I remember she once said if Teressa had been a boy, it would have been the death of her." Daniel chuckled softly. "Said she would have been outnumbered five to one, and it was more than she could handle. But we all knew she was the one who had the best of us, what with four men to do her bidding. Believe me, she had us pups whipped into shape. There wasn't an Ellers boy who wouldn't give his all for her. In the end, it was cancer that took her away to be with Dad." Daniel paused a moment, dwelling on memories of his family. "Dad passed a couple years ago. I think the only thing Ma wanted after Dad died was to be with him."

"I'm so sorry. For ye to lose both your parents so close together, it must have been hard." Her heart ached for him.

Daniel shrugged. "It was their time. They both lived good lives. I've never seen a more loving marriage. You could tell they belonged together."

"I like hearing yer stories, listening to the way ye speak. Please tell me more," she pleaded. She was thoroughly relaxed by the soothing sound of his voice and his foreign accent. Her eyelids became heavy, lulled by his curative powers.

~~~

Needing no further enticement, Daniel dove into the subject dearest to his heart. He told her about his life on the ranch and growing up around horses, relating some of the hellish pranks his brothers and he played on each other. All the while, he continued to lightly rub her feet, changing from deep tissue massage to gently soothing strokes. Kayla sat relaxed in the chair with her eyes nearly closed, quiet and smiling.

Sometime along the way, Daniel stopped talking and noticed Kayla had fallen asleep, no doubt overcome by her exhaustion. He took a moment to appreciate her peaceful appearance before he stood and gently placed her feet on the footstool. After tucking the edge of the blanket around her bare feet and ankles, he bent to place a chaste kiss on her forehead.

"Sleep well, my sweet angel," he whispered and brushed a stray curl from her cheek. Smiling, he took one last lingering glance at her angelic features before he exited the chamber, closing the door softly behind him.

CHAPTER 9

E arly the next morning, Kayla paced at the edge of the great hall, waiting for Daniel to make his appearance, her anger building. What could he have been thinking to let her fall asleep like that, so early in the evening? Hadn't they agreed she would tend to his sore shoulders? She had every intention of soothing away his aches and pains, much as he had done for her, but instead, he had left her sleeping, allowing her to shirk her duties as his healer.

It had all been so nice and relaxing, the way they had talked and laughed while he massaged her aching feet and ankles. In fact, it had been so very pleasant she had fallen asleep. And he had left her there, in her chamber, alone, and sleeping. He had even thought to seek out Bonnie, telling her to send up a tray of food to her chamber, as if she were some kind of invalid, unable to carry herself down to the hall for the evening meal. Worse, she had to hear from Bonnie what a grand time Daniel and her brothers had at supper, exchanging stories about their day in the lists. She would have enjoyed hearing her brothers tell their tales about Daniel's introduction to Michael's training. But nay, she was left sleeping, alone in her room. What must her mother and the others have been thinking? That she was lazy? Lazy and unkind to have let Daniel tend to her injury without returning the favor.

As she paced the great hall, checking first one entry for signs of his arrival and then the other, she considered how it had just gotten easier to resent the man, and not because he happened to be Teressa's brother. This time he had earned the resentment all on his own.

She was about to lose her patience and seek him out in his bedchamber when Daniel finally sauntered in through the wide front door of the keep.

~~~

Daniel flashed Kayla a warm welcoming smile. "Top of the morning to you, angel. I trust you slept well. How's that ankle holding up?"

It was a pleasure to see his little angel waiting for him. At least she appeared to be waiting for him; although, from the look on her face, she seemed less than happy. Maybe her ankle was still giving her pain this morning.

"My ankle's fine and I slept well, all thanks to ye." For such kind words, her voice dripped of sarcasm laced with anger. "How could ye tend to my ankle and then simply leave me sleeping like that?"

"Um, because I was trying to be nice?" he questioned with a shrug, his smile quickly fading. Daniel knew she was upset; her displeasure was obvious. He just didn't know what he had done to earn her wrath.

"*Nice!* Do ye think 'tis nice to leave a person sleeping alone in her chamber while the rest of the family gathers for the

126

evening meal?" She stood with her hands on her hips, a storm brewing in her deep hazel eyes.

"Yes, when she looks as sweet and peaceful as you did." *Darn women,* he thought, *they're just as perplexing in the thirteenth century as they are in the future.*

"Did we nae have an agreement that I would treat yer sore shoulders after ye tended my ankle?"

"Yeah, sort of, but you fell asleep, and my shoulders felt fine. I forgot all about them being sore. Some beers with your brothers and a good night's rest was as all I needed." Again, he shrugged his shoulders, which ironically enough were starting to tense.

"Aye. I fell asleep, and ye left me there, sleeping. Ye even had Bonnie send up a tray for my supper." She was beside herself with indignation.

She was talking in circles. This made no sense. Daniel reached the end of his patience.

"Kayla, can you just cut to the chase. Tell me what this is all about, and I'll make amends so we can all go to breakfast." Daniel tried to keep his frustration in check, keeping his voice calm, but he wasn't in the mood to placate her. He was hungry, and breakfast was getting cold. He needed to know the reason for her anger.

"Ye left me sleeping in my chamber after tending to my ankle. Ye didn't give me a chance to return the kindness, and besides that, I missed supper with my family. They must think me lazy, that I'm shirking my duties. Mother will think I took advantage of my injury. But I would nay do such a thing. Doona ye understand?" Her eyes looked a little misty, as though she were holding back tears.

Daniel needed to put a stop to that. No man likes to see a woman cry. Especially one he likes. He searched his barely awake brain for what to do. Finally, the lightbulb came on.

"I didn't let you keep your end of the bargain." His frustration washed away. He realized she had no prior experience with being pampered. A simple kindness he took for granted was something new for her, and she was finding it difficult to accept. His frustration was replaced by a desire to reach out and hold her.

A tear spilled down her cheek, and she wiped away the wetness, embarrassed by its betrayal.

Drawing her aside to a nearby alcove, he gave in to his urge and gathered her into his arms. "I'm sorry, Kayla. Really, I am." Glad she didn't resist, he held her in his arms until he felt her breathe deep, relaxing against his chest. It was the sign he needed to know she was ready to talk.

Pulling back, he gently brushed a thumb across her cheek. "I get it. You're angry because you think I made you look like a fool to your family. Am I right?"

"Aye," she nodded, her eyes downcast.

Not allowing her to cower, he raised her chin to look him in the eyes. "First, let me tell you, no one can make you look like a fool, because you're not. If anyone thinks that, they're mistaken. It's not foolish to rest when your ankle's been injured and needs to mend. You're feeling better today, aren't you?"

She nodded again in agreement.

"It's because you got the rest you needed. Do you hear me? Rest. Our bodies need rest to heal. You're a healer, you should know that."

"I do." She stood a little taller.

"Let me ask you. If it was someone else, say Janet or Shannon, who came to you with a swollen and injured ankle, what advice would you have given her?"

A reluctant half grin escaped Kayla's lips. "I would have told her to stay off her feet and rest."

"Right, because you're a caring, compassionate healer, and you want to offer what's best for someone in pain. So why won't you give the same to yourself?"

"I canna . . . ," she began.

"Why not?"

"I . . . I doona know how." Her voice was small. This wasn't an easy thing for her to admit.

"Then it's time you start learning, and I'm going to help. You can't keep giving to others and not give to yourself. Sooner or later you'll experience burnout, and then you'll be no good to anyone, especially yourself."

She stared up at him with confusion. "Why are ye being so nice to me?" she asked.

"How could I not, after all you've done for me? Besides, first impressions are hard to overcome. You'll always be my angel."

Daniel's fingers traced a path across her cheek and brushed her hair, hooking a wayward strand of red silken curl behind her ear. His stare roamed her face, trying to absorb every nuance: the freckles on her nose, the laugh lines near her eyes, and the arch of her brow. She remained quiet and still, as though frozen in place.

He was caught up in her beauty and the touch of his fingers on her skin. His gaze fell to her full, pink lips. They called to him. Slowly, he lowered his head toward hers, leaning in for a kiss. She seemed ready, willing, but before his lips could touch hers, she turned her head.

"Please, stop. My family . . . I am expected . . ." She turned to look toward the great hall, as if worried they might be seen.

How stupid was he? No doubt, her brothers would not appreciate finding their little sister cavorting with a time traveling visitor who was likely to disappear without a moment's notice. Someone like him did not qualify as good husband material, and he doubted Kayla was allowed to date. She had a no-boyfriends-allowed kind of vibe.

"That's okay. I get it," he said, trying not to sound as disappointed as he felt. "Maybe we should go to breakfast. I'm mighty hungry, and while you're a feast for my eyes, you're doing nothing for my belly." His stomach was rumbling, hungry for food, but an area just south of his belly was hungry for her, and perfectly ready to make itself known. He needed to create a distraction if he had any hopes of controlling his arousal.

Kayla looked up, and he was rewarded with a glowing smile. "Breakfast, of course. Ye need to eat. What are we waiting for?" Stepping back, she turned on her heel, grabbed his hand, and headed toward the great hall where the morning meal was being served.

Daniel had the feeling he'd follow her anywhere.

~*~

At one of the long plank tables, Daniel was finishing off the last of his breakfast, watching the flurry of activity taking place around him. The great hall of the keep was a busy place, and Kayla had deserted him to tend to her chores. Striding across the great hall, Rory approached him and greeted him with a cheery nod.

"'Tis a grand summer's day. One of the last we shall see afore the rain sets in. Let's go fishing." Rory clapped Daniel on his back.

"Shouldn't you be off doing warrior training with your brothers, or some such stuff?" Daniel drained the last of Kayla's herbal tea from his mug and stood to join Rory. The herbal tea was turning out to be a good substitute for coffee. He didn't know what she put in it, but it had a nice little kick, and was a great way to start the day.

"Nay, brother. Today, I am nay warrior, nor have I any wish to be my mother's servant. Today, I am a man of the sea."

"A man of many talents." He liked Rory's attitude.

"I play well at work and work hard at play," Rory said with a relaxed manner, grinning broadly.

They tramped across the great hall toward the exit and headed out to the stables. The courtyard was buzzing with activity in spite of the early morning hour. It reminded him of his younger days with his dad on the ranch when everything had been in full swing. Allen Ellers had rarely let his boys sleep past sunrise, and Daniel had learned early the value of a hard day's work. Seeing the bustle of the fortress, he missed those days and the feeling of home.

Before they reached the stables, Rory stepped into a storeroom to gather a few supplies, along with some woolen blankets and a couple of large leather bags. He handed a set of the supplies to Daniel.

"I remember well another time I allowed for a day of play at the bay. I hope yer nae as intimidated by a wee bit of cold water as was yer sister."

"Couldn't get her in the water, could you?" Daniel scoffed, accepting the supplies Rory selected for him. He was well aware of Teressa's aversion to swimming in a cold ocean.

"Nay, she was stubborn in her attachment to dry land." Rory paused. "'Tis hard to believe three years have passed since she was here with me, laughing in the sunshine as we gathered sea creatures for the evening meal." Sadness passed briefly through Rory's eyes as he reminisced on their time together.

"You miss her, don't you?" Daniel voiced the obvious.

"She is my love, my life, my soulmate. If she'd been able to stay, I would have made her my wife."

They entered the stables, inhaling the rich familiar scent of hay and horses. Rory led Blazer, his warhorse, from his stall while Daniel readied a grey-and-white-spotted stallion. Aptly enough, Rory told him the horse was called Spots. Out in the courtyard, Rory mounted Blazer and Daniel followed suit.

"If you had to leave this all behind, your home, your family, to be with Teressa, would you still make that choice?" Sitting astride his mount, Daniel gestured toward the courtyard and the keep.

"In a heartbeat," Rory answered, deadpan serious.

"But you knew her for such a short time." Daniel was impressed, but he questioned Rory's unwavering conviction.

"Love is nay about time. 'Tis a feeling," Rory answered with calm assurance.

Daniel studied his friend's face. Apparently, Rory had given the matter a lot of thought over the years. Teressa had written in her journal Rory would become Robert, her husband, in another life. It was how they could be together again. Maybe he could throw the man a bone.

"When Teressa came back, she told us she had met her soulmate, the man she wanted to marry. I'm guessing it's just a matter of time before the two of you are together again."

"Aye, time. That does seem to be the curse of this matter." Rory clicked his heels against Blazer's flanks, spurring him toward the castle gate.

More than you know, Daniel silently agreed as he followed Rory's lead, *more than you know*.

Daniel wanted to reassure Rory everything would be okay, someday, but he had no idea how to begin. How could he tell Rory his soul would be alive, and well, and married to Teressa seven hundred years in the future? The man would think him a crazed nut. Besides, how could he know if that were actually the truth, or just Teressa's outrageous imagination? Maybe for some crazed reason she needed to believe Robert was the reincarnation of this man from the thirteenth century, even if he wasn't. Even if he did try to explain such a concept to Rory, what comfort could it possibly give him in this lifetime? *Hang in there, buddy, and in seven hundred years, it's all gonna be alright.* Not likely a good idea. Besides, it was all a bit too strange for Daniel's simple mind to sort out.

He was certainly no expert, but he'd heard about reincarnation and had even done some reading on the subject once before. A lot had been written about it in recent years. There were reports of people having vivid memories of their past lives, even little kids. Some were able to speak ancient languages they never learned in their current lives. Often they looked a lot like the person they claimed to have been in their past life. But it was difficult to know how much was truth and how much was a case of someone's overactive imagination creating dreams of things that never were, only wished for.

Daniel was willing to concede there was enough evidence to support the *possibility* of reincarnation, but it wasn't exactly proof. How could you ever really prove such a thing? Besides, it was one thing to read about other people's stories, it was quite another to encounter it firsthand, up close and personal.

As they approached the bay, Daniel was taken in by the raw rugged beauty of the coastline. The small bay sat in a protected crook of the island, intimately situated next to the commanding onslaught of the northern ocean. Beyond the shelter of the crescent beach, harsh waves battered the coast where the surging strength of the sea rushed against the encroaching land. The cliffs of Portree stood steadfast against the embrace of its powerful lover, firmly supporting the fortress of Scorrybreac.

"'Tis beautiful, this joining of the land and sea, is it nae?" Rory breathed in the sight.

"Aye, 'tis beautiful," Daniel said, mimicking Rory's Scottish brogue.

Rory gave Daniel a hard look. "Ye would do well here." He dismounted from Blazer and headed off down the beach.

"What makes you say that?" Daniel followed close behind, carrying their supplies.

"Just a feeling. But I always trust my feelings. 'Tis well-known we MacNicols carry a bit of fae blood in our veins." Standing at the water's edge, Rory sent him a lop-sided grin loaded with meaning.

"Yeah, so I hear." Daniel grinned and rolled his eyes with exasperation as he dropped the supplies on the sand.

"What have ye heard?" Rory gave him a quizzical look.

Daniel hesitated, not knowing how much to reveal. "I've heard the stories about your great-grandmother Sophie. They say she was a fae princess who married your great-grandfather."

"Aye, 'tis correct."

"Teressa told me your mother, Lady Lydia, is her direct descendant." Well, not directly, but in so many words, even if the story were in her journal, which technically she never gave him permission to read. "If there's any truth to all that, wouldn't that make you a tad bit fae, too?" Daniel chuckled at the thought of the big Scottish warrior being part faerie.

"Why do I get the feeling ye know more than yer saying?" Rory's eyes narrowed into a scrutinizing glare.

Probably because I do, Daniel thought. He wasn't about to open that can of worms. It wasn't his place to tell Rory his mother had arranged to have Teressa brought back in time by Moezell, her faerie cousin, only to have her sent back home and away from Rory. There was no telling how much trouble that would stir up.

Daniel shrugged it off. "Couldn't say, maybe it's your faerie senses tingling." He wiggled his fingers in the air, laughing at the jest as he mimicked a modern comic book character.

"Aye, and how's this for tingling senses?" With one heave-ho, Rory knocked Daniel off his feet into an oncoming wave.

When Daniel came up for air, he was shuttering with cold. "Holy shit, dude, this makes the ocean back home seem like a freaking bathtub."

"Ye should see yer face." Rory fell to the sand in peals of laughter.

"You won't be laughing when I'm done with you." Daniel cupped his hand and shot a spray of ocean water at Rory. Rory sidestepped the worst of it then dove into a breaking wave.

"How can you stand the cold?" Daniel asked when Rory came up for air.

"I was a sailor for many years. Sailors get wet. We get used to it."

Hours later, they headed back to the keep, tired but totally satisfied. It had been a splendid day of male bonding and seafood gathering once Daniel got past the initial shock of the frigid cold of the Atlantic Ocean, which actually wasn't much worse than the frigid cold of the Pacific Ocean back home.

Entering the kitchens, Rory and Daniel plopped their wet bloated bag of sea creatures on the prep table.

"Hail Milly, I come bearing gifts," Rory greeted the head cook.

"It best be gifts ye bring me if ye come in here smelling of the sea and dripping with sand." Pushing the young warrior aside, Milly turned to examine the contents of the soggy pouch.

Daniel saw the mischievous look in Rory's eyes and knew this was a well-planned assault, one he had played out many times before. He stood back and watched, enjoying the charade.

"Only ye, my love, could I trust to turn these sea critters into a scrumptious meal." Rory teased the aging cook with a wily grin.

"Yer love is for my cooking. I am nay old fool." A slip of smile escaped the grouchy woman's lips.

"Now, Milly, doona ye be speaking so. Ye will break my heart." Mischievous humor played across Rory's face as he gathered the elderly cook into a hearty bear hug.

"'Tis yer stomach ye treasure, nay yer heart." She accepted his squeeze of affection for a brief moment before she thumped his chest with her large wooden spoon, pushing him away. "Now, be off with ye both afore ye turn this kitchen into a sodden salty mess."

As Daniel and Rory hightailed it out of the cookhouse, Rory slung a brotherly arm across Daniel's shoulders. "Ye must admit. 'Twas a grand day at the bay."

"Aye, a grand day, indeed," Daniel agreed. "All that's missing is a nice cold brew."

"Ye mean ale?" Rory dropped his arm and raised a quizzical brow.

Daniel nodded.

"'Tis nay problem." Rory grinned. "I can fix that."

CHAPTER 10

D aniel hoped to carve out some alone time with Kayla, but he kept running into missed opportunities. She was either busy with her duties around the castle, or he was being called into action by one or the other of the MacNicol brothers. One day he was training with Michael in the lists, and the next he was out foraging for seafood with Rory. Even when they gathered together for the evening meal, Kayla was always surrounded by family, most notably her mother. Lady Lydia hovered around Kayla like an overly protective mother hen.

Surely there was a way to get her out from under the watchful eyes of her protective family; Daniel just needed to find it.

When he saw her crossing the courtyard toward the stables, he figured he would give it another try. A ride out away from the keep offered the perfect opportunity for some alone time. Of course, his intentions were all on the up-and-up, he told himself. After all, he was a man of self-control and had no intention of seducing her or taking advantage of her innocence. He tried to convince himself it was only a friendly ride, even though he felt an undeniable surge of anticipation flowing through his gut.

He rushed to meet up with her just before she reached the entrance to the stables and launched into his plan of attack.

"It looks like you're headed out for another ride. My invitation to join you must have gotten lost along the way."

"Excuse me?" Kayla said, eyes blinking. "I've come to check on Sallie and to give her a treat." She showed him the carrots she held in her hand.

"Mind if I join you?" Daniel asked.

"As you wish," she replied with a shrug.

He took it as a yes and walked with her into the stable. When they reached the dimness of the building, he was tempted to reach out to grab her hand and pull her to his side but was stymied by his blasted good intentions. Best to keep his hands to himself, not that it was easy. When they reached Sallie's stall, he made a show of looking over the large brown mare.

"It looks to me like she could use some exercise. She looks a little restless." He ran a hand along the mare's back and down her flank while Kayla fed her the carrots.

"Really? How do ye know?" she asked, sounding concerned.

"I've been around horses all my life. Remember, I grew up on a horse ranch. It's important to keep your horses well exercised. Don't want them getting lazy or soft." He wanted to make it sound as though he had her best interests in mind.

Kayla glanced over her shoulder back toward the keep.

He saw her hesitation and moved in to advance his position. He gestured toward the spotted pony he had ridden to the beach with Rory. "Spots over there could also use a workout. I'd be happy to accompany you."

Before she could say no, he opened the tack box and started pulling out bridles and saddle blankets. "Here, I'll help you, and we can be on our way."

She stood her ground. "Ye must be mad."

"Why not?" he asked as he continued to gather supplies.

"I have work to do."

He stopped what he was doing and looked up, letting his disappointment show. "You always have work to do. Can't you take a little break? It'll still be here when you get back."

She smiled. It was working. "We canna be long."

"I'll get you back before sunset, I promise."

This time she laughed. "We shall return long afore that."

He had her.

Together they saddled the horses and led them out into the courtyard. After they mounted up, he asked, "Ready?"

"Aye." She gave him a curt nod.

"Then lead the way." He flashed her an easy smile that came from deep within.

Kayla gave Sallie a tap with her heels, setting them off across the courtyard and out the main gate of the fortress. She led them down the dirt road toward a gentle sloping hill covered with summer grass.

"I think Sallie could use a good run, if ye can handle Spots." She cast him a challenging look.

"Go for it," Daniel replied, still grinning.

With a brisk kick, she launched Sallie into a gallop. Daniel came up beside her and matched her pace momentarily before spurring Spots on. She in turn matched his pace. Together they raced over the ground in the late afternoon sun. The sky was a brilliant blue, laced with large cotton candy clouds, a perfect backdrop to the lush green land.

When he reached a rocky outcropping at the edge of the grassland, Daniel brought the pony to a halt, turning to watch Kayla come up behind him. Her face, flushed with pleasure, glowed from the exertion of the run. Stray strands of hair slipped from her braid and swirled about her face, dancing in the wind. The sight of her hit him square in his chest, just around the area of his pounding heart. Catching his breath, he absorbed the sheer pleasure of being with her.

"Ye won," she said, gasping to catch her breath.

"Not by much. It was a good race." He stared at her, enthralled by her beauty.

Dropping her eyes, she turned to look away. He followed her gaze, letting his eyes roam across the landscape. Thin soil clung to the volcanic rock, blossoming with the green growth of summer. A magnificent ridge of jagged stone dominated the distant view.

"It's pretty rugged out here," he said, making a rather lame attempt at small talk.

"Aye, rugged, harsh, and beautiful." Her eyes glazed over with uncensored affection for the land.

He understood her feelings. The Isle of Skye didn't offer an easy life, and yet he sensed her connection to the place. It supported her people and gave them sustenance.

"Ye should see it in winter," she continued. "When the land is covered in snow so white it hurts yer eyes. Or the sky is so thick with grey clouds it blocks the sun."

He doubted she had any idea how lovely she looked, absorbed as she was in her appreciation of the countryside and the land she called home.

"Do you miss yer home?" she questioned, turning to look at him. "Is it hard to be so far away?"

"I haven't really thought about it. Too wrapped up in being here, I guess." It stunned him to realize he really didn't miss home or his own time, at least not as much as he expected. He was displaced in a faraway land, in a long-ago time, and yet he didn't want to dwell on where he came from. His life in California seemed distant, even remote. It wasn't something he longed for. The here and now felt real, and surprisingly, even comfortable.

They began to walk the horses again, setting off at an easy gait, headed for nowhere in particular.

"Are ye enjoying yer travels?" she asked.

"Yeah, I am. This trip has turned out to be much more than I expected." A secretive grin tugged at his lips as he thought how much of an understatement that was.

"Is this a good thing?" A hopeful smile curved on her lovely lips.

"I'd say it's a very good thing. This is the first time I've traveled so far. I've always been inclined to stay close to home. But this, yeah, this is a very good thing." The best thing by far was the opportunity to enjoy her company. Every time he came within five feet of her, he felt things he'd never felt before. Like right now, he had the urge to grab her and ride off into the sunset. He guessed that was a case of one too many Hollywood Westerns.

"I enjoyed hearing yer stories about yer home and family," she said. "Ye have traveled so far. I've never left the Isle of Skye. Can ye tell me more?"

With her innocence, she had no idea how appealing it was for a man to be asked to talk about himself.

"For years, the ranch was all I knew. I lived, ate, and slept for the ranch, working with my dad and the horses. We raised horses for the rodeo circuit, barrel racers, and such. Quick, sure-footed breeds that respond well to their rider."

"Did ye ever race the barrels?" she asked hesitantly, looking somewhat confused. It was understandable, his words probably sounded like gibberish to her, but she was doing her best to not let it show.

"Ride the rodeo? Yeah, I did. I had a good time, and I usually placed well, but it really wasn't my thing. I was more interested in the horses, seeing them excel in the hands of seasoned veterans. Those guys live for the sport. I took enough falls to know I don't want to risk my life and limb for an oversized trophy and a few bucks."

"A few bucks?" she asked.

"Reward money. It's paid out to the man who performs the best at the games."

"Oh." Her face brightened with understanding. "Yer ro-de-o sounds much like our warrior games. Men seem to welcome the opportunity to display their talents for all to see. I'm sure ye did well. Ye were very capable with the fighting staff against Michael."

Ah, so she admitted she had watched him that first morning in training. The candid confirmation brought a secret smile to his heart.

"My first love was always the horses." It was an unconscious gesture for him to reach out and stroke Spots along his velvety neck. "When it came time for me to branch out on my own, I was drawn into law enforcement, keeping the peace. But I wanted to do it from the back of a horse instead of . . . um, you know, walking a beat."

He was about to say "ride around in a patrol car," but thankfully, he caught himself. There was no way he could explain an automobile, or how he had traveled through time, without looking seriously deranged. It churned his gut that he had to monitor his words, withholding secrets from her, but he couldn't reveal such trust-shattering info. He had promised Duncan and Rory.

"That's where I learned to fight, to defend myself and protect others against the bad guys in the world. There are more than enough bad guys to go around. I wanted to play for the good guys' team."

His need to help and protect others was one of the things that set him apart from his brothers. They were the guys who wanted the glory and the big bucks, seeking to excel in every high school sport they could hook their fists into. He liked being a team player, the guy who defended the quarterback. Maybe it was a thankless job, but the way he saw it, someone had to do it, or the quarterback, usually one of his brothers, would have been ground meat at the hands of the other team. He didn't mind being the defender of the land, the one who kept the home fires burning. It was his choice to stay behind when his brothers left for college and careers in the aerospace industry. He just wished it hadn't become so lonely.

His parents had passed, and Teressa was all grown up and married. It made him wonder what new home fires he would find to defend.

"What about you?" he asked, returning to the reason he had whisked her away from the keep. "What's your story?"

Daniel really wanted to know if there were any past or present boyfriends he should know about, but he didn't want to just blurt out the question. He was hoping a more subtle approach would get her to open up to him.

"Me? I have nay tales to tell. I've lived my whole life here at Scorrybreac, the dutiful daughter of the MacNicol chief, never leaving the protection of my family."

"Nothing wrong with that in my book. It seems I have a liking for dutiful daughters."

"Ye jest, I am sure," she said, but her shy smile brightened.

"In my line of work, rebels without a cause are a dime a dozen. It's the honest, hardworking folks like you and your family who give me a reason to get up each day and do my duty. Besides, I already know you're a healer. Tell me more about that."

She graced him with a beaming smile, obviously pleased by his interest. "I learned from my mother, who learned from her mother. The healing arts are passed from mother to daughter. They have been a part of our family as far back as anyone can remember. Surely ye have heard of great-grandmother Sophie?"

"From what I hear, you have a talent for it."

"Who told ye?"

"Oh, I have my ways." He thought of the amusing hours he'd spent in Bonnie's company, plying the chatty woman with his probing questions.

"It was Bonnie, no doubt," Kayla guessed. "She's a great one for boasting of our clan's accomplishments. But tending to the needs of our clan has always come easy for me. 'Tis nay a talent but a gift I was born with."

"You've said it yourself, you have great accomplishments." His grin turned devilish, happy to have caught her off guard.

"'Tis boastful to think such," she protested.

"Kayla, when are you going to learn, it's not boasting to acknowledge your abilities?"

A delightful pink colored her cheeks. She looked away.

Daniel halted the horses. Reaching across to Kayla, he cupped her chin, turning her face toward his.

"You know what I see?" he asked, looking deep into her eyes.

144

She remained quiet, holding his gaze.

"I see a woman full of compassion for her family and her people. I see a woman who seeks to serve those around her, forgetting to serve herself. I see you, Kayla, a woman full of innate talent and natural beauty." He also saw her struggling with her own sense of self and her desire to break free from the cocoon of her family. Already, there were signs of the butterfly she was about to become.

"Ye see all that?" she asked, looking wide-eyed and innocent.

"I wouldn't say it if it wasn't true." He paused for a moment and then asked, "What do you see when you look at me?" He had no qualms against fishing for a compliment if it meant learning more about her feelings for him.

Her eyes brightened, still staring into his, while her lips curved upward into a shy smile. "Possibly the best man I have ever met," she stated softly.

The extent of her praise both pleased and flabbergasted him. "Ah, no, that's going too far. I'm just a hardworking stiff trying to find my place in life." He tried to shrug off the effects of the unexpected compliment. Clicking his tongue against his teeth, he nudged Spots to continue their slow-paced journey. Kayla nudged Sallie to follow his cue, falling into step alongside him.

"It seems I am nae the only one who has trouble accepting a compliment," she teased, gracing him with an unrestrained smile. "I wouldna say it if it wasn't true." Mirth danced in her voice as she mimicked his words.

"Touché," he quipped. "You have me there. Are you always this bold with the men in your life?"

"Me, bold? Sir, ye must be mistaken. Why, I'm as gentle as a lamb. The only men in my life are my brothers, and I can assure ye, they do nay encourage boldness in their little sister."

"I find it hard to believe you have not turned your considerable charms on another unsuspecting soul." *At last,* he thought, *an opportunity to hear of the men in her life.*

"I assure ye, nay other has provoked me to the same degree as ye, my fine sir." A nervous giggle escaped her lips.

"Really, I'd think a pretty woman like you would have a dozen boyfriends by now."

"Boyfriends?"

"You know, suitors, men seeking your attentions."

"I can make nay such claim. There have been nay others. 'Tis nay allowed," she confessed.

His shock to learn she was even more innocent, more inexperienced, than he had believed was accompanied by acute embarrassment over his blunder. His jaw clamped closed on the proverbial foot he had just inserted firmly into his mouth.

"I wonder how many women ye have back at yer village vying for yer charms." Her suggestive remark surprised him. His little butterfly had just gotten a little bolder.

"Right now, considering my recent track record, I'm thinking none."

"I can only believe 'tis because ye are too busy with yer precious horses, or defending yer village. I hear ye have made a favorable impression with our serving women. Milly almost made it sound as if ye were welcome in her kitchen."

"Milly barely tolerates me and my silly stories." He laughed, relieved to be back on solid ground.

"I could spend all day listening to yer stories of home."

"I would think you've heard it all from Teressa. I'm sure she had lots of stories to tell." He wondered how much his sister had shared with Kayla without revealing her twenty-first-century origins.

"Nay. We dinna speak much," Kayla admitted.

"That surprises me, as I recall she was here for several days before she had to leave." His own words sounded an alarm in his lust-driven brain. Teressa had been forced to return home, she had no choice. Someday, so would he whenever Moezell decided to send him back. It surprised him how little he worried about his fate. Lately, it seemed his greater fear was he would wake up one day and find this was nothing more than a dream.

"I must confess, I wasn't very friendly to yer sister. I dinna take time to know her." She looked sad, regretful.

"Why not?"

"I knew she planned to leave, to return home, and when she did leave, she left Rory with a broken heart."

"She had no choice. I'm glad she came home. I would have been worried sick if she didn't. But the choice wasn't hers." A heavy dose of frustration surged through him, chilling his blood. He knew he had no control over how long he'd be allowed to stay in this time and place. He also knew Rory was heartbroken over the loss of Teressa. Disappointing as it was, his own sense of honor demanded he stop flirting with Kayla's tender emotions. It wasn't fair to put her in the same position.

"I know that now, but I dinna understand it then," she tried to explain.

Mired deep in his own thoughts, he nodded, indicating he understood, but a dark shadow crossed his face.

"Daniel, are ye feeling well?" Kayla asked.

"Yeah, I'm all right. I don't know what I was thinking. I'm sorry, Kayla. We need to go back," he stated bluntly. "I've kept you away from the keep for too long."

Daniel wanted to kick himself for his irresponsible behavior. Instead, he kicked the horse's flanks, sending Spots into a gallop toward the fortress. How could he have been so selfish and thoughtless? He had no business pursuing this innocent young woman, knowing he could disappear at any time without a moment's notice.

~~~

Kayla wondered what just happened. She wished she understood men better, especially this one.

His sudden appearance at the stables had caught her by surprise. She hadn't seen him alone since the morning after her foot massage, and she was beginning to believe he was purposely trying to avoid her. It wasn't her plan to take Sallie out for a ride. She had far too many chores waiting for her attention to indulge in such a frivolous use of her time. But when Daniel had asked her to go riding, all worries about chores flew from her mind.

She had promise to go riding with him, but until today, she had not made an effort. It felt like avoidance, which didn't feel good. The feeling was too closely akin to cowardice, and she was determined not to give in to cowardice where Daniel was concerned. For once in her life, she was determined to be brave, even bold.

Throwing off her usual caution and concerns, she had accepted his request to go riding, alone, just the two of them. If her mother had seen her leave alone with Daniel, there would have been hell to pay. Knowing she was taking such a risk made it all the more thrilling.

The experience had been pure joy as the horses raced across the land. It was exhilarating to feel the freedom of unrestrained movement if only for a while. She felt her heart race along with the horses as they moved with powerful grace across the rugged rolling hills she knew so well.

This was her home, her land, and she felt the pride of being able to share it with him. She had felt firsthand the cruel cold winters and relentless storms that often battered this island, but she had also seen the blessing of each new spring and nature's green growth as it reclaimed its place on the land. Skye was the only land she had ever known. She couldn't imagine it any other way.

She was comfortable with Daniel, more comfortable than she expected. His friendly smile filled her with a kind of self-confidence she'd not known before. The recent strain of her inner struggle against the restraints of her family, her mother in particular, had left her feeling disturbed by churned-up emotions. In the carefree pleasure of his company, she allowed herself to shed her pent-up concerns. He was an easy man to be with. His pleasant manner made it so, and she enjoyed hearing him speak with his strange accent.

Sometimes it sounded as though he were speaking a foreign language, but she enjoyed the sound of his voice too much to intervene and ask silly questions. The lilt of his accent was so different from anyone she had ever encountered on Skye. Even his sister's speech didn't carry the same tuneful cadence. Teressa spoke with polish and refinement, as if she were well-bred and well educated. Daniel's voice was friendly and carried a smile. It made it easier to relax in his presence.

She liked that he put more value on doing the right thing than seeking the glory of the winner's circle. He was an honorable man who put his home and family before short-lived rewards and accolades. Whenever men gathered to compete for fame and recognition, there would always be another who would seek to knock the winner from the lofty perch of prominence, but a man who was confident in his own abilities, that type of man would always find sure footing in his life.

When he asked about her life and her healing arts, it was tempting to retreat behind her well-established wall of modesty and indifference, but he had persisted, drawing her out. She admitted her healing arts were not so much a talent as a gift she was born with, and apparently with good reason. According to Moezell, many of her abilities were the benefit of her connection to the fae. Though she wanted to trust him, and tell him more, she had held back. Not sharing her recently gained knowledge was necessary, but it still felt deceitful. It was even scarier to think how he would react if he knew she were part fae. Some secrets were of necessity better kept to oneself.

He had looked in her eyes and told her she was beautiful. No one had ever bothered to see so deeply into her soul, much less bless her with such a compliment.

Boosted by his open show of support, she had even flirted with him a wee bit, spreading her wings and testing her ability to fly. For a moment, it felt good to play the role of a lighthearted woman. Sadly, the moment didn't last. Instead, she felt as though the effort had landed her on her arse with a painful thud.

Everything had all changed when he had asked about Teressa, and she had confessed her poor judgment of his sister. It hurt to know she had only herself to blame for shunning the woman. She had never asked Teressa about her home or family. She had not taken any time or shown any interest in getting to know her. Lately, she was beginning to realize how selfish she had been. Teressa had become the love of Rory's life, and she was the reason Daniel had come to Skye, to meet Rory and his family. It seemed her harsh judgment of Teressa was coming back to haunt her.

She had tried to explain her reasons to Daniel, telling him she didn't understand Teressa's need to suddenly return home and leave Rory behind. But she had failed.

Instead of him understanding her point of view, she had seen his disappointment and felt the conversation take a sharp downward turn. She hadn't known how to stop it.

Kayla had felt the change, felt him slipping away. Believing him to be angered by her admission she had spurned his sister, her heart sank. She couldn't blame him for his anger. Even now, as she recalled her disdain for Teressa and her presence in their keep, she felt the sting of how unfriendly she had been toward his sister. Knowing she had disappointed Daniel caused an ache in her chest that felt every bit as real as the pain in her ankle, only this time, she very much doubted he would be willing to soothe away her discomfort.

CHAPTER 11

Kayla headed out to the stables. She hadn't seen Daniel all morning, but she told herself she wasn't going there to look for him, even though she knew he liked to be around the horses. Though she told herself she was only going to check on Sallie, her instincts told her something was amiss.

As she approached the corral, she heard two guards talking.

"He raced out of here like a demon from hell. Ye would think he had the devil chasing him," the first guard was saying. His long hair hung lank about his shoulders.

"Do ye ken where he was going?" the second, older guard asked, rubbing a hand over his nearly bald head.

"Nay, I dinna have time to ask," the first guard replied. "Only heard him say, 'I have to go back.' It made nay sense to me. Guess he needs to return home sooner than expected. I hope the chief willna be missing the pony he rode out on over much."

"Who? Who raced out of here?" Kayla asked. She stepped up to the guards, fearful of the answer.

"That strange-speaking lad, the foreigner," the first guard replied.

"Did he ride out alone?" Her gut tightened, and she felt her throat go dry.

"Aye," the long hair guard answered.

Unable to dismiss her growing fear, Kayla knew something was terribly wrong. "Which direction did he go?"

"He headed out the gate and turned toward the river road. I lost sight of him soon after. I dinna ken I needs keep an eye on the wayward lad."

"Should we go after him?" the older guard offered.

Kayla immediately decided on her course of action. "Nay, 'tis nay necessary. I'll track him myself."

The guards shifted uneasily, clearly uncertain as to how they should respond to her declaration she would be the one to search for the foreigner. Standing straighter with a lift of her chin, she ordered in her most confident voice, "Help me ready my horse. I'm sure he hasn't gone far, and ye must nae leave yer duties." Though she tried to speak calmly, not wishing to reveal her worries to the guards, they surely felt her anxiety and rushed to do her bidding.

Within minutes, Kayla was heading out over the fields, past the village, and along the river road. She feared Daniel was leaving, heading back to where he had come from without even saying good-bye. *Just like his sister,* she thought, adding anger to her fear.

As she rode, she battled with herself. Should she be racing after him to ask him to stay, or was it better to let him go? In truth, she knew she had no choice. How could she stand back and do nothing? She had to at least try.

~*~

Daniel raced down the river road, second-guessing his choices. He was tired, hadn't slept well, and probably wasn't thinking straight. How could he when his mind and heart were engaged in a fierce battle? Should he stay, or should he go? His head told him he needed to leave. He had no business being here, and he definitely shouldn't pursue Kayla, an innocent young woman with no knowledge of his world. Especially when he knew the risk of leaving and losing her was allegedly at the whim of some unseen faerie. But his heart told him to stay. It offered him no logical explanation on why or how; it simply persisted in its quest, fighting to win his internal battle. His heart insisted he stay with Kayla while his brain told him to go.

The battle raged on, and reasonable doubt fought to take control. Daniel told himself such feelings of wanting to stay in Kayla's world were unreliable and illogical. He shouldn't listen to his heart. There was too much at stake. Logic told him he needed to forget about Kayla and get the hell out of Scorrybreac. It would be best for everyone. But his heart let him know in no uncertain terms it wasn't going to be easy. Trying to ignore his urge to give in to his own desires, he spurred his horse on, riding away from his feelings and away from Kayla, while he reasoned out a plausible plan to travel back to his own time.

According to Teressa's journal, she had been swept back to the future when she returned to the place on the beach where the time travel had first occurred. Was that the trick to getting back home? Were there special, magical portals located around the island that allowed the fae to move people through time? It was a crazy idea, but for the moment, it was the only clue he had. Maybe, just maybe, he figured by returning to the spot along the stream where his freaky accident had occurred, he could find the magical portal and go back to where he came from. Perhaps he just needed to recreate his arrival in reverse to make the whole thing work. It was a long shot, but his mind wouldn't let him rest until he at least gave it a try.

Even though he believed it was his duty to return home, to leave this place and time, a part of him hoped he would fail. It was his stubborn heart telling him he wanted to stay. In his head, he argued it was only because he wanted to explore the potential of this time and place, but in his heart, his feelings for Kayla told him to throw caution to the wind, take his chances, and stay.

Even more disturbing was his overriding fear, that in the end, he had no power over his fate. The last thing he wanted was for Kayla to suffer for his self-indulgence if he let his feelings be known.

When he reached the incline above the river, Daniel paused. There it was, the place where his time travel mishap had occurred. Spots pawed the ground, prancing to and fro, as if sharing the anxiety and uncertainty of his rider. Daniel hesitated a moment longer before he gave a swift kick to Spots's flanks, spurring the horse to gallop headlong toward the imaginary portal. He was surprised to feel tears stinging his eyes, blurring his vision as he raced toward his intended destination.

Horse and rider raced along the stream, heading toward his point of arrival. They passed the mark and galloped beyond.

Nothing. No gust of wind sprung up, not even the stirring of a breeze. He wasn't pulled from his mount and rendered unconscious. They passed through the area without incident. Nothing happened.

Daniel pulled Spots to a stop several yards past his point of reference. He turned and surveyed the area. Certain he was in the right place, he gave Spots another kick to his flanks and headed back along the stream, this time slower, not wanting to risk missing the mark. Again they passed his point of reference without incident.

His theory was being shot to hell.

Scratching his head, he dismounted from Spots and walked the pony back along the stream, stopping when he reached the matted grass indicating he was in the right place. He stared at the ground, as though it held clues for him to find. A sense of deep disappointment tempered by a flood of relief confused his thoughts. It made no sense, but nothing about his situation made any sense. The theory of a magical portal was only his imagination gone wild.

"Are ye lost?"

Daniel nearly jumped out of his skin. "What the hell," he cursed under his breath then turned toward the voice. A rider at the top of the incline sat watching him. "Who are you?" Daniel called out to him.

The man leisurely walked his warhorse down the incline. "Alec MacLeod," he said as he drew near, towering over Daniel. "And who might ye be?"

Daniel eyed the large claymore hanging in a sling on the man's back and figured it was in his best interest to be friendly. "Daniel Ellers," he said. "I'm staying at Scorrybreac."

"Aye, Duncan's visitor. I've heard of ye."

"You have?"

"News travels fast on our isle. What are ye looking for? Ye seem lost." The warrior returned to his earlier question regarding Daniel's strange behavior.

Lost, Daniel thought. That seemed like an apt description. "I thought I left something here, but I guess I was wrong." He might be crazy, but he wasn't stupid enough to tell someone he was looking for a magical time travel portal. "What brings you out this way?" he asked in a friendly manner, thinking he should be nice to a stranger on a large warhorse with a big-ass sword.

"I'm chasing down stray cows," Alec answered.

"Having any luck?"

Alec looked at Daniel as if he were daft. "Do ye see any cows?"

"Guess not." He was feeling dumber by the minute.

Alec looked up, listening intently, and, in one swift motion, drew his sword from his back. Daniel heard it too. Both men turned to face the direction of an approaching rider. Daniel could kick himself for not bringing a weapon.

A horse and rider appeared over the ridge of the incline. It was Kayla, and the first thing Daniel noticed was her fear. Blatant fear was stamped large across her face, marring her natural beauty. He felt small, thinking he was the one who put it there.

Alec turned to Daniel, giving him an appraising looking. Turning back to Kayla, he returned his broadsword to its sling and waved to her in greeting.

"Hail Kayla, ye are looking fine this morn," Alec said.

"Good day to ye, Alec," she returned the warrior's greeting as she approached them. "Good day to ye, Daniel Ellers. What brings ye here so early in the morn?" she asked, sounding calmer than she looked. He watched her breasts swiftly rise and fall with labored breaths.

"Just looking around," Daniel answered with a shrug, grinning. It was strange how seeing her filled him with joy.

"I found him here, looking a little lost, like one of my strays," Alec joked. "Mayhap ye should take him home."

Kayla watched Daniel, silently conveying her fear. "Is that what ye want, Daniel? Do ye want to return to Scorrybreac?" she asked, her voice small and hushed.

"That's probably a good idea. I think I'm done here," Daniel answered, mounting up on Spots. He had given his theory a try, and it had failed. But knowing she had come looking for him somehow made the failure feel like a success.

"Will ye join Duncan for the games?" Kayla asked Alec, referring to an upcoming warriors' tournament Duncan was planning. Daniel had heard the brothers talking about it as he trained with them.

"Wouldna miss it. I'll be sailing in with some of my men. Someone's got to give ole Duncan a run for his money, and it surely won't be a MacDonald," Alec answered in good nature.

"'Twill be a grand time, I'm sure." Kayla turned Sallie around to face the direction of the keep.

"I'm looking forward to it," Alec replied, spurring his warhorse to head down the river road. "Farewell," he yelled back as he cantered away.

"It was a pleasure meeting you," Daniel called after the departing warrior, hoping he hadn't made a complete fool of himself.

Alec raised his hand in a final farewell salute but didn't look back.

Soon after they had traveled out of earshot from Alec, Kayla turned to Daniel. "The guards told me ye had left. Where were ye going?"

"Would you mind if I didn't try to explain?" He was too embarrassed to talk about his theory, besides, it defied explanation.

"Were ye planning to leave?" she asked.

He hesitated, wondering what he should say. She looked so forlorn. "I can't help but question if I truly belong here." It was the closest he could come to admitting the uncertainty of his situation.

"Of course ye belong here. Ye are welcome to stay as long as ye wish." Kayla assured him.

"Yeah, I guess so," Daniel replied, completely uncertain how long that would be.

~~~

Though they were returning to the keep, Kayla was still worried. Daniel seemed distant and moody, and it troubled her. If he had an injured hand or a bleeding wound, she would know what to do, but she didn't know how to bring him out of his morose silence. She was practiced in the art of healing, not in the art of conversation.

As soon as they returned to the stables, Daniel began to tend to the horses, removing the saddles and bridals and brushing them down. Kayla stayed by his side to help, hoping he would speak, mayhap tell her how he felt, but he said nothing. They went about the task with quiet efficiency. He was still kind and considerate, helping her groom her horse and stow the gear, but his lighthearted spirit was gone. Something was wrong.

Reluctant to leave his side, she walked with him to the great hall. Before they had stepped inside, Kayla was greeted by her sister-in-law, Janet.

"Have ye heard? My family is coming to the games," Janet said with obvious excitement.

"Yer family? I dinna expect them to visit so soon."

"My parents have nae seen Amy in nearly a year. She is nearly two. The games are a perfect reason for them to visit."

A shudder of alarm raced through Kayla. Could this visit have something to do with the betrothal her mother was attempting to arrange? "Who is expected?" she asked, trying to stay calm.

"Mother and Father, of course, along with Angus and his wife. Arlin, Trey, and Beatrice are also coming, but Farley is staying behind at the keep. There's so much to do afore they arrive. Lady Lydia wants us to prepare the rooms in the high tower for them." Janet turned to address Daniel. "I am sorry to impose, but we need space in yer chamber for Arlin and Trey."

"No problem." Daniel shrugged. "I'll just move to the barracks."

Kayla spoke up, "Janet, there is nay need to bother Daniel. Surely, we can handle this."

"It's no bother, really. I don't mind changing rooms," Daniel said.

"Daniel, could ye excuse us? I need to speak with Janet."

"Sure. It looks like you ladies have your work cut out for you." Daniel gave them a parting nod and headed off toward the barracks.

Kayla rushed Janet into the keep and up the stairway leading to the family bedchambers. "Why is yer family really coming? Does this have something to do with my mother's plan to have me betrothed to Arlin?"

"Duncan and Lady Lydia invited them here for the games, but aye, they may want to discuss a marriage agreement. Why are ye so worried?"

Stepping into her bedchamber, Kayla closed the door behind them.

"Can I trust ye?" she asked, desperate to confide in someone. Kayla hadn't been able to speak with Fern, and she needed the counsel of another woman. She believed she could trust Janet, and hoped her sister-in-law could keep a secret, but she was also Duncan's wife and Arlin's sister.

Janet reached for Kayla's hands, clasping them between hers. "Of course, ye can. We are sisters."

"Please understand, I mean nay offense to ye, or to yer family, or yer brother, but I doona want to marry Arlin. Doona misunderstand; he's a fine man. 'Tis just . . . I doona want to marry him." The words rushed out of Kayla, propelled by her pent-up need to share her burden with another.

"Ye doona want him as a husband?" Janet's eyes showed no judgment, only tenderness.

Kayla shook her head. "Nay, I am sorry, I doona."

"Do ye love another?" Janet asked.

It was a reasonable question.

Kayla turned away to sit on her bed. She thought of Daniel and the way he made her feel, so special, needed, and valued. It was grand to think a man like him could love her. It was grand to think she could have a man like him to love in return. It was also impossible. A fanciful faerie tale made up of wild wishes. She knew so little about Daniel and had even less reason to believe he cared for her. Shaking her head, she said, "Nay. There's no one else."

"Have ye spoken to Duncan about this?" Janet took a seat beside her on the bed.

"Nay. I could never go against Mother. She would nay allow it." Not that she hadn't been thinking about it more and more lately. Her usually close bond to her mother had begun to feel strained by the yoke of Lady Lydia's controlling ways. Before Daniel's arrival, she had never defied her mother. Now she was treading through new territory in their relationship.

"Yer mother is nay in charge. Duncan is the chief of the MacNicols. He shall be the one to arrange yer betrothal. Ye should speak with him."

Kayla was touched to see Janet living up to her vow of loyalty to her husband. Janet felt strongly about defending Duncan's position, but Kayla was well aware her mother still believed she controlled the family. Sometimes it seemed Duncan didn't do enough to challenge Lydia's beliefs, and still honored her role as matriarch of the family. However, when it came to matters affecting the clan's future, Kayla believed Duncan was in total control.

"What can I say? I am a woman of twenty years. I should have married years ago and be raising children of my own. Instead, I follow my mother around like a little lamb and have nay prospects for a proper match."

"Kayla, ye are a beautiful young woman, with great accomplishments. Any man would be proud to have ye as a wife."

"Few have shown an interest," she said in all honesty. "Besides, Mother always sends them away; they were never acceptable. Now she wants me to marry Arlin. I hate to think I may miss the only opportunity I shall have to be married. But I have always hoped . . . I am sure ye understand . . . I have always hoped to marry someone I love." *'Tis only a dream,* she added silently, casting her eyes downward with despair.

"What about Daniel? I believe Duncan approves of him. He seems fond of ye. Have ye feelings for him?"

Kayla's head jerked up, surprised by Janet's mention of Daniel. "It matters little how I feel for Daniel. He is only here for a visit. Like his sister, he is expected to leave. Ye saw what happened when Teressa left. I have nay desire to be left behind like Rory. Besides, I can tell Mother doesn't like him. She would never approve."

It was all true, but Kayla wasn't sure if she were making the arguments for Janet's benefit or her own. She couldn't bear to state her real concerns: that a man such as Daniel would have nay real interest in her. Aye, he had been kind, but she found it difficult to believe his feelings went beyond respectful gratitude.

"This is nae about yer mother or her feelings. She is nae going to marry the man. There was a time in my life when I almost lost Duncan because my mother dinna approve of him.

It was only through the blessings of God and the help of Teressa that Duncan and I were reunited. When Mother saw how much I love him, she finally accepted the match, although I think Lady Lydia was always in favor of our betrothal. Surely, ye can see how happy we are."

"But Daniel is expected to return home, much like Teressa. And we doona even know where that is," Kayla argued.

Janet gave her a questioning look. "Are ye telling me ye would nay be willing to follow the man ye love? Would ye really risk the same mistake I once made?"

Kayla shuddered. She couldn't leave Scorrybreac. The very thought filled her with despair. "I dinna say I love Daniel. I doona know how I feel. At first, I resented him for being here, but I do find him attractive." *Mother of God, I can't believe I'm telling her this.* "I appreciate yer concern, and yer desire to help. But, I doona see how I can get past Mother's desire to have me marry Arlin."

"'Tis why ye need to speak with Duncan."

"And Mother's blatant dislike of Daniel?" Kayla asked.

"That might be a wee harder. She means well. She loves her children. She simply has a tendency to put her desires above all others."

"Mayhap ye could talk to Duncan. Or mayhap Arlin. Let them know how I feel," Kayla offered with hopeful enthusiasm. Janet was only a year older than Kayla, but it felt as though she were far ahead of her in confidence.

"Nay. That is something ye needs do. Ye need to stand up for yerself."

"I was afraid ye would say something like that." Kayla's enthusiasm sank.

Janet laid her hand on Kayla's shoulder. "Mayhap I can be there with ye, to offer moral support, if ye would like."

"Oh, would ye? 'Twould mean so much to me. I canna face them all alone."

"Kayla, ye are never alone. Yer family loves ye. In the end, they only want what's best for ye. Ye must speak yer mind, and I recommend ye start with Duncan. 'Tis best if ye avoid speaking to Lady Lydia 'til it becomes absolutely necessary."

A half smile returned to Kayla's face. Maybe there was hope after all. She was reminded of Moezell's advice. The faerie had told her to set aside her fears and seek with an open heart. She wondered if Moezell had known that to follow her advice, she would need to challenge her mother.

~*~

Kayla could hardly eat, her nerves buzzed with such intensity. She was about to take one of the biggest risks of her life, and it wasn't sitting well in the pit of her stomach. Earlier she had asked Duncan if she could speak with him after supper. It would not be easy, she feared, to tell him she did not wish to marry Arlin. There was much at stake. She could very well be passing on her last, if not best, chance for a suitable match. A fearful voice in the back of her head told her it was a grave mistake to take this risk, one she may long regret.

Even more disturbing were her conflicted feelings for Daniel. There had been an immediate attraction when she found him stranded along the river road, but his allure was quickly tempered by resentment when she discovered he was Teressa Ellers's brother, a woman whom she believed had hurt Rory beyond measure and without cause. After learning her resentment was without merit, her attraction had resurfaced. He had been kind and caring to her in ways no man had ever been before, such as when he tended her injured ankle. But as far as she knew, that was merely his way. It didn't necessarily mean he was attracted to her. Bonnie had told her he was agreeable to everyone in the kitchens; even Milly had kind words for him.

To think he might care for her was tempting enough, but to think he might love her was more than she dare dream. Even if he were Teressa's brother, he was still a relative stranger, and like Teressa, she expected him to return home anytime he chose. It would require a courageous heart and a leap of faith on words not spoken for her to pursue her deepest dreams. Was it wise to risk her future based on her limited experience with Daniel, a man she hardly knew?

While it was grand to think Daniel could turn out to be her white knight, a hero to rescue her from all her troubles, even she knew such heroes only existed in faerie tales.

The evening meal passed with stomach-churning slowness as she steeled herself for her upcoming interview with Duncan. She had little appetite and mostly picked at the hearty meal of mutton stew and crusty bread. If only she had thought ahead to brew some of her herbal tea to drink instead of the sweet spiced wine she sipped from her goblet. The warm, soothing brew would be much better for her churning stomach.

Distracted by her thoughts, she tried not to focus overmuch on Daniel as he spoke with Michael and Rory. Occasionally, she cast fleeting glances his way and was only dimly aware of their conversation as they spoke of prized horseflesh and the benefits of well-bred horses. Sometimes she would catch him watching her when she dared to sneak a peek from under her lashes, but just as often, he was too caught up in his conversation with her brothers to pay her any attention.

When Duncan stood from the dining table, he motioned for Kayla and his wife to join him in his study. Kayla breathed a bit easier, knowing her sister-in-law would be there for emotional support.

"I understand ye wish to speak with me on a matter of some importance," Duncan said, casting an intimidating look at Kayla. He poured himself a generous serving of his fine Scottish whisky before taking a seat in the large armchair near the hearth.

Kayla sat across from him with Janet on a wooden bench. She forced herself to look at her brother and not down at her hands.

"Lady Janet has informed me the MacDonald clan will be attending yer games," Kayla began.

"Aye, 'tis true they've been invited," Duncan confirmed.

The next part was a little harder for Kayla to say. Her heart pounded hard in her chest, really hard, perhaps the hardest she had ever felt. "I understand Mother seeks to arrange a betrothal between me and Arlin."

"Correct. I believe ye were there when we discussed the matter."

Impossible as it seemed, the pounding in her chest increased. Though she had rehearsed this statement several times over, the words wanted to stick in her throat. She forced herself to push on. "Duncan," she said taking a breath and lifting her chin, "as my brother and chief of this clan, I think 'tis only right ye should know I doona wish to marry Arlin MacDonald."

"Are ye nay longer interested in a betrothal to Arlin?"

"I never said I was interested in marrying him. That was Mother's idea." Kayla wondered if her brother were being difficult on purpose. His expression was unreadable.

"Do ye still hold feelings for Murdock MacLeod?" Duncan asked. A slightly malicious grin let Kayla know he was teasing her instead of taking her seriously.

She drew a deep breath, swelling with indignation. "I am well past any fondness I may have felt for Murdock. We have both moved on from our childish affections." It was irritating to be reminded of her first experience with young love. She had not yet seen sixteen summers when she spent the whole week at the Isle Faire following the youngest son of the MacLeod chief around like a lost puppy. He was nearly five years her senior and had showed only a modicum of interest in Kennon MacNicol's only daughter. The following year she learned Murdock had taken up with Merrie Lewis, putting a final damper on any desire she might have had for the handsome lad.

"What I am saying, if ye will only listen, I wish to oppose an arranged betrothal with Arlin. As chief of this clan, I am aware ye have the power to force such an arrangement. I can only hope as the loving brother I know ye to be, ye will see the greater benefit in allowing me to choose my own husband." She hoped her case held merit, but she had very little experience with dissention. She seldom disagreed with her eldest brother, and she never argued. She feared she lacked the necessary skills.

"Pray tell, what would be my benefit for allowing ye to choose yer own mate?" His smile disappeared, and his expression became serious as his jaw clenched.

"Seeing yer sister settled in a happy union that would bring honor, and mayhap joy to this family." Even as she said the words, she felt how flimsy the argument appeared. What was she thinking? He had no reason to grant her request. His primary goal was to see her wed as soon as possible to a suitable husband. Other than her idea that he was not the man she wanted to spend the rest of her life with, there was very little to dispute the fact Arlin qualified as a suitable husband.

"Do ye have a proper suitor in mind to fill such a role?" he asked.

Color rose instantly to her cheeks. She had dreaded the possibility he would ask such a question. What could she say? That she hoped Daniel found her irresistible, or even acceptable, and would ask for her hand in marriage. What a load of cow dung was that? Too stunned to know what to say, she was relieved when Janet spoke in her defense.

"My dear husband, I am doubtful Kayla is able to provide an answer tonight. She only wishes to know if ye will grant her request."

"I canna very well let her sell off one horse until we know there is another to fill the stable," Duncan answered his wife.

"Duncan!" Janet was shocked.

"Brother!" Kayla was even more shocked. "How can ye say such a thing, to compare my suitors to horseflesh? 'Tis disgusting and indecent . . ."

"'Tis the truth," he stated firmly, interrupting her. "Kayla, I care for ye, truly. But as yer brother and chief of this clan, I have a responsibility to see ye well wed. Twenty years on a woman does nae sit well with many men. Ye may find my words harsh, but I only speak what we know 'tis true."

Feeling remiss, Kayla looked down at her hands twisting in her lap. Even though she knew he spoke the truth, she had hoped for greater support from her brother. It was not her desire to remain as a single woman in his household indefinitely, and yet if she rejected this chance for a match, she was woefully aware such might very well be the unintended result.

Reacting to her silence, Duncan asked, "If Arlin comes to seek yer hand, do ye really think I should refuse?"

Her eyes shot up to catch his. "Do ye think he will?"

"'Tis possible. 'Tis time Arlin seek a family of his own. He is of an age when such is expected of him, and his plans may well include ye, fair sister. Ye should be honored."

She paused to consider Duncan's words. Was Arlin truly in favor of a match with her? They had known each other for years, and yet she had never detected more than courteous indifference from him, and sometimes less than that. She hadn't considered he might wish to pursue her hand in marriage. It occurred to her that she had based her opinion solely on her feelings for him. If she had been mistaken about Arlin, wasn't it also possible she had used the same reasoning in her attraction to Daniel, hoping he felt for her as she did for him? She began to seriously question her perceptions.

"Does this mean ye will require my betrothal with Arlin, if he so requests?" Kayla asked, as calmly as she was able, while holding back the tears constricting her throat and threatening to escape.

"We will see what develops when the MacDonalds arrive. Until then, I shall make nay promises."

Kayla felt burning tears pooling in her eyes. She blinked them away, trying not to show her weakness.

"However—" Duncan held up a hand, as if to ward off her tears, "—since ye have made yer feelings known, I will take them into consideration."

Kayla nodded her acceptance and stood to leave. Avoiding the great hall, Kayla went directly to her room and plopped down in her chair by the hearth where Daniel had massaged her injured foot only days before. She tried to take solace in Duncan's final words, but she couldn't help but feel as though she had been driven off course. It felt as if the horse she'd been riding had been pulled from beneath her and she were left to wander again on her own.

CHAPTER 12

The MacDonald family was due to arrive soon, and Daniel was doing his best to make himself scarce. He had moved from the large room in the high tower to a small cell in the barracks with the MacNicol guards. Still feeling like an outsider, he wanted to avoid the dinner celebration planned for the MacDonalds' arrival and went off on his own to explore more of the intriguing nooks and crannies located throughout the castle. The MacNicol clan was beginning to gather in the great hall in anticipation of their guests, and he had no desire to hang around to observe the reunion of the two families.

After wandering through a maze of dimly lit corridors and narrow winding stairways, Daniel reached the top level of the high tower. He hoped to be rewarded with a spectacular view once he gained access to the rooftop; he wasn't disappointed. When he pushed open the heavy wooden door leading out to the tower's roof, he was greeted with a vast, sweeping vista of endless ocean.

Daniel stepped out into the late afternoon sun slanting across the rooftop and saw an elderly man dressed in long grey robes sitting on a bench overlooking the sea. He guessed him to be Souyer, the old master druid Teressa had mentioned in her journal. More than once, he had seen the old man watching him from afar, but this was his first personal encounter with the wizard. He wondered why the old man was keeping his distance. It was obvious Souyer had an interest in him, and yet he'd made no attempt to approach him.

"So, finally we meet," Daniel greeted the old man, indicating his awareness of the subtle surveillance.

"I've been expecting ye. 'Tis a fine day for contemplating life." Souyer remained seated on the bench with his eyes focused on the endless blue of the sea.

"I figure you know who I am, and I'm guessing you're Souyer, the master druid. Teressa mentioned you." Daniel crossed the tower roof and stood next to the old man.

"Did ye enjoy learning about her time travels? Her journal must have been very helpful, considering yer unusual circumstances." His gaze didn't leave the sea, watching the constant ebb and flow of the ever-moving ocean.

"How do you know about that? Are you the one behind all this?" Daniel had been led to believe it was most likely the infamous faerie, Moezell, who brought him to this time and place, but perhaps this old wizard knew more than the MacNicol brothers realized.

Souyer finally turned his attention to Daniel. "'Tis nae my doing. I am only an observer and mayhap an adviser. When the student is ready, the teacher will appear."

Daniel cocked a distrusting eye at Souyer. "Teressa pegged you as a wizard wannabe, not a mentor."

Souyer gave Daniel an appraising look. "I prefer to think of myself as a sage; old and wise, but still somewhat mysterious. 'Tis far more enjoyable than striving to be a powerful and respected wizard, and much less tiresome. Of course, I still maintain my position as master druid. 'Tis a title I've grown quite fond of. Playing the role of wizard required a constant effort to demonstrate supernatural abilities. 'Twas mostly a lot of bluster. Since Teressa's visit, I'm much more comfortable being a sage. Nae getting any younger, ye know. So, ye have questions, am I right?"

Daniel was impressed. "Let's start with the obvious. Why am I here?" He folded his arms across his chest, doubtful he would be given the answers he was hoping for.

"'Tis yet to be seen. I expect ye have a task to perform, much like Teressa. Ye shall know when the time is right. Until then, I recommend patience. Fate and the faeries have a way of revealing themselves in their own time."

"That's not a lot of help," Daniel scoffed.

"Doona be so quick to judge. Patience, my lad. Certainly ye have other questions ye wish to discuss."

Daniel stood next to the chest-high stone wall encircling the high tower and gazed out to the ocean's horizon. Uncertainty churned through his gut. For the most part, he tried to avoid thinking too much about fate, and faeries, and mystical possibilities. Maybe it was time to accept the magic of Skye, as Rory suggested. Maybe it was time to consider his fate and why he was here. He also tried to avoid thinking about Kayla, but that was a bust. Lately, she was all he thought about.

"I read once there are no coincidences. At the time, I didn't believe it. Coincidences happen all the time. Lately I've been thinking it wasn't a mere coincidence Kayla was the one to find me lying along the road. It might have been a mean-spirited prank by a meddlesome faerie that brought me back in time, but there must have been a reason I landed in that place, at exactly the right moment so she could be the one to find me." He glanced over his shoulder to observe the druid-turned-sage. "Am I right?"

The master druid seemed impressed. "The world may appear random and chaotic, but 'twas nay mere coincidence that brought ye and Kayla together."

Daniel nodded, absorbing the druid's words. He turned to lean against the stone wall with his back to the ocean. "Okay, so tell me, do you think it's possible to fall in love at first sight, or something like that?"

Souyer cast a sideways glance at Daniel. "That's one of the funny things about love. The best time to fall in love is usually at first sight."

The old man's answer surprised Daniel. "Really? You don't think there's some advantage in taking your time, getting to know a woman first to find out if she's right for you?" He voiced his concerns though he found Souyer's comment curiously reassuring.

"Why would ye take the time unless she appealed to ye from the moment ye met? It may take some time afore the realization finally settles in and makes itself known, but from my observations, as well as my own experience, either 'tis there or 'tis not. Wishful thinking will not make it happen, nor make it go away."

Daniel could see the logic of the druid's advice. Even a long, drawn-out romance was likely to start with the all-important first impression. Either the spark was there, or it wasn't. Still, he worried his attraction to Kayla might just be a heavy dose of lust at first sight, an infatuation, or even a simple case of wanting what he couldn't have. The allure of the taboo was too strong to be ignored.

He thought about the moment when he first laid eyes on her as she was bending over him along the river road, backlit by the sun. Even then he'd known he felt an uncommon connection between them. A feeling of recognition had stirred somewhere deep in his soul, as though he were aware he was meeting someone special. And he had called her an angel.

The possibility of time travel was still beyond his understanding, and surprisingly, it didn't seem to matter so much, at least not as much as it should. He was here; it had happened; time to move on.

More important was his need to understand *why* he was here, in this time and this place, with Kayla. From the moment they met, she had slipped under his skin and into his dreams, her presence as comfortable as the well-worn jeans he had stashed in his chamber. There was a certain feeling of familiarity about her, but more than that, his desire for her was much stronger than a casual attraction to a beautiful woman.

Kayla was a lovely woman in her own right; he thought her beautiful, but he'd met dozens of good-looking women back home in San Francisco. California was loaded with more than its fair share of attractive women, and yet none had captured his attention like Kayla.

He liked the way her flaming red hair framed her face like a halo and glowed when struck by the sun. Her liquid green eyes had specks of gold that danced in tune to her emotions, flashing bright one moment and becoming dark and intense the next. They were a window to her soul, which she left open and unguarded for anyone who took the time to look. He was especially charmed by the smattering of freckles splashed across her pert little nose and dusty pink cheeks. She was a lovely little package, particularly appealing to him. And if that weren't enough, there was the alluring promise of her shapely, well-formed figure. From what he had seen—and felt—she had a lot to offer.

It may have been a prank by a freakish faerie, but it wasn't dumb luck that brought them together. There was a force of destiny at work here, well beyond his comprehension, and in that moment, he realized he was eternally grateful, and totally confused.

Still, he had more questions for Souyer. "What can you tell me about this faerie, Moezell? Why haven't I met her like Teressa did? If she really is the one behind all this, why hasn't she shown herself to me?"

"From what I know, Moezell has her own way of doing things. There was a time when she worked with Lady Lydia, but recently she has branched out on her own, taking more control of matters, or mayhap less."

"What do you mean?"

"Lady Lydia prefers to control the details of any situation. She plans every step along the way. Moezell likes to set up situations and see how they play out. The faerie has a great fondness for humans and their volatile emotions. Her greatest joy is to watch them choose their destiny."

"No way, man. It wasn't my choice to be sent seven hundred years back in time." Daniel shook his head, folding his arms across his chest.

"Mayhap ye dinna pick the method, but there must be some need, some wish of yers longing to be filled. Why else would ye be here? At some level, mayhap deeper than ye are aware, ye were seeking this adventure, or it could nay be happening. 'Twas true with Teressa. 'Tis true for ye."

"You think I chose this mess I'm in?" The idea was pure nonsense.

"Would ye prefer dull and boring? Life is messy. If it wasn't, it wouldn't be any fun. All of life is a blessing, an answer to yer prayers."

"I'm not a praying man," Daniel scoffed.

"Every thought ye think, every word ye speak, every choice ye make is a prayer waiting to be heard, longing to be answered." A pleasant smile graced the old man's features. He appeared to enjoy playing the role of a wise, old sage.

"I never spoke a word about traveling back in time. The thought never occurred to me."

"Dinna ye find Teressa's journal intriguing?" Souyer asked with a raised brow.

"Maybe, a little, but mostly I found it unbelievable. Of course, that was before it happened to me."

"Think upon it. What is the greatest risk—the one that scares ye the most?" Souyer stared into Daniel's eyes, as if searching for his soul. "Every risk ye take makes ye stronger. Ye are nay a weak man, Daniel Ellers."

Obstinate silence accompanied the steely gaze Daniel leveled at Souyer. He wanted to rail against the druid's words, call them foolish, crazy ideas, not words of wisdom. But he figured there was no use arguing with the man. This wasn't a battle he was going to win. Besides, it kind of picked at him that the old man's words might be true, not that he was ready to go there, not yet. As much as it irked him, he figured he'd just have to let it go, for now. Mysteries, like crimes, usually didn't go unsolved. The right clues always showed up sooner or later.

Pushing off with his staff, Souyer slowly rose from his bench. "A storm is brewing off in the distance. It may take a few days to reach land, but 'tis out there gathering force."

Daniel looked out at the smattering of fluffy white clouds gracing the skyline of the setting sun, relieved to be speaking on a topic as benign as the weather instead of questioning his choices in life. "Looks fine enough to me," he countered.

"Summer storms can brew up suddenly, and appear out of nowhere. Watch for the signs." With that, Souyer turned toward the tower door, muttering something that sounded a lot like scripture as he shuffled off to return to his chamber. "I have planted thy seeds in fertile soil. We shall await the harvest."

Daniel shook his head, amused. *Silly old sage.*

~*~

Having been alerted by Duncan's master-at-arms, the MacNicols stood on the steps of their keep awaiting their visitors. Front and center was Duncan with Lady Janet and Lady Lydia on each side. Janet held their young daughter, Amy. As instructed by her mother, Kayla stood behind Duncan, flanked by her brothers, Michael and Rory. When Lydia wasn't looking, she stepped closer to Rory and clasped his hand for brotherly support. He gave her fingers a gentle squeeze of reassurance. Peering around the large frame of her eldest brother, she watched the incoming procession and sighed. The arrival of Hugh MacDonald and his family was certainly a sight to see.

The MacDonald chief and his wife, Lady Evelyn, rode on a pair of large dark warhorses through the main gate of Scorrybreac, crossed the courtyard, and stopped at the steps leading to the great hall of the keep. Following close behind came Hugh's sons, Angus, Trey, and Arlin. They were accompanied by Angus's wife, Elisa, and the MacDonalds' youngest daughter, Beatrice. Following at some distance, almost as though she were an afterthought, a petite young woman with chestnut brown hair and equally dark brown eyes tagged along behind the MacDonald clan on a far less impressive mule.

Kayla had to admit, the MacDonald's liked to take advantage of situations, making the most of them to further their image as a powerful clan. As the right and mighty chief of his clan, the MacDonald used his aggressive reputation to preserve their status. Hugh, she noted, tarried a moment longer astride his mount while his wife and children dismounted. This slight delay allowed his wife and children to take their places before he moved to his prominent position in front of the collective troop of MacDonalds ready to present themselves to Duncan. Hugh led the procession, climbing the steps of the keep with slow, regal determination. A respectful step behind the chief was his wife, Lady Evelyn. She, in turn, was followed by their children, completing the grand presentation.

After a nod of acknowledgement by Duncan, the MacDonald greeted his daughter with an enveloping embrace before moving quickly to gather his granddaughter into his large burly arms. Hugh, Kayla noted, was not a quiet man. When he spoke, he nearly bellowed.

"Lady Janet, daughter of my heart, yer lovely lass is the image of her mother and grandmother afore her." Hugh smacked his lips soundly upon Amy's rosy pink cheek before she squirmed and wiggled away, fleeing his embrace to return to her mother's arms. "'Tis another blessing for an old man already blessed many times over with fine sons and grandsons to carry on the MacDonald name."

Kayla didn't miss the backhanded jab aimed at Duncan and Janet. While she knew Duncan and Janet loved their daughter completely, she understood all too well the preferred objective for any clan chief was to produce male offspring to continue the family name. Apparently, Duncan chose to ignore the rudeness of Janet's father for the sake of his wife and to keep peace in the family.

Rather than succumb to petty insults, Duncan greeted the elder chief with an appropriate level of respect for the father of his wife, even if it was undeserved in Kayla's opinion. "I welcome the MacDonald chief and his clansmen to my keep. Ye look to be in fine health. I trust yer journey went well."

"Well enough, thanks to my fine set of horses," Hugh boasted, motioning toward the dark stallions standing at the foot of the stairs.

Fulfilling her role as matriarch, Lady Lydia stepped forward to greet their guests, grasping Lady Evelyn's hands in hers. "Lady Evelyn, such a joy to see ye again. It has been too long. Look how our granddaughter has grown." She motioned toward Amy. "Hugh, ye are looking hale and hearty. 'Tis our pleasure to welcome yer family to our keep."

Her mother's greeting bordered on disrespect. Lydia hadn't acknowledged Hugh until after she had greeted his wife. This was one time Kayla approved of her mother's actions.

Lady Lydia extended her hand to Hugh, who brought it to his lips for a slight brushing kiss. Upon his release, her mother returned her hand to her side, covertly rubbing her knuckles against the folds of her gown. With growing interest, Kayla noted the telling gesture.

From the edge of her vision, Kayla watched as the last rider dismounted at the foot of the steps with vivid relief. Judging by the younger woman's appearance, she guessed her to be Lady Evelyn's personal chambermaid, since she was dressed in a plain brown wool skirt and muslin tunic. Nonetheless, something in the woman's expression and the way she carried herself brought questions to Kayla's mind. Even as she dismounted from the mule, she kept her eyes focused on the MacDonald men. It looked as if she were waiting to be introduced, or maybe even announced. Lydia must have also noticed the maid.

"Am I right in thinking ye have found a replacement for Matilda?" Lady Lydia asked, referring to the young maid. She directed her question to Lady Evelyn, while her eyes tracked the younger woman's movements.

"Aye, and lucky for it. That's Becky, Matilda's niece, almost one of the family," Lady Evelyn replied.

"Really, how very fortunate for ye." A half smile graced Lady Lydia's lips. "I'll have Bonnie see to her needs. She can sleep on a pallet in the chamber assigned to Beatrice, if ye've a mind to keep her near. Otherwise, Bonnie will find space for her with the servants." She motioned to Bonnie waiting inside the great hall.

"Beatrice's chamber would be preferred," Lady Evelyn confirmed. "Becky has only recently taken on the position of my chambermaid. I'm sure ye heard of Matilda's passing. She was my personal maid since I was a young woman, and I miss her dearly. I couldna bear the prospect of losing another chambermaid to old age. Thankfully, Arlin convinced me to enlist the services of Matilda's niece. She's the daughter of our blacksmith."

In Kayla's opinion, the young servant displayed an inordinate amount of pride and self-confidence for someone in her position. Even if her father was the blacksmith, one of the more respected positions in the keep, this lass was still only a maid. Maintaining a look of disinterest, Kayla was pleased when Bonnie took the lass off to the kitchens where she would work with the other servants of the keep.

With a wave of his hand, Duncan directed the gathering of travelers into his great hall. "Come, let us relax and refresh after yer long journey. Food and ale await yer arrival."

One after the other, Duncan and Hugh led their families into the warmth of the great hall, which had been well prepared for their guests' arrival. Banquet tables laden with food and drink stood ready to provide for their pleasure. Duncan took his seat at the head of the head table, joined by his wife and mother on his right. At the opposite end of the table from him sat the MacDonald chief with Lady Evelyn to his right. The respective family members followed in step around the long banquet table. Michael, Shannon, Rory, and Kayla sat on the MacNicol side of the table, with Angus, Elisa, Trey, Arlin, and Beatrice on the other.

Duncan signaled for the ale to be poured, and the feasting began.

An hour later, Kayla surveyed the remains of the meal being cleared from the large plank tables. It appeared their guests had enjoyed the full bounty of the MacNicol's hospitality. They had eaten their fill and then some. She noticed barely a spoonful of the hearty seafood soup or a morsel of the mutton roast remained by the end of the banquet. Duncan's best ale and cider had flowed freely to wash down the filling feast. Having enjoyed the abundance of food to his fullest capacity, Hugh MacDonald motioned to a nearby servant for yet another refill on his tankard of ale before sitting back to relax.

"I am pleased to see the MacNicol chief is able to provide an adequate meal for yer guests," Hugh said. "I trust this has nae overly taxed yer provisions." It seemed the MacDonald chief had a natural ability to flavor every comment he made with a heaping spoonful of insult, often to the point where any hint of a compliment was effectively lost in the bitter spice.

"I am equally pleased to see ye spared nay effort in partaking of our hospitality." Duncan retorted, eyeing Hugh's platter as it was cleared from the table. It was all but licked clean.

Hugh seemed to ignore the reference to his gluttony.

"I'm surprised to see Roderick still unattached." His gaze rested on Rory at the far side of the large table. "Last I recall, he was quite smitten by that saucy lass who accompanied ye to the Isle Faire a few years back."

Rory was speaking to Michael and appeared to be ignoring the MacDonald. Kayla doubted the MacDonald chief was unaware of Teressa's departure from Skye. Their lands were not a far distance apart, and the island was too small for gossip to be confined to any clan's keep.

"Rory keeps his own counsel. To my knowledge, he is satisfied with his current situation," Duncan said.

"What is his current situation?" Hugh inquired, his brows raised.

While it clearly took some effort, even if such effort chafed mightily against his preference, it appeared her brother was determined to be considerate to the elder chief, whether he deserved it or nae.

"Ye would be best served to ask Rory such a question," Duncan replied. Leaning back to relax, he accepted a refill to his tankard from an attentive servant.

Picking up the thread of the conversation, Lady Lydia spoke up, directing her question to Lady Evelyn. "How fare yer other children? 'Tis unfortunate not all were able to accompany you on this visit."

Kayla was glad for it. The visiting MacDonalds were already filling their limited number of guest chambers, forcing Daniel to move into the barracks. The Scorrybreac keep was modest compared to the accommodations available at the MacDonalds' larger compound, but her mother had done all she could to ensure their comfort. Lady Lydia would not have Lady

Evelyn spread gossip that the MacNicols lacked in providing hospitality to their guests.

Never one to miss an opportunity to boast of her family, Lady Evelyn readily gave an accounting of her children and their offspring. "Angus and Elisa have already been blessed with two fine sons, Hurley and Nevin. They chose to remain at our keep with their cousins. Farley and his wife have a brood of three to keep them busy, and Trey's dear young wife is already heavy with their first bairn."

"I'm so happy for them," Janet said, turning to catch Duncan's eye. "They've been married far longer than us. I'm sure this is a welcome relief for them." She reached out to cover Duncan's hand, clearly proud of their young offspring, Amy, who had been born weeks shy of a full year after their marriage.

"We expect it to be another lad," Hugh broke in. "Our sons have proven quite successful in that area," he boasted once again.

Kayla rolled her eyes. Was there no end to his bluster?

"It appears only yer youngest, Arlin and Beatrice, are without suitable matches," Lady Lydia said, ignoring Hugh's comment.

"I'm sure Arlin will have his pick of young lasses when he is of a mind to wed. And Beatrice has only recently come into an age to make a match," Lady Evelyn said, quick to defend her youngest children.

Aware Beatrice had reached her nineteenth summer, Kayla considered her to be a bit further into the marriage market than Lady Evelyn wished to convey, but she couldn't very well argue such a point, knowing she herself was all of twenty.

"What of yer Kayla? Has she nay suitors?" Lady Evelyn turned the topic back to Lady Lydia.

This was the moment Kayla had been dreading, becoming the subject of their conversation.

"Kayla has chosen to focus on learning the healing arts. She's well respected in our village for the talents she has developed. We find her a great asset to our keep, as she will be to any clan she chooses to marry into."

For a moment, Kayla was surprised to hear her mother rush to her defense. But she quickly realized it was only because Lady Lydia believed it was important for the MacDonald chief and his wife to see her as a desirable wife for their son.

"Thankfully, we have been well served for many years by our midwife, Astra. She has been there for the birth of each of our grandsons," Lady Evelyn said.

"Wasn't she also the midwife for the births of yer children, Lady Evelyn? I should expect she's quite experienced by now. I wonder how much longer she can continue to be in yer service," Lady Lydia rebutted.

"Actually, Clara, one of my younger maids, has begun her training with Astra. She's progressing well, and we expect when the time comes, she will be able to take on Astra's duties."

"What a relief that must be for ye, considering Astra's advancing years. As ye may know, Kayla has nae only assisted our midwife, Bettina, but has delivered a number of bairns on her own. Aye, she'll be a welcome addition to any clan of her choosing," Lady Lydia reiterated.

"At her age, I'm surprised she hasn't already found a suitable match," Hugh mumbled into his tankard before taking a long deep draw of the amber brew.

Kayla was taken aback by the direct insult to her honor.

"I can assure ye, Kayla has had her share of suitors," her mother retorted, her voice raising a notch higher than before.

"We once considered a match with Murdock MacLeod, but we found him nae in our favor."

"Murdock MacLeod joined with Merrie Lewis years ago. Surely there have been more recent suitors since him," Lady Evelyn remarked.

"Ye canna expect me to give a complete listing of all who have shown an interest in my dear sweet Kayla." Indignant, Lady Lydia held her ground.

Kayla was both grateful for her mother's arrogance and appalled by the nature of the conversation. She'd been watching the interplay between her mother and the MacDonalds long enough to realize the MacDonald chief and Lady Evelyn had no intention of proposing a betrothal between her and Arlin. Her mother was only making matters worse with her blatant efforts to promote her. If the conversation were allowed to continue much longer, she was apt to appear as damaged goods. Although it was impossibly impolite to leave the banquet table before her elders, Kayla profoundly wished she could melt into the floorboards.

The only thing she had to be thankful for right now was that Daniel had declined to join them for the evening meal. Having him watch her mother try to pawn her off to the MacDonalds would have been more embarrassment than she cared to endure. Surely it would have diminished any attraction he felt for her.

She wished she understood the twists of fate that repeatedly deposited Ellers on their doorstep, only to have them depart as quickly as they arrived. She wondered if it were a blessing or a curse bestowed upon her family. For Rory, she could see it had been some of each. She was beginning to understand why it had been such a blessing for her brother to experience such heartfelt passion with Teressa, even if only for a limited time. However, it had also been a curse when Rory experienced the heartbreak of their separation.

To his credit, Rory refused to view the separation as a curse. He had once told her, "How could I feel such pain unless I had known such pleasure. One cannot exist without the other." At the time, she hadn't understood his remarks. Now they were taking on a whole new meaning.

"I have every faith in my sister's ability to attract a proper suitor," Duncan spoke up, interrupting his mother and Lady Evelyn. "In fact, she has spoken to me recently on where her interests lie."

Kayla gave her full attention to her eldest brother, wondering what he would say next. She hadn't exactly shared with Duncan whom she had in mind to replace Arlin as a possible suitor, but she figured her brother had a pretty good idea.

"She has?" Lady Lydia asked, sounding slightly suspicious.

Lady Evelyn leaned forward, as if ready to catch some juicy piece of gossip. Apparently Kayla wasn't the only one caught unaware by Duncan's announcement.

Catching Lady Evelyn's keen interest in her surprised reaction, Lady Lydia quickly amended her words. "I'm surprised she would speak to her brother of such intimate matters."

"I am the chief of this clan. 'Tis only proper she share her preferences with me," Duncan said.

"Why, of course, Duncan, I only meant to convey . . ."

Before her mother could dig her hole any deeper, Janet broke in, "Mother, Lady Lydia and I are planning a picnic for Amy tomorrow. I am hoping ye will join us."

"Of course, my dear." Lady Evelyn responded to her daughter's invitation.

"If the weather holds, we can walk over to the meadow. 'Tis well protected from the wind, and Amy can play in the wildflowers."

Silently, Kayla blessed Duncan's wife, relieved to be leaving the subject of her marriage prospects.

"I've arranged with Milly to have baskets of treats prepared for the outing," Lady Lydia chimed in, finally seeing the necessity to abandon the previous conversation. "We expect Elisa and Beatrice will join us, and of course, Kayla will be there."

Kayla sent a grateful glance at Janet. She may have remained silent throughout the ordeal, but she was painfully aware of being the topic of their conversation. It was unsettling to hear them discussing her, as though she wasn't even in the same room. Such treatment had the effect of making her feel more like a possession to be disposed of than a person with opinions and preferences of her own. She understood it was her mother's desire to strengthen clan ties and provide for her well-being that drove Lydia to pursue a betrothal for her with Arlin; however, Kayla couldn't help but feel like a lamb being sold at market.

Hoping to engage Arlin in a pleasant conversation, Kayla turned her attention toward him. Much like his father, Arlin had been more focused on devouring the well-prepared feast than engaging in polite conversation.

"Did ye fare well on yer travels to Scorrybreac?" she asked him.

"Our travels were uneventful," Arlin answered, his tone anything but engaging. He immediately turned his attention back to his elder brother. "Angus, have ye decided which games ye will compete in tomorrow?"

"Archery is my strongest talent. I expect to take the field," Angus replied.

"I expect to fare as well with the fighting staffs," Arlin boasted. "I doubt the MacNicol clan has a man who can best me."

Michael glanced over at the arrogant young man. "I wouldn't be so sure if I were ye. I've picked up a few new moves that may surprise ye," he said with a knowing smirk.

Nothing would please Kayla more than to see Michael take down the loudmouthed Arlin. Though the words nearly stuck in her throat, she tried one more time to draw Arlin's attention. "Ye sound rather confident. Have ye trained long with the fighting staffs?" she asked.

"Of course, I'm confident. I'm the best in my clan," he answered gruffly. He dismissed her with a look of disdain, turning his attention back to his brother as they continued to discuss the upcoming games.

Kayla took a sip of wine to clear the bitter taste from her mouth and focused on keeping her face expressionless. She would not give Arlin or his siblings the satisfaction of seeing her cringe. Silently, she hoped Michael would do her the honor of knocking their rude guest on his backside tomorrow at the games, perhaps with a few ugly welts thrown in for good measure.

Looking away from Arlin, Kayla caught Beatrice's snide expression. The younger woman made no attempt to hide her condescending smirk. It was obvious she enjoyed watching Kayla flail in the wind.

"Which games will ye compete in, Rory?" Beatrice asked, her voice dripping with sweetness as she turned her gaze to Kayla's brother.

"Nearly all of them," he answered, giving her his attention with a pleasant smile.

"I'm sure a strong man like thee will do well in whatever games ye play," Beatrice offered coyly, providing little chance for misunderstanding her innuendo.

"Aye, I'm sure I will." Rory nodded, grinning. He acknowledged her comment with elusive politeness, but he didn't offer more. Apparently, he had no desire to be pulled into her flirtations.

Beatrice looked as if she were about to say more, but Michael spoke first.

"Have ye spoken to Alec MacLeod?" Michael asked Rory. "Do ye know how many men he plans to bring to the games?"

"Nay, he has nae given me an exact number, but if I know the MacLeods, we can expect them to come in full force."

"I expect they shall give us a run for our coin, as always," Duncan interjected.

This sparked a new round of male-centered discussions, and Kayla was again left to sit and observe in silence.

Throughout the evening, she kept an observant eye on Arlin and his siblings, hoping to detect his mood. For a man who was being sought by her mother as a possible suitor, Arlin displayed a discouraging lack of interest in her.

However, there was one advantage to being thoroughly ignored. It gave her an opportunity to freely observe the interactions of those around her. She noticed the younger generation of the MacDonald clan had formed a tight-knit alliance, slightly distancing themselves from their parents. The MacDonald siblings banded together, keeping close company to their eldest brother, Angus, the hereditary chief, confirming his role as the anticipated chief and master of their clan. She wouldn't go so far as to say Angus actually snubbed the hospitality of the MacNicol clan, but it was obvious he preferred the attentions of his brothers and sister, who were never far from his side.

The one noticeable exception was Beatrice. In Kayla's opinion, Beatrice displayed an inordinate interest in Rory, repeatedly trying to engage him in a conversation. While Beatrice was never far from the company of one or the other of her elder brothers, her eyes seemed to follow Rory wherever he went. Rory, too occupied with his ale or the boisterous conversation of menfolk, did little or nothing to encourage the attentions of Beatrice, but Kayla noticed the younger woman's actions. Kayla noticed and took heed.

CHAPTER 13

Lady Lydia paced her chamber, barely able to contain her anger. Things were not going as she planned, and she was not pleased. Furious as she was, it was hard to decide who irritated her more: her cousin Moezell for bringing Teressa's brother to their keep, or Daniel for becoming such a thorn in her side. It was bad enough he encouraged Kayla's willfully independent behavior, but apparently he was also becoming the focus of her attention. She wasn't accustomed to such blatant disrespect for her opinions, or failure in her manipulations of her family's affairs.

Wrapping her arms across her middle, Lydia did her best to rein in her anger, refusing to allow it to get the best of her. She needed a plan, and she needed to think; anger would only muddle her thoughts. Though she had already tried confronting Moezell directly, that course of action had proven useless. Perhaps it was time to confront their unwelcome visitor. While such an idea was distasteful to her, it also carried considerable risks. Lydia might not know why Moezell had brought Daniel to their keep, but she had no doubt her fae cousin was behind his appearance. A confrontation with Daniel had the potential of causing more problems than it fixed.

She had to consider the situation carefully. As long as he was under the protection of her cousin, a true faerie and granddaughter of the Faerie Queen, she had no power over him. It was possible Moezell had summoned him back in time to perform a specific task, much as they had with his sister, Teressa. If that were the case, she wondered if Daniel knew what the task was and if he were willing to share such information with her.

His confiding in her was highly unlikely, since they hadn't exactly become the best of friends, but hopefully, it wouldn't hurt to ask. If he were here to perform a specific task, she could offer to help him along and speed his return to his own time. Perhaps such an arrangement would benefit them both. It would take skill and a wee bit of luck to win him over to her way of thinking, but the reward was worth the risk.

Regardless of his willingness to confide in her, there was one thing she needed to make perfectly clear. She had no intention of letting a time traveling, short-term visitor from some unknown family disrupt her plans for her daughter. She needed to make a suitable match for Kayla with reputable kin from one of the neighboring clans to strengthen their alliances. Daniel certainly did not fit those qualifications. Nevertheless, even she couldn't overlook the fact Arlin had shown a complete lack of interest in her daughter.

What was wrong with the lad? Was he completely draft? Kayla was pretty, talented, and intelligent. Lydia knew her daughter was shy, reserved, and had a tendency to live with her head in the clouds; but Kayla was *her* daughter, for goodness sake. That should count for something.

Pacing in her room would accomplish nothing. She needed to take action, so she returned to the great hall to search out Bonnie. As she passed through the room, she saw all of the MacDonalds except Beatrice had retired to their chambers. Even from across the room, she could see Beatrice was attempting to beguile Rory; what a disgraceful show of indecency. However, Beatrice's flirtation suited Lydia just fine. Let the young woman have at him. If she wanted him badly enough, she could have her dear father, the grand MacDonald chief, request a betrothal. Lady Lydia would welcome the opportunity to encourage such an arrangement. Maybe Beatrice's youthful beauty was just the thing Rory needed to get his mind off his long gone Teressa and back among the present.

Focusing back on her priorities, Lydia pulled Bonnie aside as she was returning to the kitchens. "I know the hour grows late, but I'm concerned for Daniel. He was nae at our evening meal," Lydia said, though she knew perfectly well he hadn't been invited or expected.

"Daniel took his supper in the kitchens with the servants," Bonnie explained. "He offered to help with all the extra work we had, and a real fine help he was, minding the roasting pits all eve. Many hands lighten the work, and Daniel says he is nae against helping out where needed. Milly tried to shoo him away more than once. She told him it wasn't his place to work in the kitchens, him being a guest and all, but he would have none of it, claiming he was happy to be assisting wherever he was needed."

"Thank you, Bonnie, that's all very interesting," Lydia interrupted her servant. She was well acquainted with her chambermaid's tendency to ramble on. "I would like ye to find Daniel and tell him to meet me in Duncan's solar. I want to thank him personally for his troubles." Her servant might ramble, but at least she could use Bonnie's information to her advantage.

Happy to do her bidding, Bonnie scurried away to find Daniel as requested while Lydia went to wait in Duncan's solar. Thanks to Bonnie's diligent efforts, Lady Lydia didn't have to wait long.

~*~

Daniel had been wondering if he would ever get an opportunity to speak with Lady Lydia, alone, but he hadn't expected her to request a private meeting. It seemed as though she were intentionally avoiding him, and he highly doubted the MacNicol matriarch was suddenly interested in expressing her appreciation for his aid in the kitchen. This was an intriguing turn of events, and he looked forward to hearing what she had to say.

Trying to clean up as best he could without the benefit of soap and water, Daniel wiped his hands down the front of his pants. He looked pretty scruffy after a long evening manning the roasting ovens, but he doubted it mattered very much. Past experience with Lady Lydia assured him he was well past making a favorable impression. Taking a moment to gather his composure, he drew a deep breath and knocked on the door before entering.

"You called." Daniel bowed, greeting her in his best imitation of an on-screen butler.

Lady Lydia, of course, did not get the jest and ignored his strange tone.

"Aye, Daniel. Thank ye for joining me. I heard ye have been helping in the kitchens, which is rather unusual, and I wanted to express my appreciation." Lady Lydia sat regally in one of the leather armchairs facing the large fireplace. Shadows flickered across her face. The faint glow from the banked embers of the fire and a brace of candles on the sturdy wooden desk provided the only light in the room.

"No problem," he answered. "No thanks necessary. I like to help where needed."

"That is quite kind, but typically we doona ask our guests to earn their keep."

His brows drew back in surprise. *Your guest!* This was news to him. Since he arrived, Lady Lydia had treated him as if he were an unwanted intruder in her life.

"I like to keep busy," he said. "Helping out in the kitchens is a lot better than mucking out horse stalls, not that I haven't done my fair share." It was also gossip central and, from a cop's point of view, one of the best places to gather information.

"Surely ye have other *tasks* that deserve yer attention." She looked at him pointedly.

"None that I know of, other than training with your sons in the lists. Michael's a fine taskmaster, but you know what they say, 'all work and no play . . .'" Daniel was still standing, evaluating the situation and wondering how to proceed. For now, he figured it was better to let Lady Lydia take the lead.

"But if ye do have a special task to perform, something that would speed ye along yer way, mayhap I can offer ye my assistance."

Yeah, I bet you'd like to speed me along my way, he thought. "That's very kind of you to offer, but really, as far as I know, I'm just kinda hanging out. And let me say, it's a right fine place you've got here." Daniel was starting to enjoy her discomfort. She hadn't offered him a seat, but thinking this may take a while, he settled into an armchair near the hearth. He could see her cringe as she drew back on her chair. It seemed she preferred to have him standing before her like one of her servants. He might be helping out in the kitchens, but he was no servant, and he wasn't about to play that role with her.

"Ye must have a reason for being here. Ye canna expect me to believe ye know nothing."

"Haven't a clue, other than a nice friendly visit. It's been great getting to know your sons." *And your daughter*, but he figured it was best to leave Kayla out of this for the moment.

"Ye truly doona know why ye are here? Have ye nae been informed?" She eyed him suspiciously. Obviously this wasn't what she expected, and it wasn't good news.

"Informed by whom? Where would I be getting this information?" He stretched out, crossing his long legs in front of him.

She turned in her chair, moving her body away from him. "Surely ye have heard of Moezell."

"I've heard a lot about the little lady, or should I say faerie, but I've never had the pleasure of meeting her." He held his hands near the glow of the banked embers, examining the dirt accumulated under his fingernails.

"Ye jest." She glared at him.

"No, I don't." He glared back at her.

"Doona deceive me. I want to know why ye're here." Lady Lydia's eyes grew dark with anger.

"Yeah, well I'd like to know why I'm here too." Daniel sat forward in his chair. "Come on, Miss Lady Lydia, you can't fool me. I know you're half fey. I also know you have a meddlesome faerie for a cousin, who goes around sticking her nose into other people's business, usually on your behalf."

"Ye have nae proof." Lady Lydia shrank back into her chair, stunned.

"You think Teressa didn't tell me? I know everything. I know how you had Moezell bring her back here to hook up

Duncan and Janet. I also know you had her sent back home when you were done with her, even though you knew she was in love with your son. Now she's gone and he's brokenhearted. He won't even look at another woman."

"I'd advise ye to mind yer manners. If ye know so much, then ye also know I have access to magic." She tilted her chin and glared.

"What're you going to do? Turn me into a frog?"

"Faeries doona turn people into frogs," she huffed.

"No, you just send us whipping back and forth through time, as if we're your effing playthings. A regular cat with a mouse."

Putting on a regal expression, she said, "Then let me tell ye something, Mr. Daniel Ellers. Eventually, ye will be sent away, just like yer sister. Until then, I want ye to stay away from my daughter. Do I make myself clear?"

"And if I don't?" Daniel leaned forward, invading her space.

"I will make it my personal *task* to make yer life miserable."

"Yeah! Like being whipped through time without knowing why isn't bad enough."

"I wasn't the one who brought ye here," she admitted in anger, before quickly looking away, thoroughly displeased.

He could tell she hadn't intended to let that one slip out. "Right. If it were up to you, I'd already be gone. Which means it's not up to you," he gloated over her misspoken confession. "I wonder how much more is out of your control."

"Be gone. I have nay more to say." Lady Lydia threw her hands up in frustration.

For a moment, Daniel thought he might go spinning back to the future, but nothing happened. No wind, not even a breeze. She just wanted him to leave the room, and would probably be even happier if he left her keep and the Isle of Skye. The latter was out of his control, but he could do her the honor of leaving her presence.

Standing, he mocked her with a courtly bow. "As you wish, my lady," he taunted her and headed for the door. *Faeries my ass, that woman's a witch.*

~*~

It had been a long day and an even longer evening spent in the company of the MacDonald clan. Kayla was greatly relieved when she finally was able to return to the sanctuary of her bedchamber. She breathed deep, soaking up the calming quiet of her cozy room. Blissful solitude—what a blessing.

Sinking into the chair next to the hearth, she willed herself to summon enough energy to stir up the fire and add more peat to the blaze. Settling back to enjoy the fire's warmth, her thoughts once again turned to Daniel. This newly developed habit, she noticed, occurred with increased frequency.

She had missed the pleasure of his company at the evening meal. She missed hearing the sound of his strangely unique voice, and she missed his kind manners. They stood in sharp contrast to the unpleasant conduct she received from Arlin and his kin. Time spent with Arlin and his family only served to increase her desire to avoid being married to the man. She saw no appeal in becoming one of the MacDonald clan.

"Oh Moezell," she spoke aloud to the empty room, "what am I to do? Why can't I have Daniel? Why does he avoid me? If only Daniel wanted me, all would be well. Why can't I have him instead of that beastly Arlin? Has my harsh judgment of his sister truly lost me any hope of gaining his affections?"

She was certain she could sense the faerie's presence, but Moezell remained silent and concealed.

Thinking back to the night the faerie had appeared in her chamber, Kayla tried to recall Moezell's words. The faerie had advised her to seek love with an open heart. Hard as it was to admit, even to herself, Kayla knew it was her fear of failure that consistently held her back. She feared being rejected by Daniel. If she could even find the courage to tell him she cared, which she highly doubted, he could easily reject her. If that happened, she would be without hope, with nowhere to turn. The unknown was scary enough, but knowing the truth was more than she could risk. It left no room for illusions. If Moezell were here, Kayla was sure the faerie would tell her to take control of her fears and follow her heart. The idea sounded so simple, and yet as Kayla was beginning to learn, it was also devastatingly hard.

CHAPTER 14

Morning was giving way to midday when Daniel wandered over to the training fields to watch the men competing in the highlander games. Several warriors from the MacNicol keep and the surrounding villages were on hand to participate in the quest for bragging rights and the few coins bestowed upon the winners. Earlier that morning a group of men from the MacLeod clan had arrived by way of a fishing vessel. News of the games had spread to the Dunvegan keep, and they were anxious for the opportunity to compete. Among the MacLeod warriors was Alec, the second son of the MacLeod chief and a trusted friend of Duncan's.

Officially, it was every man for himself, but Daniel knew the MacNicol clan was particularly intent on besting the MacDonalds, and from what he could see, the feeling was mutual.

While he was anxious to learn more about the various contests the medieval Scottish warriors would wage with each other, he didn't plan to participate. He'd already been asked and had respectfully declined Michael's requests for him to join the games. Besides feeling like an outsider to the proceedings, he was intelligent enough to know he didn't have the experience or expertise to do the games justice. He also had no desire to look foolish competing against men far more experienced and skilled in their ancient competitions. Rookie status didn't appeal to him.

Since the arrival of the MacDonald clan, he'd been giving the MacNicols and their visitors a wide berth, preferring to spend his time training with the other men or hanging out in the kitchens with Bonnie and Milly. He plied them with friendly flattery and flirted with them in a way intended to remind them of their younger days when they could still turn the heads of many a young warrior. In return, the elder serving women had taken him under their wing in a way not many had benefited from before. They fussed over him, plying him with special treats, and laughed at his easy humor.

It was in the kitchens where he had met Becky, the young chambermaid accompanying Lady Evelyn. Daniel had offered his services to help Milly oversee the grilling of the roasted meats on the large indoor fire pit, since it was a lot like his experience as a backyard barbeque chief. It wasn't hard to notice the shapely figure and pretty face of the new arrival as she toiled in the midst of the controlled confusion flowing through Milly's domain. Becky had barely stepped through the wide-open door of the kitchens before Milly put her to work refilling the heavy ceramic jugs used to serve the guests ale and spiced cider. Several times during the evening, Becky had returned to fill her jugs from the large storage barrels kept in the cool of the kitchen larder, and each time, Daniel had noticed she lingered longer and longer in the great hall before returning to her duties.

As the night wore on, her pretty young face and shapely figure were damaged by her observable sense of self-importance. Her conceit went far beyond anything he'd seen from the other serving staff he had encountered. All she could talk about was how important she was, claiming she was a valued assistant to Lady Evelyn and was loved by everyone in the family. The young woman reminded him of a San Francisco socialite, struggling to prove her self-worth by putting on airs. In the end, she failed to impress anyone with her attitude.

When Daniel passed through the kitchens early the next morning, he was informed by Bonnie, who was none too happy, that Becky had hardly put in an appearance before she offered a flimsy excuse to head off to the training fields to deliver bread and ale to the menfolk. Bonnie was not one to be fooled by the young woman's antics. In fact, as she had informed Daniel, she knew very well the lazy young maid was off gawking at the men participating in the games. Daniel did well to hide the smirk tugging at his lips. He had the distinct impression Bonnie would welcome an opportunity to join the young lass for a pleasurable bit of male gawking, not that she would ever admit to having such a thought.

As Daniel approached the edge of the training field, he spied Kayla returning to the keep with Shannon's two boys, Tanner and Torrin. They'd been out at the women's picnic, and it seemed the boys had decided to return before the others. He couldn't say he blamed them. Young lads seldom wanted to hang out with the girls in a field of wild flowers, at least not until they were older. When the boys saw Daniel heading toward the lists, they ran ahead of Kayla to greet him.

Torrin burst ahead of his younger brother. "We're going to watch the games. Do ye want to come with us?"

"I was headed there myself," Daniel informed him, rustling the young lad's russet hair.

"Are ye going to compete?" Tanner wanted to know as he caught up with his brother.

"I'm here to watch, like you. It's their party," he begged off.

"I'm sure ye would be welcomed if ye wanted to join the games," Kayla offered as she joined the trio.

"Michael offered his invitation. I respectfully declined." Daniel flashed her a warm, welcoming smile. It was accompanied by heated blood racing toward his groin from the core of his body.

"Why?" she asked, looking surprised and slightly disappointed. "Doona ye want to show off yer skills?"

"It wouldn't be right. I'm an outsider here. Besides, I'm not familiar with these games. I'm content to be an observer and cheer for your brothers. Competitors always need a cheering section." Turning to the boys, he added, "Would you like to join me?"

Both boys shouted their agreement at once. "Can we, Aunt Kayla? Can we stay with Daniel? Ye can return to the picnic."

"'Tis nae Daniel's job to be watching ye two young lads," Kayla admonished the boys.

Daniel interrupted her refusal to their request, "I don't mind. It would be my pleasure."

"But 'tis my job to watch the lads," she argued. "And truly, I have nae desire to return to the picnic."

"Well then, if they're in your charge, maybe you should join us and make sure I don't run off and sell them to pirates or talk them into becoming black knights." He teased her with a provocative grin. For a moment, the boys fell silent with wide-eyed wonder. Before Kayla could answer, he added, "Seriously, it would be my pleasure to hang with the boys, and it'd be nice if you want to join us."

He was being honest; he wanted her to stay. All he wanted was to spend time with her, to hear her laugh, and see her smile. It didn't matter whether Lady Lydia approved of his actions or not, his affections for Kayla were real.

"It would be my pleasure," she agreed with a tentative smile.

"We doona need a silly girl to help us cheer," Tanner disagreed.

"Ah lad, you say that now, but someday you'll be proud as a peacock to have a woman cheering for you. Besides, if your aunt joins us, maybe later I'll teach you some of my fighting moves." Daniel threw a couple of air jabs at the boys, who scurried to avoid the pulled punches. "Then I'll have a woman to show off for, and she can cheer for me. What do you say?" The last question was directed at the boys, but his eyes quickly darted to Kayla for her reaction. She graced him with a glowing smile. It settled warm on his heart. Even better, she seemed pleased by the idea.

"Look, they're starting the caber toss. Let's go." Torrin's attention was already distracted by the action on the field. Excited to see the competition, the boys ran ahead, racing toward the training fields.

"Lads, stay back, doona get in the way. I doona want ye getting hurt if one of those men should toss their long pole in the wrong direction," Kayla cautioned the boys.

Daniel held back a snicker at Kayla's inadvertent pun. She had no idea how easy it was for a man to toss his long pole in the wrong direction. Placing a hand at the small of her back, Daniel escorted Kayla to the edge of the training field, where they could see the games and keep watch on the boys.

Kayla fell into step beside him, turning for a moment to smile with approval. She seemed relaxed as she walked beside him, registering his hand at her back. He had to resist his urge to hold her hand, she was so comfortable to be with, or even better, take her in his arms. Daniel very much wanted to gather her into his arms, to pull her into a loving embrace and feel her soft, pliant body mold into his. He wanted to touch her soft auburn curls and run his fingers through her hair. His eyes dropped to her lips graced by her soft smile. How he would love to touch his lips to hers, to taste her, to know the full pleasure those lips might hold.

But he resisted. Restraining himself, he waged his own private battle against his base desires while his body buzzed with craving. He wanted this woman. It tore at his innards how much he wanted her, and yet every reasonable thought in his head argued against getting involved with her. It might feel right for him, but it would be so very wrong for her.

He knew he wasn't alone; he sensed her interest too. With very little encouragement, she could be his for the taking; she was too naive and inexperienced to resist, but he could never do that. The "good cop" in him wouldn't let him.

It was temping to take whatever pleasure life offered him, but he doubted they had much time together. As it was, he didn't know if he'd be here next week, next month, or even tomorrow, and he couldn't do that to her. She deserved better than a momentary lover passing through her time.

So he maintained his polite composure and continued to play the good cop, a role he knew well. Daniel knew the rules. He knew how to act nice, how to treat a woman well, and while it wasn't easy, he also knew how to control the passion-driven fiend that crawled in his belly.

Daniel, Kayla, and the boys joined the rest of the spectators gathered to watch several rounds of caber tossing, stone throwing, and archery. Daniel was interested in seeing the types of competitions these ancient warriors engaged in. He knew the local fairgrounds back home held Scottish highland games each year, but he had never felt the need to check it out. Now he was getting a firsthand look at ancient Scotsmen doing their best to strut their stuff. Regardless of the time or place, it was obvious these men took their competitions seriously.

Alec MacLeod and Duncan ended up very nearly tied in the caber toss. That event fascinated Daniel the most. It seemed rather crazy for men to heave a long pole end over end to see who could land the darn thing the closest to the straight-up twelve o'clock position. Most guys couldn't even get the thing to do the end-over-end thing. He figured it wasn't a skill he would be practicing anytime soon. He'd rather stick to martial arts or the fighting staff.

Hugh's eldest son, Angus, proved to be an excellent marksman during the archery competition, easily beating all the other competitors in the field. Archery would be a useful skill in these times, and one Daniel would seriously like to pursue. A bow and arrow seemed to be the next best thing as a replacement for the department-issued firearm he had carried on duty.

During a break in the action, as the training field was being set up for the next event, the boys began to grow restless.

"Aunt Kayla, I doona want to sit here anymore," Tanner whined.

"Can we get closer to the warriors? I want to go out on the training field," Torrin requested.

"Yea, let's go out on the training field," Tanner cheered, supporting his older brother.

"Nay, you need to stay and watch from here. 'Tis nae safe for ye on the field. The men are too busy to look out for ye," Kayla rebuked their attempt to leave her side.

"If you boys are tired of watching the games, how about a warrior game of your own?" Daniel offered.

"Yea, can we, Aunt Kayla, can we?" the boys sang in unison.

It looked as though Kayla were going to deny the boys, but as she looked from one young lad to the other, she seemed to realize it would be a losing battle. "Are ye sure, Daniel?"

"No problem; it'll be fun," he assured her. "I've got an idea. How about a game of defend the castle?"

"How do we do that?" Torrin asked.

"Follow me." Daniel led the boys and Kayla away from the training fields to a nearby grassy knoll. Along the way, he picked up a blunt fighting staff for him and a couple of wooden play swords of the boys to use.

"Okay, boys, see this group of boulders here? That's going to be your castle."

"Our castle?" Torrin asked. "Seems kinda small to be a castle."

"It can be as grand as your imagination. Think big. Now, Kayla, you stand back here behind the castle walls. You'll be the damsel in distress." Daniel grasped Kayla's hand and directed her where to stand.

Turning to the boys, Daniel continued, "Torrin and Tanner, it's your job to defend the castle and your lady from the clutches of   the   evil   black   knight."

"Who will be the black knight?" Tanner wanted to know.

"Me, of course," Daniel answered.

Torrin poked his younger brother in the ribs. "Who did ye think?"

It was only fitting the boys should defend their aunt against the black knight, Daniel told himself, for truthfully, if given the chance, he would come and steal her heart away. But hers was a heart surrounded by beauty and grace and unblemished innocence, and to wound such a heart would truly be a grievous and unforgivable crime.

With all the props in place, he instructed the boys, "Okay, show me some of your fighting skills before I make my attack. But be careful not to really hurt each other."

Torrin and Tanner immediately took up fighting stances, raising their hands, holding their swords as their father and his warriors did during training. They clicked and hacked their play swords against each other, making all the right grunting noises one would expect to hear from men in training. Daniel had to chuckle at their natural ability.

Watching from the sidelines, Kayla gently admonished the older boy, "Torrin, ye must be careful of Tanner. He's nae as big or strong as ye."

"I'm fine, Aunt Kayla," Tanner assured her. Although Tanner was younger, Daniel was sure he didn't want to appear weak, even as he backed away from his older brother's assault.

"Keep your guard up," Daniel coached him. "Look for an opening." He was enjoying their swordplay and the opportunity to mentor the boys.

Without warning, Kayla stepped around the outcropping of boulders and headed toward the boys. Daniel raced over to her, bobbing and weaving back and forth to block her way. "Where do you think you're going?" he asked.

"I need to watch the lads," she gasped. A smile spread across her face, amused by his movements.

The boys stopped what they were doing to watch.

"Oh no, you don't." Daniel grabbed her around the waist, pulling her back up against him. "The boys are just fine."

Kayla started laughing, disarmed by his actions. Struggling, she made a halfhearted effort to wiggle away. When Daniel wiggled his hands across her belly, she broke into uncontrollable giggles as he tickled her sides. Squirming even harder, Kayla intensified her attempts to break away.

"I've got you, you feisty little thing," Daniel said, holding her fast in his arms.

Kayla continued to squirm, causing Daniel to lose his balance. He wrestled her to the ground as he fell, rolling onto his back to break her fall.

"Feisty, ye say? Aye, I can be feisty," she managed between laughs as she continued to squirm in his arms.

Daniel used his weight to roll her onto her back as he pinned her wrists to the ground. "I have you now," he chuckled, caught up in the moment of play. "There's no escape."

Kayla gasped, trying to catch her breath. Her heaving chest pressed against Daniel. For a moment, time stood still as they each focused on the other. Staring into her eyes, Daniel thought about kissing her. His eyes dropped to her lips. He began to lower his head.

Just as suddenly, the spell was broken when Torrin and Tanner jumped onto his back, beating him with their little fists in defense of their aunt, their damsel in distress.

"Stop, knave," Tanner yelled.

"We have ye now, Black Knight," Torrin shouted, grabbing Daniel around his broad shoulders.

Their valiant efforts were enough to squash Daniel's desires and return him to his senses. It had been tempting, all so tempting to ravish her there on the grass, but thankfully her nephews had done their duty to protect her innocence. As he rose to stand, Daniel reached behind him and grabbed each of the boys around their waists football style. Their little hands continued to pelt him as their legs thrashed about. "Okay, enough you two. You have me. I'm beaten," he said as he deposited them on the ground.

The boys continued to squeal and shout with glee over their victory. "We won. We beat the black knight," they boasted.

Kayla had scrambled to her feet and was brushing grass and dirt from her skirt as she returned to her place behind the boulders. Her breathing was labored, and her eyes shone from the excitement of their tussle.

Brushing dirt from his clothes, Daniel turned his attention back to the boys, but his body was still vibrating from feeling Kayla lying beneath him. He still wanted her, but now was certainly not the time.

While they played, Daniel taught the boys some of the basics of martial arts, showing them how to take a fall and tumble correctly so they wouldn't get hurt. They were able to master the skill fairly quickly, showing no fear. He also showed them how to fend off an assailant, using the momentum of the attacker to deflect his blows.

Next, he demonstrated how to spring back after an attack to catch an assailant off guard and how to use the proper kicks and punches from his martial arts training. Most of the moves were too advanced for the young boys, but they tried to mimic him and cheered at his display of skill. Along the way, he cautioned them that as true warriors they were to only use their newly developing skills when it was necessary to protect themselves or their family.

"You are becoming fine young warriors," he told them. "It's important to use your might to defend, not offend. Do you understand?"

"Aye, Sir Daniel," Torrin and Tanner responded in unison. In the course of the afternoon, Daniel had gained their youthful admiration for his fighting expertise, and they took his advice quite seriously.

~*~

Duncan watched as Kayla and Daniel engaged in playful games with his nephews. It was obvious she enjoyed his company. He couldn't recall when he had seen her so relaxed or laugh with such ease, and with an outsider. *He'd be a good man for her,* he thought, *far better than Arlin.* After the way Hugh and Lady Evelyn had talked about her at dinner the night before, he could no longer support his mother's efforts to marry off Kayla in a loveless match solely for the purpose of strengthening an alliance with the MacDonalds. It was true they were a larger and stronger clan, but his sister deserved better than to serve as a bargaining chip against future battles.

As chief of the clan, and more importantly as Kayla's elder brother, Duncan needed to ensure his little sister entered into a proper marriage with a proper husband. However, unlike his mother, it wasn't particularly important to him if she wed Arlin or another. The important thing was she be wedded, and soon. If they delayed much longer, she'd be edging toward spinsterhood.

Still engrossed in his assessment of possible husbands for his sister, Duncan was shocked when he saw Michael take a bone-jarring fall during the final round of footraces. Seeing the pain etched across his brother's face when he hit the hard-packed dirt was enough to send Duncan racing to Michael's side along with Rory.

"What be the matter?" Duncan questioned when he reached his fallen brother. Michael's face was pinched with pain, his jaw clenched, and his eyes were squeezed shut. Michael was not one to give in to pain, and the look of agony displayed in his face gave Duncan significant cause to worry.

"I must have twisted my knee. 'Tis a minor thing," Michael spat out through clenched teeth, holding the injured leg.

"'Tis nae how it looks to me," Duncan contradicted his brother. "It looks as if ye will need to sit out the rest of the competition."

"Nay, I canna. I'm slated to compete with the fighting staff. 'Tis the last contest we need to ensure our win against those bloody MacDonalds. I'll nae be letting down my clan."

Duncan turned to look toward the direction of Daniel and the boys playing down in the grassy field. "Daniel can take yer place. He's the only one we know who can best ye," he offered, recalling Daniel's first day of training.

"Nay, Daniel has declined," Michael countered, sucking in breath.

Though pain was stamped across Michael's face, Duncan knew he'd resist admitting defeat.

"If he knows ye are injured, I'm sure he'll reconsider. 'Tis only fitting we should ask." Duncan placed a calming hand on his brother's shoulder. He understood the trepidation his brother felt about letting down his clan, but Michael's well-being was far more important than bragging rights. "Give him a chance," Duncan said. "Let him know he's one of us."

Michael hesitated a moment longer afore nodding. "Aye, 'tis fitting," he finally acquiesced.

~*~

At Duncan's request, which was adamantly supported by Rory and Michael, Daniel found himself squared off against Arlin MacDonald as the last two competitors with the fighting staffs.

"Hah," Arlin scoffed. "I see they bring in the retainers to do their work. Just like the MacNicols, always picking up strays; like Rory did with yer sister."

Arlin's pointed sneer made Daniel's blood boil, but he said nothing. His contempt for his opponent only served to strengthen his resolve to kick his butt. He'd fight fair and square, but he definitely intended to do the man some serious damage.

The two men circled each other with their long blunted staffs in hand. Daniel felt the heat of the competition surging through his blood. He was pumped and primed, ready to put his energy into action. Watchful, he evaluated Arlin's strength.

"I saw ye with Kayla, playing yer silly games. Did ye know they wanted to hand her off on me?" Arlin continued to badger Daniel, poking at him with verbal darts.

"I'm sure you are mistaken. No one would give a prized jewel to a beggar like you." Though he'd overheard enough comments from the servants to know Arlin was referring to Lady Lydia's desire to arrange a betrothal, he refused to believe Duncan would allow such a thing. Kayla deserved so much better. He also knew Arlin was trying to bait him, looking for a weakness in his defenses. Daniel refused to take the hook, drawing on an inner well of self-discipline to maintain his composure.

Daniel's eyes narrowed, his mind focused on Arlin's every move. Arlin danced around the ring, lunging and swinging his staff to test the strength of Daniel's defenses. Each time, Daniel parried but held back, watching and waiting for the right moment to present itself. Knock, swing, jab, swing again; he emulated Arlin's moves, testing the other man's skills and letting his opponent show his hand before he took decisive action.

Arlin's blows were powerful, but he was letting his emotions and his desire to win overrule what skill he possessed. Daniel felt strong. He wanted to beat Arlin, if only for Kayla's sake, but he tried not to focus on clan honor or protecting his reputation. It was simply a matter of his skill against another's, and he felt confident in his abilities.

The parry and thrust wore on, blow against blow, each man giving little ground to the other. Arlin delivered a bruising blow to Daniel's left shoulder. Daniel countered with a well-placed jab to Arlin's chest.

Finally, Daniel saw the opening he needed and jabbed at Arlin's left side before swiftly swinging his staff in a circular motion that caught Arlin in mid motion, delivering a mind-numbing blow to his rib cage, followed by a brutal pounding across Arlin's back just below his shoulder blades. They were powerful hits, and highly effective.

Arlin gasped and shuddered, arching backward in pain. His loss of composure was all Daniel needed to finish him off. With one final swift swoop of the staff, Daniel knocked Arlin off his feet, and the man's arms flailed helplessly as he fell backward.

Daniel spiked the long rod into Arlin's chest as his opponent lay splayed on the ground. The pressure he levied against the fallen man's chest was more than enough to let him know Daniel had him pinned and beaten. He was tempted to smack Arlin upside his head with the blunted staff for his earlier comments, and he almost did. But he resisted the urge, knowing it was the mark of poor sportsmanship, something he considered to be beneath him. Still, it was tempting, and he was only human. After he was called victor, he released the fallen man, and seemingly accidentally, let the end of the staff knock against the back of Arlin's head. Another minor victory.

~*~

Kayla cheered along with the rest of the MacNicols as she had never cheered before. As far as she was concerned, Daniel had just become her champion. She even allowed herself to laugh when the MacDonalds' servant girl, Becky, tripped over her skirts as she ran out on the field to assist the fallen Arlin. She was still cheering when Rory came to her side.

"That was a fine thing Daniel did for us, agreeing to take Michael's place." He draped his arm comfortably across Kayla's shoulders. "He really came through when we needed him." His smile was one of brotherly pride.

Kayla gazed across the training field to where Daniel stood, talking to Duncan and Michael. The three men were exchanging congratulations in that boisterously happy way men did when they'd just bested another in competition, especially one so easily disliked.

"Aye, 'tis lucky he was here to take Michael's place." She was happy for her brothers, as well as for Daniel. With his help, the MacNicols had won the day. He was one of them.

Feeling another thought tug at her heart, she turned to focus on Rory, a sad smile gracing her eyes. "How was it for ye when Teressa went away? I mean, I've never really asked ye about her, and even worse, I never listened." It was hard for her to ask such a personal question, even to her own brother.

Rory let his arm slip to his side and turned his gaze upon Kayla. "I'll nae lie to ye. It was heartbreaking."

"I was afraid of that." Kayla allowed her gaze to fall to the ground. She wasn't comfortable opening up old wounds.

"I would have been, too, if I had allowed myself to believe she would really go away. Even though she told me over and over she had to return home, I never allowed myself to believe she would actually leave me or I wouldn't be allowed to follow. I wanted her to stay, and I believed I could make it happen. I may have been a fool in love, but at least I was a fearless fool." He flashed one of his signature grins at Kayla.

"Are ye still brokenhearted?" she asked, determined to learn the truth. She had allowed this matter to be ignored for too long, believing it was better not to know.

"Nay, sister. I'm simply a patient man waiting for my love to return." His smile faded, replaced by a look of longing in his eyes.

"Return? Did Daniel say Teressa will return?" This was news to her.

"Nay, 'tis something my heart tells me, that we shall be together again, someday. It's the one thought I hold on to, the one holding me together. Believing we'll be together again allows me to face each day and do my duty."

"Is that why ye've changed? I noticed Beatrice seeking yer attentions. She's a pretty young lass, and yet ye give her nay mind. In yer younger days, ye would have encouraged her, but now I see nae interest in yer eyes."

"I believe I have changed. It's called growing up." He chuckled, a roguish grin returning to his face.

"When did ye become so wise?" she wondered.

Rory grew serious. "Teressa was a woman tied to her home and family. 'Twas her anchorage. I see that clearly now. I have to say, Kayla, I doona see Daniel as a man with an anchorage. For sure, he has a love for his kin and home. Ye can hear it in the stories he tells. But he has nay haven as Teressa did. He's a lone ship afloat in his life without a true rudder to steer by or star to light his way. It seems the man has nay anchor to hold him where he's been. I believe he may be looking for his safe harbor. The question is where will he find it?"

The look in his eyes said he was worried for her, as well. Her feelings for Daniel were growing stronger day by day, and she understood he would not wish her to suffer the same heartache he had known. She also knew, no matter how much her dear brother wanted to protect her, he could not protect her from her own heart.

Duncan and Daniel approached from the training field, carrying Michael between them to spare him from having to use his injured knee. Following close behind was Duncan's friend, Alec MacLeod, with his troop of warriors. It appeared they had every intention of celebrating with the winning clan.

True to his nature, Rory quickly became boisterous and cheered with the other men as they drew near. "Our hero approaches. Let us find some fine ale and do some fine drinking," Rory hailed the men. "MacLeod, I hope ye brought some of that fine ale your clan is known for."

Kayla recalled many nights of celebration when Rory had overly appreciated the MacLeods' ale.

"I travel with nothing but our finest," Alec boasted.

"Aye, 'tis time for celebrating," Duncan announced. "Alec, I insist. Ye and yer men must join us in the spirit of goodwill."

The men gave a rousing cheer of "Scorrybreac! Here's tae us!" as they slapped large calloused hands on each other's shoulders. Pushing Duncan aside, Rory took his elder brother's place in supporting Michael along with Daniel.

Alex MacLeod draped an arm over Duncan's shoulder. "Ye know, Duncan, I've seen that wee lass of yers. I believe yer Amy will make a fine match for my son Iain someday. What say ye? 'Tis never too soon to make plans."

Kayla looked at her brother, hoping with all her heart he would agree. She believed the MacNicols would be far better served by a clan alliance with the MacLeods than the hateful MacDonalds. Even though the MacDonalds were known for being the larger and more powerful clan, the MacNicols had just proved they could get the best of them in a fair fight.

"'Tis something to think on—a dozen years from now." Duncan laughed. "Tonight we drink in celebration of our games."

Carried away in the wave of excitement over their well-fought victory, Duncan led the men toward the keep. Of course, he would invite the MacDonalds to join in their wee drinking party. While Kayla doubted they shared the MacNicol's joy, she also doubted the MacDonald's would miss an opportunity to join in the celebration. After all, several of them had performed quite well in the games, and Angus had won at archery.

Daniel was being swept up in the merriment of the moment, but he turned to catch Kayla's eye for one quick glance and gave her a wink. She had cheered for him when he won the match, and now, with the way he looked at her, it felt as if he were her knight in shining armor.

CHAPTER 15

After a long evening of drinking with Rory, Duncan, and the rest of the warriors, Daniel headed back to his room in the barracks, making a pit stop at the garderobe along the way. He stepped out of the primitive toilet facilities and adjusted his breeches, checking everything was where it belonged. The clothes Rory had given him were comfortable enough, but the one-size-fits-most design required some nips and tucks to keep him looking presentable.

As he turned toward the barracks, a flash of brilliant blue light caught his eye. It came from the direction of the training field. Had he not known better, he would have sworn it was caused by an electrical light. Certainly, no candle or torchlight could have produced such a brilliant flash. Too curious to simply ignore the eerie image, Daniel headed off in its direction.

Cautiously, he stalked off across the shadowy courtyard with only the glow from the moon above and the sparsely spaced wall torches lighting his way. When he reached the entrance to the training field, where he thought he had seen the flash of blue light, no one and nothing was there. He wandered around the field, thinking maybe a highly polished shield or gleaming broadsword could have reflected a ray of moonlight in some freakishly bizarre manner, but he couldn't find anything that remotely explained the bright flash. There was nothing. Daniel began to feel a bit foolish, wondering if the bright flash of light had only been a figment of his ale-enhanced imagination.

He was about to return to the barracks when another bright flash of blue light caught his eye. This time it came from the direction of the stables. Whatever it was, it was definitely signaling him, as if it wanted him to follow. Feeling as though he were being led on a wild-goose chase, he grabbed the only weapon he could find—a fighting staff left propped up against the wall—and continued on toward the stables.

As he neared the entrance, he heard noises coming from inside. Most of them he could identify as typical animal sounds, but there was one noise, a kind of rustling, that indicated there were more than just animals lurking inside.

Daniel held the fighting staff braced in front of his body with his back against the wooden frame of the building. He listened for a moment longer and heard the rustling again, this time muffled and farther away. Taking a deep breath, he quietly stepped through the stable doorway then quickly retreated into the shadows. After giving his eyes time to adjust to the darkness of the stable, he could just barely make out the shadowy outline of a hooded figure hunched down in the straw at the far end of the shed row. It took him a good long moment, but he finally figured out who it was.

Kayla, wrapped in a heavy wool cloak, was huddled alone in the straw.

He straightened up and dropped his shoulders. *What the hell is she doing out here at this hour,* he wondered.

Setting aside the fighting staff, he started down the shed row, checking the gates at the front of each stall to announce his presence. He didn't want to spook her, but he wanted her to know he was there. Speaking loud enough to be heard, he called out to the horses, "Hey, Spots. Hey, Blazer. How you boys doing tonight?"

He kept an eye on the hooded figure of Kayla, checking her reaction. Did she want to remain hidden? Or would she accept his intrusion? If it looked as though she were trying to hide, he'd respect her desire for privacy and head back out, as if he hadn't seen her. Instead, he noticed as he got closer, she sat up a little straighter and adjusted her cloak, dropping the hood away from her face. It looked as though she were sitting there waiting for him to see her.

Daniel stepped up to the stall next to where she sat, made his inspection of Sallie, and then looked over at her, as if seeing her for the first time. "Hey, Kayla, is that you?"

"Aye, Daniel," she whispered.

"Um, have you been sitting in the dark this whole time?"

Kayla looked down at her hands. "'Tis quiet here."

"Mind if I join you?"

"I'd be pleased."

He heard a smile in her voice and sat down on the hay beside her. "What're you doing out here?"

Kayla shrugged and sighed, "I've had enough of the celebration. I wanted to check on Sallie. 'Tis better than sitting in the hall with my family and the MacDonalds."

"Won't they miss you?" Daniel picked up a blade of hay and stuck it between his teeth. Just like old times.

Kayla looked up at him as if he had two heads. "I doubt it. Why should they? They never notice me when I'm there. How can they notice me when I'm gone?" He could hear the pain in her voice.

"It seems to me like your mother always has her eye on you, especially when I'm around. You know, I don't think she likes me very much." He spoke in a conspiratorial tone, as if sharing some great secret, trying to sound lighthearted. His reward was her tinkling laughter. Unfortunately, it was short-lived.

"I'm sure ye heard she wants me to marry Arlin." Kayla glanced up at him but quickly looked away.

"Yeah, I've heard. How do you feel about that?"

She seemed surprised he would ask such a question. "I doona believe Arlin wants to marry me. Have ye seen the way he acts?"

"That's not what I asked. How do *you* feel?"

Kayla turned sullen again. "It doona matter how I feel. This is nae about my feelings. 'Tis about what's best for the clan." She nearly spat out the last two words.

"I beg to differ. This is all about how you feel."

"'Tis easy for ye to say. Ye are a man. Ye do as ye please. Ye've nay one to tell ye what to do or whom to marry. Yer life is yer own. Mine is not."

He was tempted to argue with her. Lately, it didn't feel like his life was his own, but this wasn't about him. "You still haven't told me how you feel. What would you do if it were up to you?"

"I would nae marry Arlin. I would send him and the whole MacDonald clan away tomorrow."

"Can't say I blame you. I haven't found them to be all that grand myself." Daniel gave a lighthearted chuckle. In the dim moonlight, he could see her smile. Barely, but he'd gotten a smile out of her.

"It does nae matter. They doona listen to me."

"I'm listening." Daniel reached for her hand and brought it to his lips.

She remained perfectly still, her eyes large and searching, her lips slightly parted. Holding her hand in his, he placed the palm of her hand to rest against his chest. Alone with her in the dark, it was too easy to give in to the temptation that had been plaguing him since the moment he met her. He dropped his head, placed his lips over hers, and kissed her. Ever so softly, he kissed her.

Dear Mother of God, she was sweet. He could feel her melting on his lips like warm milk chocolate, and dang if her taste wasn't every bit as delicious. He brought his free hand up to cup her cheek. Her lips parted, welcoming, inviting, and he delved deeper. He felt her fingers on his chest grab at his shirt, bunching the fabric in her fist, hanging on and pulling him close.

Pulling back for only a second, he checked her reaction. Longing and desire filled her eyes. It was enough for him. He reached for her again, pulling her close. Almost immediately, she responded to his kiss, her body seeking his, and he laid her down beside him as he rolled over on the hay, aligning their bodies in a lover's embrace.

Though she was innocent, and slightly awkward in her movements, he felt the heated need in her response. He held her close, allowing his hand to roam freely over her body, exploring her lush curves, imagining the soft naked flesh concealed beneath the layers of her clothing. Thank God for her clothing. It was thin but vital protection from his blatant desires. However, it didn't protect her from his kisses. He smothered her with his kisses, and she yielded. Holding nothing back, she took as he gave.

When had he last made out with an innocent woman like her . . . ten, maybe twelve years ago? The sensation was unnerving. He wanted to pull the clothes from her body and ravish her right then and there. For one primordial moment, he nearly gave in to temptation. Burying his face in the softness of her neck and bosom, he breathed in her scent, earthy, and fresh, and totally woman. Daniel had to stop; he had to control himself. But it was so damn hard. He was so damn hard.

He had just reached a hand up under her skirt, seeking naked flesh, when suddenly he heard a noise. She heard it too and stiffened. Almost as bad as being allowed to continue his ravishment of her body was the embarrassment of being interrupted. His first thought was for Kayla. Daniel couldn't let anyone find her like this.

Though he motioned for her to be quiet, he realized it was a rather needless gesture. She had no intention of making any noise. Softly, silently, he rolled away from her into the dark recesses of the narrow stall. He reached out to help straighten her clothing, pulling bits of straw from her hair and clothes. She understood. Pulling her close for one last kiss, he whispered into her ear, "You have to go."

She nodded.

Kayla impressed him with her stealth. Moving with quiet efficiency, she made her way to the stall holding her horse and began to brush the animal's hide. She then began to whisper words of endearment, as if speaking for Sallie's ears only. Daniel appreciated her ingenuity. Within seconds, he heard a man's voice call out to her.

"Hey, Kayla, what're ye doing out here?" It was Rory.

Daniel breathed a little easier, but maintained his hiding place deep in the shadows of the last stall, his back against the wall. Rory was by far the more easygoing of the brothers, but

Daniel had no doubts Rory would obligingly kick his ass if he thought Daniel was trying to take advantage of his little sister.

"I couldn't sleep, so I took a walk to check on Sallie," Kayla replied.

"Alone?" Rory questioned.

"Aye, alone." Daniel heard the trepidation in Kayla's voice. He wondered if Rory heard it too.

"'Tis late. Ye should be up in yer chamber."

Kayla yawned. "I'll be going there now. Will ye walk with me?"

Good girl, Daniel thought.

"Aye, come along now."

When Daniel heard Kayla walk away, headed toward Rory, he crawled to the edge of the stall and very cautiously peered through a space in the boards. Rory wrapped an arm around Kayla, and they started to walk away. Daniel let out the breath he'd been holding. A moment before they stepped out of the stables, Rory paused and turned to look over his shoulder.

"Ye best get yerself to bed too, Daniel," Rory called out.

Kayla gasped. Rory laughed. Daniel beat his fist against the wall. Dang, they were busted.

CHAPTER 16

Daniel had just finished training with Michael, and he was missing Kayla. He hadn't seen her all day. Before he had even finished his breakfast, he had heard from Bonnie she was busy working with the women cleaning the keep from the previous day's revelry. Meanwhile, he'd been recruited to return to the lists to practice with the other warriors. Duncan and his men had enjoyed the festive break the sporting games provided and the chance for some heated completion, but now it was time to get back to work.

Immediately after the games Daniel had offered to help bind and immobilize Michael's injured knee, but Michael had refused. Instead, after receiving a healing massage from Kayla, he claimed it no longer hurt, or at least not as much. She had simply laid her hands on Michael's injured knee after rubbing it down with some of Lady Lydia's curative salve, and about thirty minutes later, he was up and walking with hardly a limp. It was almost as if he'd never been injured.

Daniel was skeptical about Michael's quick recovery. He wondered if the warrior's injury were really as bad as he'd been led to believe or if Michael had used it as an excuse to get him to participate in the games. Michael and Duncan had both disclaimed such a notion, stating more than once how grateful they were Daniel had stepped in to take Michael's place when he was no longer able to compete. When questioned about his quick recovery, Michael claimed it was simply due to Kayla's healing powers and soothing touch. Still skeptical, Daniel simply marveled at how quickly the allegedly wounded warrior had been able to recover.

After their night of revelry, many of the guards had wanted to sleep in, but by midmorning, Michael had his men back in the lists, training hard as always. He'd allow no rest, even if they were the momentary victors. There would always be challengers to take the champion's place if they were allowed to go soft. Besides, he argued, he could still direct his men through their drills even if he did have to lean on his fighting staff occasionally to relieve the strain. Injured or not, there were no excuses to miss a day of training.

By the time Daniel headed back to the barracks, he had put in another hard day of training. It felt good to be out on the field once again, but now he was looking forward to a few hours of quiet relaxation. All day he'd done his best not to think about Kayla and how close he'd come to taking her innocence the night before, and was grateful for the mind-numbing distraction of a hard workout. At one point, Rory had made a sly comment about Daniel getting lost on his way back to his room in the barracks, but thankfully, nothing else was said.

"I see Michael has put ye through another day of hard training, my friend." Souyer, the wizard, greeted him when they met as Daniel was on his way back to his room. "What do ye think of yer time here? It must be greatly different from the life ye once knew."

"More different than I could have imagined." Daniel slowed his pace for the benefit of the old druid. "It's one thing to read about history; it's another to be physically forced to experience it." Daniel rubbed at a pain in his shoulder. "Don't get me wrong, I'm actually enjoying the hell out of this."

"Are ye now?" Souyer looked more pleased than surprised.

"Sometimes I catch myself feeling lost and confused, worried about when I'm going to pop back to my own time, but for now, I'm just doing my best to enjoy this whole darn thing." Daniel was grateful to have someone to share his thoughts with. Considering Souyer's unique understanding of Daniel's circumstance, the old wizard was turning out to be a respected confidant.

"Are ye nae looking forward to returning home to yer family?" Souyer asked. He motioned for Daniel to stop so they could sit on a nearby bench and take advantage of the waning warmth of the late afternoon sun.

Taking a seat beside the old wizard, Daniel stretched out his legs and relaxed, welcoming the opportunity to speak his mind. "You know, truth be told, I'm not really worried about going back home to hang with my brothers. I rather like the camaraderie I'm enjoying here with the MacNicols. Besides, my brothers have all moved away and have families of their own. I hardly ever see them anymore."

"Am I to believe ye are nay longer interested in going home?" Souyer sounded intrigued by Daniel's change of heart.

"It's not like that; it's just that I don't have much to go home to. The family ranch is too big for me to run by myself, and I don't have anyone who wants to share the load. I've lost my job; they've done away with the mounted police, and if I stay with the force I'll just be another cop with a beat, chasing down the bad guys and rounding up the homeless off the streets." Daniel ran his hand across his forehead, wiping off beads of sweat, and turned his face toward the light afternoon breeze.

"So, what do ye want?" The old druid leaned on his staff, casting a sideways glance at Daniel.

"A job I enjoy going to every day and a family to go home to every night. Isn't that what everybody wants?" Daniel stared off toward the horizon, picturing what a home and family might look like. A redheaded woman with dancing green eyes slid easily into the picture.

"How do ye see that happening?"

"That's a good question." Daniel shrugged and directed his attention back to the old druid. "But I don't know the answer. Not while I'm expecting to leave, and who knows when." Right now it wasn't a question Daniel wanted to dwell on too long or too hard.

"Are ye certain yer going to leave here?" Souyer asked with pinched brows.

"Of course, I'm going to leave. Teressa returned home, and I expect I will too. The only difference is Teressa knew why she was here and what she needed to do before she was sent back. I don't have any idea why I'm here or what I'm supposed to do. Lady Lydia thinks I have some task to perform."

"Did she say what it was?" The look on Souyer's face told Daniel the wizard was more than just interested. He was downright concerned.

"No, but it sure would be nice if someone could clue me in so I'll know what's expected of me and when I have to leave." As much as he tried not to think about it, the frustration of not knowing was never far from his thoughts.

"When ye *have* to leave? How interesting."

"Might be interesting, but it's not doing me any good. Not as long as some freaking faerie is in control of my life. Except for the not knowing part, I really like being here."

"What do ye find so enjoyable?" Souyer asked.

"Believe it or not, it's the unavoidable raw, physical, in-your-face kind of reality that's hitting me the hardest. I mean, I thought living on a ranch, raising horses, and doing chores with Dad was physically demanding, especially compared to the kind of chores the other boys who lived in town had. The hardest part of their day was spent out on the sports field. Here, every day is a new challenge. There's no getting away from it. The only drawback is there's no hot shower at the end of a long, hard day." Daniel also knew Kayla was a big part of why he wanted to stay, but there was no use going down that dead end.

"A hot shower?" The druid gave him a quizzical look.

Daniel thought about how to describe a modern-day shower in a way that would do the experience justice for the old man. "Imagine a steaming hot waterfall being brought conveniently to a corner of your own bedchamber for you to enjoy."

"In the future, man learns how to control the flow of water?" Souyer seemed amazed by such a wondrous idea.

"That's only a minor feat of modern plumbing. It pales compared to the marvels man will accomplish. Someday we'll build castles that reach to the sky and fly across the land." Seeing the look of stark astonishment on Souyer's face, Daniel reined in his futuristic prophecies. "But today, I'm simply a man in search of a hot bath, even if I have to fetch and heat the water by myself."

"Well now, I believe a hot bath is something I can assist ye with. I know the whereabouts of a large wooden tub, often used for washing garments. I'm quite certain it could support the cleansing of yer body. I'm also quite certain Bonnie would be happy to secure the necessary servants to fill the tub with the heated water you require. I've observed she's quite taken with yer friendship. I believe she would deny ye little in the way of creature comforts. All ye need to do is ask," Souyer informed him.

Within an hour, thanks to Souyer, and with Bonnie's help, Daniel found himself pleasantly ensconced in his cozy little room with a large tub of steaming hot water. "Finally," Daniel murmured as he relaxed into the comfort of the bath. It had taken a near-Herculean effort to secure the large tub and heat enough water to facilitate his bath, but Bonnie had proven to be a champion in her efforts to provide the luxurious gift to her favored friend. The moment he slipped into the relaxing water, he knew their efforts were worth the results. Several days of sponge baths had forced his personal hygiene standards to be woefully compromised. This luxury afforded him a thorough and much needed cleansing, not to mention the good ole pleasure of soaking away his aches and pains in a soothing tub of wonderfully hot water.

If I was stuck in this time, Daniel mused, *I'd get Duncan to build a communal bathhouse.* He could picture the structure and its components in his mind. It would have large wooden tubs, big enough to hold a full-sized man, with a fireplace to warm the building and heat the water. And it would need to be located near a source of water.

Then his mind circled back on his words, *If I was stuck in this time . . .*

What if I am stuck in this time? he wondered. *How would I feel about never going home again?*

Daniel contemplated the idea as he scrubbed the grunge off his body, digging deep into his thoughts and feelings. He had already considered the idea more than once, but that was before he got to know Kayla. Then, the idea of not returning to his own time had felt like a curse, a dreaded outcome, but now it felt more like a choice. Unfortunately, it wasn't his choice to make.

In all honesty, he admitted to himself, the possibility had its appeal. Living in the thirteenth century on the Isle of Skye would never be dull. It would be a hard life, for sure, but it wouldn't be dull. He'd never have to worry about having a dead cell phone battery or falling behind on the latest electronic technology. Though, he'd also have to do without all the other modern conveniences he used to enjoy, like supermarkets, fast food, and fast cars.

And then there was Kayla. Always there was Kayla. The idea of being able to pursue a relationship with Kayla held the greatest appeal of all. He certainly wasn't fool enough to believe it was some idealistic notion of a warrior's life that appealed to him, at least not enough to hold him here. No, it was all about Kayla. She was the one who would make it all worthwhile.

Because Daniel had never met a woman he wanted as much as he did Kayla, he really wanted to know her, talk to her, and understand what made her so unique. He wanted to learn more about her ability to heal with just her touch, and what made her happy or sad.

Enticed by her innocence, he found her refreshing; she wasn't jaded by the world around her, nor was she boastful or full of false pride. If anything, she suffered from a case of acute modesty, not only for her innate healing talents, but also regarding her natural beauty. Hers was a beauty that radiated from her soul.

He could understand her modesty, even her lack of self-confidence. She had grown up with the loving protection of her three large, elder brothers. No doubt they cast rather daunting shadows, long and wide, which were reinforced by Lady Lydia's mothering and smothering ways. It was understandable why Kayla had chosen to live in the comfortable shade of their love and protection rather than seek the limelight for herself. It was an easy place for her to dwell.

But he also saw beyond her modest facade to the spirited woman held deep within. She had the ability to take charge and know her own mind. He'd seen glimpses of it over and over. It was her spirit that resonated with him most. Something about her truly grabbed his interest, and like an old dog with a bone or a miser with his money, it refused to let go.

A voice spoke in his head. *Right woman, right time.*

Disheartened by the thought, he shook his head. It wasn't possible. How could she be the right woman if he was in the wrong time?

~*~

Souyer sat alone on his bench, perched high on the roof of his tower, watching the never-ending ebb and flow of the ocean below. He heard Duncan approach before he saw him, but then, he'd been expecting the chief. Over the past few years, as he progressed deeper into his new position as wise old sage, he and Duncan had grown closer. Souyer had to admit, he appreciated the transformation.

"Dinna see ye at the games yesterday. Did our warrior contest nae interest ye?" Duncan asked as he approached the druid.

"I watched yer games and was quite pleased by the outcome. I simply chose to watch from the comfort of the battlements." Souyer pointed with his staff to a prime spot along the fortress wall. It afforded a fine view of the whole bailey and training fields. From his perch above the crowds he'd been able to see not only the warrior games, but he had a ringside seat for the courtship of Daniel and Kayla, even if they weren't admitting such intentions to themselves, at least not yet. "'Tis a better view from up there, and it dinna require me to mingle with yer horde of visitors."

"Now ye mention it, ye've made yerself more scarce than usual since the arrival of the MacDonalds. Are ye nae missing the company of the MacDonald chief? Ye did help him become my father-in-law, after all." There was a bold smirk on Duncan's face.

"Doona be hanging me with that rope. 'Twas Teressa's doing from start to finish. I was as much at her mercy as ye when it came to her ability to manipulate a situation. That woman has a true talent. I'll give her that." Souyer thought back to the day Teressa talked him into playing his part to get the MacDonald chief to agree to Duncan's marriage to Janet. He could've kicked himself for not seeing through her little ploy, but her charm had worked its magic. He had fallen right into her plans to ensure Hugh MacDonald would not stand in the way of Duncan's marriage proposal and his daughter's happiness. But now, three years later, seeing the happiness of their union, he was more pleased than he was likely to admit at the success of Teressa's matchmaking skills.

"Apparently, 'twas her successful completion of the task that got her sent back to her time. I sometimes wonder if she sacrificed her happiness in exchange for mine." Duncan leaned against the battlement wall and folded his arms across his broad chest. "I've enjoyed these years of quiet happiness with Janet. Now I must deal with another time traveling Ellers as well as a botched betrothal between my sister and Arlin MacDonald."

"From what I know, Teressa had nay choice in the matter. Moezell never planned for the lass stay in our time. She had a family who needed her back home, and to home she had to return." Over the years, Souyer had learned of Lady Lydia's participation in Teressa's time travel experience, but in loyalty to the matriarch of the clan, he had agreed to keep her involvement a secret.

"Now her brother shows up, but we doona know why he's here," Duncan said.

"Ye would think a faerie wouldn't be displacing a person seven hundred years in time without a good reason." Souyer was fairly certain, this time, Moezell was acting alone. His observations of Lady Lydia told him she wanted no part of Daniel's unexpected visit from the future.

"'Tis as though he's searching for something," Duncan said.

Souyer gazed off over the churning blue of the ocean, his mind searching for the missing clues that continued to elude him. He recalled asking Teressa the same question, wondering what she had been searching for. The wizened man was certain a person didn't travel halfway around the world and seven hundred years back in time if they weren't searching for something. He often wondered if she had found it.

A strange thought came to him, followed by a peculiar feeling in his chest. His instincts were telling him something, and over the years, he had learned to listen to his instincts. He had also learned to keep such thoughts to himself until he knew more.

"Mayhap 'tis time I paid the lad a visit." Slowly, Souyer stood up from the bench with the aid of his staff. His bones had grown stiff with old age, and the chilly winds off the ocean while refreshing often added to his discomfort.

"From what I've seen, ye have become fast friends." Duncan offered the elder man a hand, but Souyer waved off his assistance.

"'Tis time for me to use our alliance to my advantage." Souyer paused a moment to lean on his staff while he got his legs under control. His left knee had a nasty habit of giving out on him, and he would rather not have Duncan see him lose his balance, especially after he had declined the chief's assistance.

"What do ye have in mind?" Duncan asked.

Even though Souyer had resisted, the chief placed a firm hand on the druid's elbow, guiding him toward the rooftop doorway.

"Just a friendly little visit." Though he preferred not to show it, Souyer was pleased to be accepting Duncan's assistance. "By the way, what are ye going to do now that the plan for another marriage into the MacDonald clan seems to have failed?"

"Mother was the one most in favor of their betrothal. There's nay use beating a dead horse. It appears neither Kayla nor Arlin has any desire for the match. As I see it, we've nay need for another alliance with the MacDonalds. I've talked with Alec MacLeod. He has a fine son, Iain. The lad is nearly five years older than my Amy. Mayhap in a dozen years from now, we'll find a MacLeod alliance more to our liking."

"A far smarter way to go, I would say. The MacLeods have always proved to be strong friends and allies to the MacNicols. Together, yer clans will have the strength ye need."

"And plenty enough ale to service even Rory's needs." Duncan laughed.

"Aye, plenty enough ale indeed," Souyer agreed.

Duncan and Souyer made their way down the long spiraling staircase of the high tower and entered the keep before parting ways. Duncan had guests to attend to, and Souyer had plans of his own.

Souyer's timing couldn't be better. As he approached the barracks where Daniel had taken a room, he saw the large washtub being removed by two of the stable lads. It took both of the lads to heft the large tub back to the laundry room. Daniel would be washed and refreshed from his day of training in the lists with Michael and the guards. A relaxed man was usually more open to a meaningful conversation, but just in case he needed reinforcements, Souyer had grabbed a jug of ale when he passed through the keep.

Daniel saw Souyer coming and held the door to his room open for him.

"From the looks of ye, I would say the bath was a success," Souyer greeted Daniel as he entered the small cell. He took a look around before setting the jug and pewter cups on the lone table.

"A fine success indeed. You have my debt of gratitude." Daniel smiled as he closed the door. "Here, take a seat. I don't have much to offer. You can choose the bed or the stool; take your pick." Daniel's gesture encompassed the whole of the confined space.

Souyer chose the stool, which sat higher than the low rope-framed bed, and it would be easier to stand when he was ready to leave. It also allowed Souyer to avoid sitting where another man slept.

"I brought ye some ale to aid in yer relaxation." Souyer pointed to the jug.

"Care to join me?" Daniel offered.

"I would be pleased."

Daniel retrieved the jug from the table and poured them both a drink.

Souyer accepted the offered mug with a nod. "Let's drink to our health."

Both men took long deep swallows of the strong brew. It was one of the jugs left behind by the MacLeods, and it lived up to their reputation.

~~~

Daniel sat on the edge of the bed, and even though he stood a good five inches taller than Souyer, the resulting seating arrangement had him peering up at the wizard. Grabbing the meager bed pillow to stuff behind his head, he leaned back to relax. He'd spent enough years being a cop to know when someone was looking for information. He figured the old druid had an agenda; he just needed to sit back, relax, and wait for the conversation to unfold.

"I understand ye have been shunned by Lady Lydia. From what I've seen, she's nae happy to have ye here. Do ye know why?" Souyer jumped right into his inquiry. Daniel respected that.

"I think simply showing up was enough to piss her off. I get the feeling she wasn't expecting me, if you know what I mean." Daniel took another deep swallow of ale. *They sure don't brew stuff like this in the future.*

"But she was expecting Teressa. She welcomed her with open arms," Souyer said.

"Yeah, and she also sent her away and had Moezell take all the heat for her disappearance. How much do you know about that whole business? Teressa wrote in her journal Lady Lydia wanted her involvement kept secret."

"Aye, I doona think anyone else in the family knows. Teressa kept her word while she was here and respected Lady Lydia's request for secrecy."

"Professional courtesy for confidentiality. Teressa doesn't discuss her client's cases with anyone. I understand she didn't even tell Rory." Daniel respected his sister's professional integrity but wondered if she had made the right choice.

"Which brings me to my next question. Rory and Teressa seem destined to be together. Moezell told Rory they'd be reunited. It has been three years, and instead of Teressa, Moezell brings ye back in time. I'm thinking ye know something. Am I right?"

Daniel figured Souyer was probably better than most at reading people's thoughts. He also figured he was better than most at hiding his. For a good long while, he sat there stone-faced, contemplating how much he should share with the elder druid. To his mind, Souyer had proven to be a loyal friend and counselor, but best of all, he'd helped him organize his bath.

"Yeah, I know something, or at least I think I do. But let me ask you first; why do you want to know?"

"I believe it may help me understand why ye are here." Those were magical words. Souyer couldn't have picked a better incentive to get Daniel on his side.

"I've thought it over and over, and I don't know how it can help, but I'll tell you what I know. When Teressa came home from her vacation, she didn't come alone. She brought home a fiancé, the man she married."

Souyer nearly choked on his ale. "Teressa's married?"

"Yeah, to a Scottish sea captain from Skye. He transferred his job to San Francisco. They got married on New Year's Day. His name is Robert MacNicol, but she calls him Rory. And here's the kicker. These two guys, her husband Robert and your Rory, they could be identical twins. When I first landed here and was introduced to Rory, I thought he was Robert."

"What are ye saying?" Souyer stared at Daniel with wide eyes, mouth agape.

"I'm just telling you what I know."

Souyer gave himself a shake to regain his composure. "Is Rory going to travel to the future?"

"No, I don't think so," Daniel said, shaking his head.

"I doona understand. How does he get there?"

Daniel peered into his cup of ale, as though searching for answers. "Well, we all die sooner or later," he said. He'd already been through the death of his parents and as a cop fatalities were part of his job. Like it or not, he accepted death as a fact of life. "None of us get out of here alive. Maybe Rory just has something to look forward to when he goes. I'm not sure I agree, but Teressa believes Robert MacNicol is the reincarnation of Rory. As far as she's concerned, they have been reunited—in the twenty-first century."

Souyer drank his ale then rolled the empty cup between his hands. He gestured toward the jug, requesting a refill. Daniel jumped off the bed, happy to oblige them both.

"Have ye considered if this," Souyer made a vague gesture with his hand, indicating the subject they'd been discussing, "could have something to do with the task ye need to perform?" The grave look on the wizard's face let Daniel know how seriously he viewed the idea.

"I don't like what you're saying. Makes it sound like I'm tied to his death, and I can tell you, that's not going to happen. I'd give my life to save his."

"Even if it meant ye could never go home?" Souyer's words hung heavy in the space between them.

"You don't know what you're saying." Anger bit at Daniel's words. "You're just making stuff up. Rory could live to be an old man. You don't know how any of this stuff works."

"If Moezell brought ye here, and if ye have a task to perform, and if Rory has to die . . ."

"Stop right there. Too many ifs and no probable cause. Doesn't hold up." Daniel didn't like what he was hearing.

"Ye think a faerie needs probable cause? Besides, if her goal is to reunite Rory and Teressa . . ."

"She wouldn't need me to do it. And if she does, she's going to be sorely disappointed."

Souyer took another long drink before he responded, "This puts a whole new light on yer situation."

"Now that I've shared, how's this information going to help me?" Daniel asked, feeling they were no further along than when they had started this god-awful conversation.

"I told ye afore; I felt a storm brewing. It's the kind of storm that will bring more than just rain. I'm nae sure what it means; I have to give it some thought. If I come up with anything, I will be sure to let ye know." Souyer rubbed his head, already deep in thought.

"Yeah, you do that. Anything you can do will help. But I'm telling you right now . . ."

"I know how ye feel." Souyer gave a shudder. "Aye, there's a storm coming. I can feel it in my bones." The old wizard hoisted himself up from the stool and headed for the door. He left the jug of ale on the table.

Daniel couldn't hide his disappointment. He'd been hoping for more, but he couldn't blame Souyer for being dazed by his revelation. Frankly, he was finding it all pretty hard to believe himself.

CHAPTER 17

Kayla retreated to the comfort of her room to indulge in the rare pleasure of a hot, soaking bath; the perfect excuse to avoid lingering in the great hall with the rest of her family and their guests. It had only been a few days since the arrival of the MacDonald clan, and Kayla was already weary of their presence. Arlin in particular wore on her nerves. The man had openly insulted her womanhood.

Baths were a luxury not to be wasted. After Kayla had scrubbed her body clean with an efficiency borne through years of habit, she took a moment to indulge in the lukewarm water while she reviewed the events of the previous day.

She had seen how Beatrice MacDonald had blatantly cheered for Rory at the warrior games. Everyone had noticed. Rory had seemed flattered by the young woman's attentions, but he hadn't appear to be unduly attracted to Beatrice, despite the young woman's best efforts to make her feelings known. Kayla understood his heart still belonged to Teressa and probably always would.

Kayla recalled her brief conversation with Beatrice. It hadn't gone well.

"'Tis a wonder to see a MacDonald cheer for a MacNicol. Why would ye show support for my brother and nae yer own?" Kayla had asked Beatrice.

"Because Roderick would make a wondrous husband. Is that nae obvious?" Beatrice had frankly admitted.

"Doona ye think ye are rushing things a wee bit?" She had been taken aback by Beatrice's aggressive manner.

"Nay, I am nineteen and wish to be married. I have nae intention of waiting 'til I am too old to be desired." Her eyes had swept over Kayla in a manner that spoke volumes.

Beatrice didn't have to say the hurtful words for Kayla to know what the younger woman had been thinking. *Too old like me.* She had wondered if all of the MacDonalds shared her opinion. It would seem so, based on the way they treated her with their poor pretense of civility.

Brushing aside the intended insult, she had continued to question Beatrice. "Ye believe Rory is the right man? The right choice for yer husband?" Setting aside Beatrice's natural arrogance, it had impressed her how the younger woman could make such a monumental choice so easily.

Beatrice had laughed. "Of course. He's strong and handsome, and he makes me laugh. I find Roderick to be a most pleasing prospect for a husband."

"Aye, as would most any other young lass he should encounter. What makes ye think he will notice ye above all others?" Kayla had found her usual politeness slipping away.

"I'm the daughter of the MacDonald chief. An alliance with our clan carries great value. I happen to know he has shown nay interest in a match since his affair with that strange woman ye brought to the Isle Faire three years ago. Everyone knows she has disappeared from Skye, mayhap never to return." Beatrice had directed her gaze back to the action taking place on the training field.

"She may have disappeared from the isle, but she has nae disappeared from his thoughts. I know he still cares for Teressa." Kayla had been highly pleased to share that wee piece of information with the MacDonald's daughter.

Scornfully, Beatrice had turned her attention again to Kayla. "He may as well be in love with a ghost. He can nae love a memory forever. When he seeks a real woman for his comfort, I plan to be the one he finds, ready and waiting for him."

"Yer words prove ye doona know my brother very well."

"Yer words prove ye doona know me very well. I always get what I want," Beatrice had made her last spiteful remark before moving off toward her mother, turning her back on Kayla.

Kayla had felt certain such a smug display of superiority could only be expressed by one so young and so mistakenly sure of herself.

"Time will tell," Kayla had quietly dismissed the younger woman. Time had a way of being a grand and arduous teacher. Her own experiences were teaching her that only too well.

At the games, Kayla had also noticed Becky, Lady Evelyn's chambermaid. Everyone had noticed her as she cheered for Arlin. And in return, he had made no effort to hide his affection for the serving girl, claiming to be her champion. Not much of a champion, Kayla had thought, considering he had lost to Daniel. How ridiculous his antics appeared as he had strutted about, trying to impress the young maid.

He had even gone so far as to refer to her as "poor old Kayla." Not that she cared what he thought, but his words carried the stinging ring of truth. It had been a sweet victory indeed when Daniel had knocked the wind out of his overblown sails, defeating him with the fighting staff.

Such a pleasure it had been to share the day with Daniel. The more time she spent in his company, the closer she felt to him, and yet she could tell he was holding something back. She sensed a part of him was on guard, as if he feared to release everything he felt. She worried if it were just her imagination wanting to believe he really cared for her.

During their playtime with Torrin and Tanner, he had called her "feisty." She thought about his use of the term. No one had ever called her feisty before. Hardworking and determined, aye, but never feisty. She realized she rather liked the idea. For a moment, she had believed he was going to kiss her; she had seen it in his eyes, but then her nephews had pounced upon his back, and the moment had passed, and they had continued on with their play.

Kayla admired how easily Daniel interacted with her nephews, how quickly he had gained their respect and affection. He'd make a great father someday, and to some woman, a fine husband. A husband a woman would be pleased to build a life with. More and more, she knew she wanted to be his woman. She wished she could be the one he loved, but he insisted on maintaining a polite distance, pulling back at the slightest hint of affection. Even today, after their kisses in the stable the night before, which had hinted at more than simply affection, he had chosen to avoid her. Daniel had trained with the men in the lists rather than seek her company in the keep.

He was always polite and kind, but usually he treated her more as a well-respected friend than a lover. Last night in the stable, the way he had kissed her, she had known he felt something more. Something he wasn't saying that begged to burst free. For one passionate moment, before Rory found them, she had felt how much he wanted her. The way he had kissed her and touched her in ways no man had ever done before, and their stolen kisses in the dark, had awakened something in her that could no longer be denied.

Rising from the cooling water of her bath, she stepped out and rubbed a drying cloth over her body before she wrapped her long wet curls with the fabric. Pausing as she reached for her night shift, she took a moment to appraise her appearance in the small mirror on her table.

The sight that greeted her was not unpleasant. Her honest assessment acknowledged she was no longer a blushing young beauty, but she believed her face still held some appeal. Standing naked in the warming glow of the fireplace, her critical eyes examined the length of her body as the flames of the fire cast a golden light dancing over her skin. It was true she no longer carried the slender young body of an adolescent girl; instead, she now boasted the lush curves of a well-formed woman. Her breasts sat ample and firm on her chest. She believed her backside and hips were not overly large and added a pleasant roundness to her appearance. Without doubt, she had a body ripe for bearing children.

I can still be attractive to a man, she thought as she ran her hands along the curves of her body. In truth, the only man she truly hoped to attract was Daniel. She wondered what it would be like to have Daniel make love to her, to take possession of her body and soul.

Standing naked as she was, she felt the temperature of the chamber drop rapidly as the wind rustled at her window. Pulling aside the heavy fabric draped across the opening, she gazed out upon an approaching summer storm. Thick grey thunderclouds led the storm front. Off in the distance, rain poured down over the ocean as it treaded its way toward land.

Suddenly, filled with determination and a bold plan, she dropped the drying cloth where she stood. Grabbing her thin nightdress, she pulled it over her head, then reached for her cloak. Wrapping the heavy grey wool mantle over her shoulders, she quietly slipped from her chamber. Her destination was Daniel's room.

If she hurried, she could make it to the barracks before the downpour of the storm hit the cliffs of Portree. In silence, she made her way down the stairs and out the back passages to the barracks. Pulling the hood of the cloak over her still-damp hair, she dashed across the final few yards to the wooden building and quickly located Daniel's door.

Her heart thumped boldly in her chest as she knocked upon his door with three quick taps. Daniel greeted her naked to the waist, wearing only loose drawstring breeches. Her pulse raced as she took in the sight of him; bare chested, bronzed, and beautiful. His startled expression left her unsure if he were surprised or pleased by her visit.

"Kayla, what are you doing here so late?" he asked, pulling her into the warmth of his narrow chamber and out of the cold night air.

She brushed the hood of her cloak back from her face as she stepped in from the cold. It fell to her shoulders, revealing curling ringlets of damp hair, indicating she had just finished her bath. It would only take a fleeting look for him to see, beneath her cloak, she was dressed for bed.

"I need to speak with ye. I know this is impulsive of me, but I've waited all day. We never seem to have any time alone. I mean, except . . ." She paced the short length of the chamber, fearful of his reaction or that her nerves would desert her.

"Is this about last night? Because, you know, I really need to apologize. I shouldn't have taken advantage of you." His usually cheerful expression had faded, replaced by remorsefully sad eyes.

Kayla stopped her pacing. He hadn't meant to kiss her. It had all been her fault for encouraging him. "Ye doona need to apologize," she stammered.

"Yes, I do. What I did wasn't right."

Her mind nearly froze. Had she misunderstood his desire? This wasn't at all what she expected, but what could she do? She couldn't leave now, not yet. Not without trying. She fumbled for an excuse. "I'm sorry Daniel, I shouldn't have come. I only wanted to ask ye a favor, but mayhap I should go."

"No. Stay. What do you need? I'll do anything."

What did she need? "Well, umm, I need a defender." *Aye, a defender*, she thought. Hopefully, he wouldn't refuse to defend her honor, even if she had misread his intentions.

"A defender? What do you mean? Has someone hurt you?" He took a protective step toward her, and then stopped.

"Arlin has insulted my virtue. Well, mayhap nae my virtue, but certainly my honor. He called me an old maid, nae worthy to be wed." However, if Daniel refused her, Arlin's claim might very well be true.

"You can't believe him. You know it isn't true. What does Duncan say about this?"

"I canna go to my brothers. 'Tis expected my family would defend me, and that would only reinforce Arlin's claim that I'm too old to find a proper suitor."

"Kayla, it's not that easy." He ran his fingers through his hair, looking wretchedly frustrated.

"I doona ask for much, just some of yer time."

"My time? What do you mean, my time?" He sounded curiously angry.

Realizing the horrendous mistake she was making, she became defensive. She lifted her chin. "Never mind, 'tis nay important. I know ye will be leaving soon."

It was stupid of her to make the same mistake as Rory, wanting him to stay when she knew he would leave. At best, all she could hope for was a brief moment of his affection, and then he would be gone. So be it, she would gladly take whatever he had to offer, without regrets.

Daniel's eyes narrowed, focusing on hers. "Why do you say that?" he asked.

She met his eyes. "That first day, when we met, ye said ye were just visiting and planned to leave in a few weeks." She remembered well the first day they had met along the road. So much had changed since then.

"Oh. Well, that was before." He shrugged, looking away.

"Before what?" she questioned.

"I mean, I don't know when I'll be leaving. I kinda like it here, and I want to work with Michael for more training."

Her heart soared. He liked it here, and maybe he was staying. It was enough to give her hope.

She suddenly recalled Moezell's words. "The greatest risk is to take no risk at all." Kayla found herself contemplating an idea holding great possibilities, but it also held great risks for her self-esteem and emotional well-being. The mere idea made her tremble.

Kayla nearly gave in to her long-held fears, but the greater part of her, the part that already loved him, needed to know. If his answer were no, fearful as it was to consider, she'd be no worse off than she was now. She would merely be aware of his true feelings. But if his feelings were anywhere near to her own, it would give her something to hope for. Hope he would stay at

Scorrybreac. Hope her prayers had been heard and her wish would be granted. Hope he could someday love her.

Searching for just the right words to say, she took a deep breath. Slipping her cloak from her shoulders, she let it drop and drape across the bed. "Daniel, do you find me attractive?" she asked. Rushing on, she added, "Mayhap I speak too boldly, but ye—ye did kiss me. Do ye care, even a little?"

"Of course, I do. More than you seem to know." His voice came out husky, laden with desire.

The light of the single candle burned from the bedside table. Surely it revealed her curves through the thin fabric of her nightgown. His eyes bore into her skin, but he didn't move.

"Are ye interested in me as more than a friend . . . mayhap as a lover?" This was proving to be harder than she had expected. Her emotions were so strong, so close to the surface, and her nerves felt raw with anticipation; so much depended on his answer. She risked a great and painful fall, and yet she knew she could not hold back from seeking the answer.

Stepping forward, he framed her face with his hands and rested his forehead against hers, still holding her at bay. He closed his eyes for a long, hard moment.

The scent of his freshly washed skin was more arousing than she would have imagined, and she could feel the heat of his naked torso so close to hers. Giving in to her newfound sensuality, her hands instinctively rose to touch the hardened muscles of his chest.

Flinching, as if he'd been burned, he grabbed her shoulders and plopped her down on his bed, then stepped away, putting distance between them. "Kayla, you need to sit down."

"On yer bed?" It wasn't proper, but then again, being alone with him in his room dressed in her nightgown was already highly improper.

Running his fingers through his damp hair, he took another step back. "Sit anywhere you want. There's something I need to tell you, things you need to know, and I'll feel better if you're sitting down."

Oh my, this must be serious. What could he possibly need to tell her that would make him so somber? He had just said he was planning to stay, that he liked it here, but he didn't say he wanted her. He'd spoken no words of love or affection. Had she read too much into his attentions? Were his kisses no more than a momentary pleasure? Perhaps he had another woman back home, someone waiting for him. She damned herself for her rash actions, her mind racing with all the fearful possibilities she could imagine.

Daniel began to pace the length of the small room. "I want you, Kayla. I won't deny it, but I won't compromise you to get what I want."

After being nearly frozen with fear, her heart once again sprang into action. *He wants me,* her mind shouted with joy. *He wants me.* Holding her emotions in check as best she could, she fought to maintain an appearance of composure.

"That's quite respectable of ye, Daniel, but what if I compromise you?"

He stopped pacing. "Now, Kayla, just what do you have in mind?" Daniel took a step back, a nervous look on his face.

She smiled, fully aware of the effect she was having on him. This was a first for her, this feeling of power over a man. Kayla stood and took a step toward him. "Ye say ye want me. Is this true?"

"God, yes, it's true."

"Then kiss me, Daniel. I want ye so much. Please kiss me."

In an instant, his resistance was shattered, and she was in his arms, feeling the strength of his passion fueled by her own.

The force of it, she thought. *Oh my God, the amazing force.* It was so powerful, like nothing she could imagine. It went beyond her wildest dreams, taking her to the moon and the stars on dazzling sparks of light.

His mouth was warm and fierce upon hers as she melted into his embrace. How could she have waited so long for this passion? The days and nights of wanting, the sensation of their first kiss—they had only created a warehouse of unspent energy that ignited the moment their lips touched. Daniel's hands blazed a hot trail across her skin, igniting her fire. This was no mistake, no deception of desire. There was no denying their passion and desire. It burned too bright.

~~~

It seemed too good to be true. Daniel had waited so long for this; he wanted her so much. To think Kayla had come to his room to offer herself to him was more than he could imagine and yet everything he had dreamed of. He wasn't one to refuse what was offered, not when it felt this good, this right. Though he knew he should have sent her away, that she was taking too great of a risk showing up in his room alone, the minute she dropped her cloak, any thoughts of chivalry dissipated into thin air, replaced by blatant burning lust. Lust and desire fueled by feelings yearning to be set free. His attempt to maintain a tight rein on his actions was lost when Kayla asked to be kissed. How could he possibly deny her? After all, he was only human, and she was so blessedly beautiful, so desirable.

As much as he wanted her, Daniel hadn't expected the quake that ripped through his body. With the first gentle touch of his lips, her body responded in a quest for more. He felt her response and deepened his kiss, covering her lips with his and slipping his tongue between her smooth, velvety lips. Quickly the kiss progressed from slow and tender to deeply passionate.

Her body melted against his, and he held her tight, increasing their physical connection. She wrapped her arms around him, as if seeking an anchor. *Hot damn*, this was grand; this was glorious; this was effing fireworks. Was there music in the air? Their kiss seemed to go on and on.

Suddenly, Daniel heard the sounds more clearly. That wasn't music; that was the baying of frightened horses. Their whinnies of alarm had finally reached through his passion-driven mind, alerting him to the danger. Pulling himself away from Kayla, he announced, "Something's wrong. We must go." He grabbed his long shirt and wrestled into it as he made his way into the courtyard while Kayla grabbed her cloak then followed close behind.

Out in the courtyard, they encountered rampant chaos. Fierce winds whipped through wild flames engulfing the stables. Frightened horses were scattered throughout the bailey. Through the smoke and flames, Daniel saw Rory heading back into the burning building, intent on releasing the horses from their confines. Seizing one of the horse blankets that had been dragged into the courtyard, Daniel dunked the heavy fabric into the nearest watering trough. He draped the soaked blanket across his head and shoulders and raced into the firestorm after his friend.

Rory was releasing the last stallion from its stall when the large animal panicked and bucked. It heaved its massive weight against Rory, knocking him firmly to the ground. The horse's hoofs descended with brute force, hitting him square in the chest, ripping flesh and shattering bones. A gut-wrenching scream tore from his lungs. His body clenched into a ball as he lay, gasping for air in the smoke-filled room. The horse bolted as burning timbers fell from the roof.

Dodging the path of the last stampeding animal, Daniel headed toward the screams of the fallen man until he found Rory crumpled in a bloody heap surrounded by flames. Pulling him from beneath the burning wreckage, he hastily draped the sodden blanket over Rory and heaved him over his shoulder. The scent of blood and burning flesh shocked his senses. Drawing on an adrenaline-fueled burst of strength, he quickly fled the burning building.

When Daniel reached the safety of the open courtyard, he saw Duncan and his men in the throes of fighting the fire and rounding up the horses. Dodging the onslaught, he raced to the far side of the open yard, well away from the danger of the ensuing chaos. Gingerly, he laid Rory on the ground, still wrapped in the sodden blanket, and sent up urgent prayers of hope. He wished there were something he could do to minimize Rory's pain.

"Help him. We must help him," Kayla sobbed, reaching for Rory. She was nearly hysterical by the sight of her brother's burned and bleeding body.

Daniel had enough experience with medical emergencies to know Rory's wounds and blood loss were too much for his body to endure. His heart and lungs were failing. Daniel held Kayla back, wishing with all his soul it could be different. "I'm sorry. I can't save him," he said. "There's nothing I can do."

She dropped beside Rory, sobbing. "Ye must let me try. I have to try." She reached out and placed her hands on his chest then pulled back with a jerk. "Dear God, it's worse than I thought." She tried again, and this time she held her hands in place. Her touch seemed to offer Rory some comfort.

Daniel stared into the eyes of the man who had become his brother. "You understand, don't you, Rory?"

With a look of brutal determination, Rory nodded his acceptance. Yes, he understood. "'Tis time," he coughed. "Teressa's waiting."

Daniel's eyes blurred with tears. He squeezed them shut, trying to hold back the flow. The effort was useless. Tears rolled from his eyes, wetting his cheeks. "I'll see you in another life, bro," he offered with a sad, broken smile.

Kayla shook with fear and grief. "I must save him; I must try." Tears streamed down her face.

Daniel looked up. He saw her pain. "I'm sorry, Kayla. He's already gone."

She looked into the face of her brother and saw Daniel was right. The light of Rory's soul was gone, leaving only his lifeless body.

CHAPTER 18

Sunlight was unable to break through the grey skies as the thick cover of clouds released a steady mist of showers. The MacNicols solemnly weathered the dampness as they laid Rory's body to rest in the clan's graveyard. The occupants of Scorrybreac were in a deep state of shock and mourning over the loss of their beloved son, brother, and friend.

The MacDonald chief and his assembled kin also attended the burial, showing heartfelt respects for Rory and his family. Soon after, they withdrew to their chambers to prepare to leave as soon as the summer storm passed. Any pleasure their visit might have offered faded and fizzled in the shadow of Rory's death.

After the burial was done and they had returned to the keep, Lady Lydia approached Daniel as he passed through the great hall on his way back to the barracks.

"Daniel, a moment of yer time, if ye please," she asked. The politeness of her address was unexpected, conveying previously unknown respect. The passing of Rory had left its mark. It seemed the loss of her favored son had broken through her hard-held prejudice.

"Yes, Lady Lydia," he answered. He gave her his full attention and mutual respect.

"I want to thank ye for yer efforts. Kayla told me how ye pulled Rory from the fire. That ye tried to save my son's life." She held herself proud and erect. Lady Lydia was the kind who shed her tears in private.

"I did it for Rory. I only wish I could have done more," he said without malice.

Nodding with understanding, she took no offense. "He's at peace now, I suppose." Her words came softly. He could see it wasn't easy for her to speak.

"He's with Teressa," Daniel declared.

"Are ye sure?" There was hope in her voice. Hope her son had found the happiness he deserved.

"Yeah, I'm sure. They were together before I left. Rory and Teressa are happily married and living in the future," Daniel confirmed, acknowledging his final acceptance of the soulmates' reunion.

Lady Lydia breathed deeply as water welled in her eyes but did not spill over. "Thank you, Daniel."

They parted, each going their separate ways with newfound acceptance. Lady Lydia had finally accepted his presence in her time, and in her daughter's life. While he couldn't agree with her actions, knowing how deeply her choices had hurt Rory, Daniel accepted she'd been blinded by her love for her son. Right or wrong, selfish or not, she'd done what she thought was best.

Later in the evening, after everyone had retired to their rooms, Daniel sat alone under the eaves of the great stone archway leading into the keep, nursing a tankard of ale while keeping watch on the grey gloomy skies. Night had fallen, and still the storm showed no sign of ending its tearful showers anytime soon. It were as if the heavens and earth were also morning the loss of Rory. Daniel welcomed the summer storm as a quiet companion for his foul mood. He needed to feel its cold brush of wind against his skin and breathe its chilly damp air as if the mere presence of the storm to reaffirmed his existence.

Unexpectedly, Daniel was pulled from his silent contemplation by the sounds of booted footsteps approaching from inside the keep. He was even more surprised to see it was Arlin.

Through his contacts in the kitchens, Daniel had learned all he needed to know about Arlin. He knew about Lady Lydia's aspiration to arrange a betrothal between Kayla and the youngest MacDonald. He also knew the asshole wanted nothing to do with Kayla, preferring to bestow his affections upon that stupid servant girl, Becky. Apparently, Arlin's preferences had stirred up bad blood between him and his parents. Bonnie had confirmed Arlin wanted to marry Becky and work with her father as a blacksmith. In fact, he was the one who had arranged for his mother to take Becky as her personal maid.

"Drinking alone, are ye?" Arlin asked.

Daniel didn't look up and hoped the uninvited gate-crasher to his private pity party would move on. He said nothing.

Arlin deliberately ignored Daniel's snub. "I understand ye were close to Rory."

"As far as I'm concerned, we were brothers." Daniel's eyes remained fixed on the summer storm.

"No wonder ye show such a preference for Kayla." There was no mistaking the undertone of malice in Arlin's words.

"Just what do you mean by that?" Daniel cast a steely look toward Arlin. He wouldn't mind releasing his sorrow and pent-up anger in a good knockdown brawl, and he wouldn't mind at all if Arlin were the one to take the fall.

"The way ye've been acting around her, pretending to be her suitor. I figure it must be for show, as a favor to Rory. The rumor is ye will be leaving soon, just like yer sister, leaving Kayla high and dry." His words were accompanied by a sneering laugh.

"I should warn you, you're treading on very thin ice." In all fairness, Daniel believed he should give the younger man his warning to back off. But by God, if he didn't take it, Daniel was perfectly willing to once again knock the snot out of the bastard.

Arlin foolishly disregarded the warning. "These are nae yer people. Ye doona belong here. Ye're passing through on yer way back to wherever ye came from. Why should ye care? 'Tis nae yer problem."

Unfortunately, that was exactly his problem, not knowing how long he could stay, fearing someday soon he would be forced to leave. As far as he knew, he could be sucked back in time without any warning, the same way he had arrived.

He wanted Kayla; of that, he was certain, but he had no reason to believe he was the right man for her. She was a woman worthy of marriage, a marriage that would serve her and her family, and that didn't include a man with an unknown future.

"Kayla is my friend. My *dear* friend. If you know what's best, you'll leave her be." He struggled to remain civil toward the man. *Walk away*, he thought. *One of us needs to walk away.*

"Such nice words, 'my dear friend.' Ha! She's been a little too long on the shelf, if ye ask me. I prefer them younger, like my Becky. Now there's a woman worth taking."

Daniel clenched his fists, his anger brewing just below the surface.

Speaking with smug confidence, Arlin taunted him, "Or mayhap ye've already had yer way with yer *dear friend*. Has she given into wantonness in her old age?"

That was the final straw Daniel needed to push him over the edge. His tightly coiled anger and frustration burst forth with a satisfying release of brute force as his fist shot out across Arlin's chin, hitting its mark with bone-crunching power. Before Arlin could flinch, a second blow was delivered in rapid succession. It knocked Arlin several steps backward, sending him reeling toward the hard stone walls of the archway.

Daniel lurched at Arlin, grabbing his tunic as he stumbled backward. Together they rolled down the stairs of the keep, the hard stones biting into their backs. Rain-induced mud greeted them at the bottom, making it difficult to secure a sure footing.

Slipping in the sodden mess, Arlin did his best to rise to his feet. Without gaining proper balance, he lunged forward toward Daniel and slipped again, falling face-first into the mud.

Daniel had let the momentum of the fall take him away from their landing site. He drew on the energy of his rolling tumble to position himself into a crouch before he stood to recover his footing. Gaining a momentary advantage, he executed a swift high kick, bringing his foot to connect with the side of Arlin's head as he was trying to stand. The man went down into the mud for a third time.

Daniel stood over him, ready to pounce again.

Duncan suddenly appeared at the door of the keep. "What the blaze is going on here? What the hell are you doing?" he demanded of Daniel.

Daniel didn't speak. Instead, he reached down to help Arlin to his feet with gruff assistance.

Bloodied and bruised, but still defiant, Arlin stared at Daniel, silently daring him to reveal the nature of their fight to Kayla's brother.

Still furious, Daniel struggled to recover his senses and rein in his emotions. It was a mess. A dirty, ugly mess, and he was in no condition to discuss what had transpired between them with Duncan or anyone else. He wouldn't lower himself to repeat Arlin's hateful words.

"Trust me, Duncan," he stated flatly, "you don't want to know."

A look of understanding flashed between the two men. Regardless of the reason, the MacNicol chief understood. Daniel had been defending the honor of his clan. Giving a nod, Duncan turned to haul Arlin back into the keep. Daniel held his ground for several minutes longer, allowing the chill of the light summer shower to wash over him and cool his temper. Finally, he turned on his heel and slowly walked away.

Daniel stepped into his room and kicked the wooden stool, sending it flying across the room. He thought about picking it up and smashing it to bits to help release his frustrations, but he didn't. Instead, he grabbed it and set it upright, returning it to its spot beside the table.

After stripping off his wet and filthy clothes, he threw them in the corner. They were a sodden muddy mess. He'd have to see if he could get Bonnie to wash them in the morning. Naked, he stepped back out into the rain and ran a washcloth over his face and body, doing his best to clean up after the fight. It was a cold and sorry replacement for a shower, but it would have to do.

After drying off, he threw himself on the small bed of his dimly lit room and stared at the ceiling with his hands entwined behind his head. A single candle kept him company in the dark.

It was late, and he was tired, but his mind was restless, busy assessing all that had happened since he first arrived on Skye. One by one, he endeavored to sort through his emotions. It wasn't an easy task, but it needed to be done.

He didn't feel bad about losing his temper, it had felt too damn good to kick Arlin's butt. The man deserved a good thrashing for the way he talked about Kayla. Usually, Daniel was in better control of his emotions; he knew he should've walked away. With grudging acceptance, he admitted his emotions had been too strong, too raw, and too ready to boil over. Though the slight about Kayla was grievous, he had welcomed the opportunity to smack the crap out of the offending MacDonald.

Lying there alone in the nearly dark room of the thirteenth-century barracks, he felt a strong connection to the MacNicol clan. Rory had been like a brother. He felt much the same about Duncan and Michael. Souyer, the old druid, had become his friend and confidant. And there were Bonnie and Milly; they fawned over him like dear maiden aunts. His list went on and on. Even Lady Lydia had shown him respect. The people of Scorrybreac were becoming his people. Daniel had come to feel a true connection to this time and place.

And God help him, he could finally admit it, at least to himself, he'd fallen in love. He was in love with Kayla, and nothing about it was easy.

With so much connecting him to Scorrybreac, he wondered why he still felt like an outsider, like he didn't belong.

Then it hit him, smack-dab in his face. Fear. It was agonizing to admit and impossible to deny. Fear was holding him back. Fear he'd lost control of his life. Fear he could be sucked back in time at any moment without any warning and lose it all. Fear prevented him from living fully in the moment—and now all he wanted was to stay.

It was an exciting adventure, the thrill of a lifetime to experience ancient history, and yet it all seemed meaningless unless Kayla were a part of his life.

Unlike Teressa, he had no idea why he'd been brought back in time. Obviously, he wasn't brought here to cause Rory's death, and he certainly wasn't able to prevent it. If he'd been brought here to assure Rory someday he would be reunited with Teressa, he had failed. He had never shared that information with his future brother-in-law. Besides, that alone seemed too weak of a reason to displace a man over seven hundred years in time.

He knew Teressa had been brought here to act as a relationship coach, a matchmaker for Duncan and Janet. She'd been given clear instructions on what was expected of her and when she would leave. His time travel experience seemed to be completely without reason.

As he continued to dwell on his dilemma, he realized there was one aspect of this experience he shared with his sister. They had both met someone with whom they felt a special connection, and like his sister, his first reaction had been to fight the obvious attraction. Unlike Teressa, his efforts to fight the attraction weren't so much for his sake but for Kayla's. He had believed he could protect her from a painful loss if he avoided getting too close. Then again, by trying to protect her from such pain, it seemed very likely he had actually created another problem, a different type of disappointment. All because he had refused to tell her he cared.

He felt the attraction between them, and knew she felt it too. It was there in her eyes, in her smile, the way she looked at him, and the way she reacted to his kiss. He might have been trying to keep their relationship light and friendly, but in the end, who was he kidding? There was a connection, an attraction, and he was simply trying to avoid the obvious.

By denying their attraction, wasn't he simply exchanging one agony for another, inadvertently choosing the pain of undeclared feelings over the pain of a possible loss? For now, that's all it was, only a possibility, but the feelings were so real.

He'd come to accept that Teressa and Rory had found a way to be reunited across time. Rory had become Robert, and Teressa believed nothing else mattered. As far as Teressa was concerned, she was with her soulmate.

Was it possible some unknown solution existed for him and Kayla even if he didn't know right now what it was? Teressa had written in her journal, 'Love is the strongest magic of them all." Because of Rory, she had learned to let go of her fears and live, and yes, even love in the moment. Couldn't the same be true for him?

Daniel's head ached. He had lots of questions, but he still had no answers. His mind was dancing in circles, going round and round. Unexpectedly, he recognized he was truly following his little sister's footsteps, too afraid of what might be to enjoy what was already right in front of him.

Leaning back, he laughed. It was a cold hard chuckle, but he was laughing at himself. *Here I am, the biggest fool of them all.* Hadn't Rory told him? "The pleasure of love was worth the pain." And Souyer had once said, "The greatest risk is to take no risk at all." This truly was a grand adventure, he mused. One hell of a journey right through life's toughest lessons.

With renewed resolve, Daniel realized Kayla needed to know how he felt. She needed to know he was from another time and be given an opportunity to choose for herself. It was only fair they both be included in this adventure. He'd been trying to manipulate the relationship all by himself, to maintain his illusion of control, forgetting she was involved. Kayla had a right to know about his situation. And she had a right to make her own choices. Now he just had to figure out how he should go about telling her.

CHAPTER 19

Early the next morning, Kayla waited for Duncan in his study, sobbing. How many times had he found her like this? Not often, if ever. It wasn't like her to pour her heart out to anyone, especially her eldest brother. She pulled the handkerchief she carried with her from the sleeve of her gown to dry her eyes and wipe her nose.

As soon as Duncan entered the room, he sat down beside her and gathered her into his arms, offering what little comfort he could. "Ye grieve for Rory, little sister?"

"Aye Duncan," she nodded. "Rory and everything else." She could barely speak between sobs, her head burrowed into his shoulder. Kayla had been close to Rory, and it was only natural she would deeply grieve for him, but his death wasn't the only reason for her tears. The events of the past few days had proved too much for her emotions, and she was sorely in need of a good cry to release from all the frustration and pain lodged in her soul. She told herself, one good cry and then she'd be done. It was the reason she had sought the quiet comfort of

Duncan's study, hoping he would soon arrive to provide his brotherly support.

"Tell me what pains ye so."

"My life. 'Tis a mess. I know I shouldn't think of myself at a time like this—but Rory's death, it could have been any one of us."

"It was a horrible accident, but Rory died trying to save those horses." He patted her on her back, trying to soothe her pain.

"It could have been Daniel. He was there, trying to save Rory." She rubbed a hand across her eyes in an attempt to dry her tears.

"Ye care for him?" His voice softened with concern.

"I do. And I hate that vile Arlin. I want nothing to do with him. If ye and Mother push for a betrothal, I shall flee. I promise ye, I shall flee. I could never be married to such a dreadful man." She needed to let it all out. All the anger and pain her grieving heart had brought to the surface.

"Ye need not worry. No one is going to request a betrothal between ye and Arlin," he assured her.

"Arlin said I was all alone, and old, and nobody wants me." Her voice took on a woeful sound.

"What a bastard. Kayla, ye canna think such a thing. Many women yer age are able to find a suitable husband," Duncan offered.

"Duncan!" With a pained look, she let him know that hadn't been the right thing to say.

"I mean, surely there are others who find ye attractive."

"But I want Daniel." She looked up at her brother with weepy eyes, wiping her handkerchief across her nose.

"I know. I've suspected it for some time now," he confirmed.

"But I fear he doesn't want me," she confessed. Daniel had been avoiding her since her visit to his room, and now she feared the worst. Kayla struggled to regain her composure and sniffed back her tears. Lord knows, she had needed the release, but crying didn't solve anything. It was time to dry her eyes.

Duncan gave a weary sigh. "Are ye sure about that? It looks to me as though Daniel has a very strong interest in ye," he said.

A glimmer of hope tiptoed across her heart. "Do ye think so? Has he said something?"

"I have eyes. I've seen how he is when ye are together. I believe he cares for ye." Duncan paused, and she could see he was gathering his words, as if he had something important to tell her. "If he hasn't told ye, 'tis because, well ye see, there's a problem."

Her eyes opened wide as her imagination spun out of control.

"He's from the future," Duncan stated plainly.

What! "The future? Whatever can ye mean?" Confusion and disbelief swelled in her belly. She fought back the nausea.

"Teressa and Daniel . . . they're both from the future, about seven hundred years. I've always known. Teressa was sent here by a faerie."

"Moezell?" Kayla interrupted.

"Ye know her?" Duncan's brows shot up in a look a stark surprise.

"I've met her," Kayla admitted.

"And you never—"

"What has Moezell done?" she asked, interrupting his question.

Duncan gave her a scowl but continued to explain, "'Twas Moezell who brought Teressa here to secure the match between Janet and me. When her job was done, she was sent back home.

We think Moezell is also the one who brought Daniel here, but we doona know why."

"Did Rory know Teressa was from the future?"

"Not until she left. He saw her disappear on the beach when Moezell sent her back to her time. That's when Moezell showed herself to Rory."

"But why? Why would she do that?"

"We doona know. We weren't told. All we know is when her task had been completed, Teressa was sent back to her own time. Rory was told he would see her again someday, but now, that no longer seems possible."

"What about Daniel? When will he leave?" Kayla's tears threatened to well up again, but she fought to hold them back.

"I doona know. We think Moezell brought him here, but we doona know why or for how long. Daniel believes 'twas to bring news of Teressa, but that has long since been accomplished, and still he remains."

Kayla gasped. "Mayhap he was brought here to save Rory from the fire, but he failed. You should have seen him. I think he would have given his life to save Rory." She reached out to grasp Duncan's hands, adamant in her conviction.

"Rory thought of Daniel as a brother," Duncan said. "I believe Daniel thinks the same of Rory. I know he grieves the loss."

"If that's true, if he was sent here to save Rory and he failed, he'll be sent back, like his sister. Oh Duncan, 'tis all my fault. What shall I do?" Her hand rose to cover her mouth, striving to hold back her anxiety.

"'Tis nae yer fault. None of this is yer fault."

"I was there, in Daniel's room, at the time of the fire. If it hadna been for me, he might have gotten to Rory sooner. He might have been able to save his life."

"Kayla, ye doona know that to be true. Ye are only guessing. Ye could very easily be wrong."

"But I was there. . ."

Duncan's glare turned dark. "As much as I'd like to question ye about yer presence in Daniel's room, this isna the right time. We need to speak with Daniel. 'Tis time we discussed this, together." He rose and stepped to the door. "Wait here," he instructed.

Kayla could hear Duncan out in the great hall. He ordered one of the servants to go fetch Daniel. When he returned to his study, he took a seat at his desk.

"While we wait, mayhap ye can tell me what ye know about Moezell. How did ye meet her?"

Kayla took a deep breath. Her moment of truth had arrived. She had some confessions of her own to make.

"Moezell came to my bedchamber the night Daniel arrived. I was feeling resentment toward Daniel, being Teressa's brother. She told me I should nae judge Teressa and Daniel so harshly; that I dinna know all the facts. Then she told me how much Rory loved Teressa, and 'twas nae Teressa's choice to leave. The faerie, Moezell, confirmed everything ye have told me; that Teressa had to return home. Only she dinna tell me Teressa's home was in the future."

"Was that all?" he asked, looking somewhat unconvinced.

Kayla was unsure about what more she could say. She couldn't tell him she was related to Moezell and the faeries. Her mother had asked her to keep that information secret.

"Nay," Kayla admitted after some thought. "She also told me to find love, I must seek with an open heart. She told me my fear of pain is what keeps me from my greatest pleasure."

It was embarrassing enough to disclose to her brother how Moezell had counseled her on love. She wasn't about to admit she had wished for true love, although he could probably guess.

Then an idea hit her, filling her with renewed hope. If Moezell were the one who brought Daniel back in time, maybe he was here to grant her wish. Moezell had said she would provide the right opportunity; it was up to Kayla to do the rest. It was too grand to be true, but she had to believe. What else could it be? Renewed excitement bubbled up inside her.

A knock on the door announced Daniel's arrival.

~~~

Daniel stepped through the door and surveyed the room. *This should be interesting,* he thought. He wondered why Duncan wanted to see Kayla and him together. He saw her red swollen eyes and knew she'd been crying.

Dropping onto the chair next to her, he asked, "Kayla, what's wrong? Are you all right?"

"We've been discussing Rory," Duncan began. "Now we've moved on to ye."

"Me?" Silent alarms went off in Daniel's head. He quickly recalled his earlier visions of the MacNicol brothers exacting their revenge for his seduction of their little sister.

"I had to tell her," Duncan remarked.

"Tell her what?"

"That ye are from the future."

"Is it true?" Kayla asked.

He paused, his eyes switching back and forth between Duncan and Kayla. So here it was, his moment of truth. Drawing a deep breath, he answered, "Yeah, it's true." Relief washed over him, and he realized he was grateful Duncan had told her. It was time she learned the truth.

"Why dinna ye tell me?" Her voice was soft and low. She sounded hurt and betrayed, and rightfully so.

His chest constricted, seeing her so upset. "I wanted to protect you."

"Protect me! Protect me from what? The truth?"

Daniel shrugged. Suddenly, his answer didn't sound so good. In fact, it sounded rather lame. He knew secrets were a bad idea. They had a way of kicking you in the ass at the worst possible time.

"I was going to tell you," he said.

"When?" She glared at him through red swollen eyes.

"Today, actually. I decided I should tell you today. And now you know." There was no saving this runaway pony. It had already left the stable.

"Were ye sent here by Moezell?" Kayla asked.

"I guess so. I don't really know. I've never met the woman, or faerie, or whatever she is."

"Ye have never met her? She hasna spoken to ye?"

"No. Have you?" He looked from Kayla to Duncan for their response.

"She visited my chamber," Kayla confirmed.

"I have nae, but she has shown herself to both Teressa and Rory," Duncan offered.

"If she's responsible for bringing me here, why hasn't she shown herself to me? Damn, this is frustrating," Daniel groaned.

"I doona know." Kayla shrugged. "She just appeared in my chamber. I dinna summon her, at least nae directly."

"Summon her? You mean ask her to appear?" Daniel questioned, feeling a flash of inspiration.

"It seems she only appears when she chooses, which isn't often," Duncan said.

"Really! Well, we'll just see about that." Daniel had enough of the fear and frustration from not knowing. It was time for a showdown with this elusive faerie.

Daniel stood and began to shout, his voice echoing off the stone walls of Duncan's office. "Moezell, get your faerie butt out here. It's time to do some talking. I've got questions, and by God, you're going to give me some answers. Do you hear me? Show yourself, and do it now," he demanded.

For a moment, the room was silent, buzzing with the stillness. Then it grew as bright as the sun at midday, and a woman appeared, stepping through the veil of the unseen. She was beautiful to behold, dressed in a long liquid blue gown, with flowing blond hair and ice-blue eyes. She had to be Moezell.

"Greetings, Daniel." Moezell smiled. "I was wondering when you would get around to calling for me."

Duncan and Kayla gasped, while Daniel stared at her in wonder. He'd never seen a faerie before, and until now, he'd never truly expected to meet one. It took a second to regain his composure.

"You mean, I could have summoned you at any time?" he asked.

"No. Not until you were ready to face this moment. And now you are." Moezell whispered, her voice like a calming breeze through the great hall.

"You sure are one mean-spirited meddling faerie." He spat at her. Daniel had no fear of her power, believing the worst she could do was send him back home, which he fully expected her to do anytime her fickle faerie soul desired.

"Such anger," she mused in amazement. "'Tis to be expected when one feels they are out of control."

273

"Yeah, like how Teressa wasn't in control when you sent her away from Rory. You didn't even let her say good-bye." Daniel felt his anger rise. He wasn't about to back down.

"That was not of my doing. I was honor bound to fulfill a request. We are all bound by our agreements. You may not be aware of it, but your souls have agreed to these adventures, or you would not be here," Moezell graciously informed Daniel.

"When did I agree to all this? That's something I still don't understand." Daniel was beyond frustrated. He'd had enough of her faerie games.

"Did you not wish upon a star? Did you not ask to find a place where you belong?" The faerie gazed deep into his eyes.

Daniel slowly nodded, remembering his whispered words as he traveled toward Scotland.

"To fulfill your wish, I provided you with an opportunity to find your destiny. Now you must choose," Moezell advised.

"You're telling me I can choose to stay or go, to return home?" Daniel's anger began to fade, replaced by new thoughts, new questions, and new possibilities.

"That is correct. The choice is yours," Moezell confirmed.

"If I choose to go back home, will I be returned to the same time as when I left, like Teressa was?" He wondered how much control she had over his time travel.

Kayla pulled back, stepping away. "Ye want to leave, just like yer sister. Ye want to leave and return home. Ye doona want to stay."

He reached out and grabbed her hand again, not letting her go. "No, Kayla, wait. You're wrong. I just need to know." He turned to glare at Moezell. "So tell me, will I return to the same place and time?"

Moezell answered his question with a smile, "Aye, be it an hour, a day, or a year from now, if you choose to go back to your time, you will be returned to the moment when you left."

"If it was ten, twenty, thirty years from now, would that still hold true?" he questioned further.

"Aye," the faerie acknowledged with a slight nod. "However, you will still age and grow old with the passing of time, regardless of when or where you live your life."

It was as he had hoped, but he realized it no longer mattered. He already knew exactly where he wanted to be. There was only one other question left to be answered before he made his choice. "There's only one good reason for being anywhere, and that's to be with the ones I love." Turning to Kayla, he continued, "Kayla, if you think you could ever love me, could ever want me, well, then I'll know where I belong."

"Love ye?" she asked. Anxious fear danced across her innocent features.

"Yes, do you think you could love me, as I love you?" Daniel asked, his voice unsteady with the weight of his emotions.

"Of course, I love ye." Tears threatened to spill from her eyes but she looked happy so it was okay.

For a brief powerful moment, Daniel silently connected with Duncan's watchful gaze. The eldest MacNicol brother gave his nod of approval. Corny as it might seem, Daniel knew it was important for him to do this right. Reaching for Kayla's hand, he dropped to one knee. "Kayla, will you marry me? Will you be my wife?"

She looked stunned. It took her a second to answer. "Are ye serious? Are ye sure this is what ye want?"

"I couldn't be more serious. What do you say? Will you have me?" A pensive look sheltered Daniel's emotions as he gazed into the depths of her bright green eyes. He wasn't known to be a betting man, and yet here he was, taking the biggest risk of his life, giving up all he had known for all that might be.

"Aye, aye, a thousand times aye." Tears of pure joy filled her eyes and spilled down her cheeks.

Daniel stood and gathered her in his arms, holding her body close as she melted against him. Home, she felt like home. Taking her face gently in his hands, he turned her face up so he could see the golden specks dancing in her sparkling green eyes. "Then I have no more questions. I know exactly where I belong."

"You choose to stay?" Moezell asked.

Daniel turned to face the faerie. "I choose to stay," he confirmed, holding Kayla close in his arms.

"As you wish," Moezell said. She turned to speak with Kayla. "I expect I shall see you again. We have much to discuss. You have much to learn."

Flashing a radiant smile upon the lovers, Moezell stepped back behind the veil and disappeared.

Epilogue

A soft patch of tufted grass cushioned the back of Daniel as he awoke near the river. He wore a plain white linen shirt with faded old blue jeans and a well-worn brown leather jacket. The jeans were tighter than before, and the leather jacket had seen better days. These items had been tucked away in storage, waiting for this day. If you looked closely, his footwear might look a bit out of place. His old riding boots had worn out long ago, and the soft but sturdy leather boots he now wore were stitched by hand.

Daniel opened his eyes to the face of an angel. Backlit by the sun, she was framed by a halo of glowing red hair. Her pale white skin took on an iridescent glow. Innocent green eyes peered back at him. He smiled, knowing she came from heaven.

"Are ye all right?" she asked.

"I think so," Daniel replied, still grinning.

"That was powerfully scary. I hope never to do that again." The lovely young woman reached out to help him sit up.

"Thanks, Bree." Daniel rolled to his side and welcomed the assistance of his strong, beautiful daughter as she helped him to his feet. "And thank you, Moezell," Daniel whispered. He turned his face to meet the fluttering breeze dancing through the air. "You've brought us both back, safe and sound. I appreciate the favor."

Years of hard and rugged living had taken their toll, and Daniel felt the stiffness in his bones as he rose to his feet and looked around. Several years had passed, but everything seemed much as he remembered. Brushing himself off, Daniel took a moment to confirm he was still whole and in one piece.

Not far downstream, Wilbur stood grazing along the riverbank. The sudden summer storm must have spooked the animal, but thankfully, he hadn't run back to the stables. It seemed Garrett had chosen a strong and reliable mount, just as he promised. Daniel was grateful the horse was still there, waiting, although he understood he'd only been gone for a moment.

Father and daughter slowly walked over to the horse, and with a fair degree of effort, Daniel vaulted into the saddle. *Old age is a bitch,* he thought, *no matter where you are.* Lending a hand to his daughter, she mounted up behind him, then Daniel spurred the horse into a gentle walking pace, taking the trail heading back to Portree. There was no hurry, he had all the time he needed. He figured they would head directly to Robert's cottage instead of the Skyeland Stables. It was probably best if he let Robert return the horse for him. That way, there would be fewer questions to answer.

Reaching into the inside pocket of his leather jacket, he pulled out a scroll of parchment and unrolled it. Blinking back tears, he gazed with undying love at the portraits sketched in charcoal. The artist had done a superb job of capturing the faces of his wife, son, and four daughters. His youngest daughter, Breanna, was the one sitting behind him. Missing from this family portrait were his five grandchildren, and there had been another one on the way. Lord, how he missed them, but there was no turning back now.

Together they had lived a good long life, but in the end, it had been the MacDonalds who had taken his wife, and nearly everyone else he loved. With the grace of God, and some assistance from Moezell, he had managed to save Breanna.

Looking up to the sky, he whispered to the wind, sending a little prayer to his dearly departed wife. "We did good, Kayla. You and me, we did good."

His daughter's hands griped the waist of his jacket, letting him know she was there, and maybe a bit scared.

"You all right back there, Bree?" Daniel sent another silent prayer of thanks to Moezell that his daughter had been allowed to accompany him back to the future. Scorrybreac was lost, taken by the MacDonalds, traitors to their kinsmen. He couldn't have left without her.

"Yea, Da, I'm fine," she assured him, but he could hear the quiver in her voice.

"I'm sure you'll be just fine. You're young and strong." Strong enough to travel through time. Daniel rubbed his hands over hers, wishing he could do more to comfort her. But his youngest daughter was brave; she would survive. "You know, I couldn't leave you back there, Bree. There was nothing left. The MacDonalds have seen to that. You'll be fine here. Safe. You'll see." When his daughter remained silent, he looked over his shoulder and added, "If I could do it, so can you. It'll be easy."

"If ye say so, Da," Bree replied, putting on a brave face.

Daniel patted her hands again and laughed, thinking what a surprise this would be for Teressa and Robert. For his sister and her husband, it would seem he had only been out riding for a few hours, but for him it had been over thirty years since he had last seen them. He'd always known this day would come, a day when he would return to the future, his long-ago past, and say his final farewell. Daniel had some explaining to do, along with a lifetime of stories to tell.

The End

Now that you've met Breanna Ellers, if only briefly, I hope you'll continue reading to take a peek at the 4th and final book of the MacNicol Clan Through Time.

A Time To Forgive

CHAPTER 1

Breanna stopped brushing the gelding's warm chestnut hide for a moment and listened as the rumble of a motorcycle reached her ears. The sound was definitely a motorcycle—not a car or a truck—and not only was the sound notably distinctive, it was unexpected. Far enough from the beaten path to make an unexpected visitor a bit of a concern, Over-Yonder ranch sat nestled against the foothills of Diablo Valley at the end of a long and narrow country road.

Sunnyside, the horse she was brushing down, turned his ears, pointing them in the direction of the roadway, his big brown eyes watching her.

"You hear it, too, don't you, boy?" Bree spoke to the horse, rubbing his long brown nose. They had just finished his morning exercise, and she was in the process of rubbing him down, first along his back and then down each leg. Front to back, left to right, the process always stayed the same. She had rescued Sunnyside from an abusive owner, and this daily routine was part of his treatment.

Bree registered the sound of the motorcycle growing closer as she methodically completed her task. It would take a lot more than the lure of an approaching visitor to pull her away from Sunnyside. For the moment, this horse was her priority. Nothing and no one was more important.

She had just finished brushing Sunnyside and was setting aside her tools, when she heard the motor bike roll into the parkway in front of the stables and come to a stop. Bree turned to give the horse a parting hug. "You're loved, Sunnyside. Now and always, you are safe, and strong, and loved." Bree gave the horse a final pat.

Sunnyside bobbed his head in approval and nickered, nudging her gently away with his nose. She could almost hear him say, "I'm all right now. Go greet your visitor." Sensing his contentment, she smiled.

As she headed down the shed row toward the front entrance, she dusted off her hands along the front of her snug-fitting jeans before she rolled the long sleeves of her plaid flannel shirt up to her elbows. In a futile effort to contain her wayward curls, she ran her fingers through her thick copper-red hair and readjusted the elastic band holding it away from her face. Though it was a never-ending battle to contain her hair, she refused to admit defeat.

When she reached the shadowed entrance at the wide double doors of the stables, she stopped to observe her visitor.

The rider had already dismounted from his bike and was removing his helmet, a sleek black orb with a tinted face plate that when worn would obscure his features.

Still standing in the shadow of the doorway, she watched as he set the helmet on the seat of his bike and ran his fingers through his dark auburn hair, releasing his disheveled curls from the dreaded curse of helmet hair. His profile revealed a strong, nearly straight nose, bold cheekbones, and a well-formed jaw.

Bree watched a moment longer as the man unzipped his black leather jacket and tucked his shirt into his faded black jeans. The tight fit of his dark tee shirt revealed the type of rock hard muscles that came from long hours of hard work. He was one nice-looking man.

After she finished checking out the man, she checked out his bike, a sleek black-and-gray Ducati Multistrada. The model looked to be a few years old, but the Italian motorcycle was in mint condition. He obviously took good care of his toys. His Ducati was one nice-looking bike.

She judged her visitor to be in his late twenties, maybe six or seven years older than her. When he started to walk toward the front of the ranch house, Bree stepped out into the bright sunlight and shouted, "Can I help you?"

The man turned with a startled jerk. Squinting, he reached a hand up to shield his eyes from the glare of the sun. "Sorry, I didn't see you standing there."

"Looking for someone?"

"Yeah, Breanna Ellers. Know where I can find her?"

Bree walked forward to greet him. "I'm Breanna Ellers."

The man fished a card from his back pocket and looked it over, then looked back at her. "You're Breanna Ellers, the animal trainer?"

"Yeah, that's me," she confirmed. He was holding one of the business cards her cousin Jack had designed for her and insisted on handing out to everyone he met. Jack also had a habit of leaving them at every pet and feed store in the area, which meant this guy could be anyone.

Her visitor looked skeptical. "It says here you have twelve years of experience."

"That's right. I trained my first puppy when I was ten years old." She moved closer so he wouldn't have to squint into the sun.

"Professionally?" He raised a doubtful brow. She noted how he gave her a quick once-over.

"Did I get paid? Sure, there's always a reward." She'd been down this road before. It was always the same until they saw what she could do. "I take it you're in need of a trainer?"

He took a few steps toward her, stopping with the bike still between them. "I've got some horses that are giving me trouble. Frank McGregor said you could help."

Her face relaxed into an easy grin. "You know Franklin?"

"Yeah. He gave me your card, but..." He flipped the card back and forth against his other hand.

"Let me guess. He didn't tell you my age."

"Nope, never mentioned that." The man gave her his first honest smile.

"That sounds like Franklin." The elder man was like a grandfather to her, part of a strong network of friends and family she had created to replace the family she had lost back home on Skye.

Though it was still early spring, the day was unseasonably warm, and the sun was approaching its zenith. She motioned over to the covered patio at the back of the house. "Why don't we go sit down in the shade? It's a little hot to be standing out here in the sun. Especially with you all dressed in black."

Now it was her turn to give him the once-over. For a second, he reminded her of a dark warrior, ready to ride into battle, mysterious and romantic. She quickly reined in her overactive imagination, but she couldn't dismiss the thought, not completely.

"All right," he nodded, stepping around his bike.

"Would you like something to drink?"

"Cold water would be nice." He met her halfway as they walked toward the table and chairs under the latticed awning.

As they drew closer, she noticed his stunning hazel eyes. Swirls of browns and greens created a kaleidoscope effect, mysteriously drawing her in. She drew in a quick, sharp breath while her heart pumped iron for a few fast beats. For a brief moment, his eyes reminded her of William Gregory, a boy from back home on Skye; but William was dead. He had died when he was only twenty, fighting to protect her ma. She blinked hard and shook her head, willing the image to fade as quickly as it had appeared.

Still dazed, she looked down and noticed the man had reached out his hand. "I'm Alex. Alex Connor," he said.

"I'm...I'm pleased to meet you, Mr. Connor," she stammered.

"Just call me Alex," he said. His beguiling smile washed over her like fresh sweet cream.

"And you can call me Bree." She shook his hand, fighting back her memories. This man wasn't William, and she was no longer in Scotland. She needed to relax.

"Here, take a seat while I get us both something cold to drink." Hoping he hadn't noticed her sudden flare of nerves, she stepped quickly through the back door and into the kitchen,

285

seeking refuge within its cool, shadowy interior. Leaning against the kitchen counter, she forced herself to remain calm.

Bree hadn't felt this way since she arrived in California nearly four years ago. No man had affected her this strongly since William. She hadn't believed a modern man could. These men seemed wimpy and weak compared to the warriors she had grown up with on Skye. But Alex didn't appear wimpy or weak. He looked like a man who didn't back down from a challenge, and something told her she was about to be challenged in ways she wouldn't expect.

~~~

Alex watched as Bree disappeared into the darkness of the house. *Damn.* She looked good coming and going. Not at all what he had expected, and that had thrown him for a loop. He had expected to meet an old crone who didn't know how to use the internet considering she hadn't responded to any of his emails. Instead, he had encountered a pretty, young woman who grabbed the attention of body parts well south of his brain.

Damn McGregor for not telling him. It felt like he'd been set up. Too late now, he'd just have to make the best of it, which was fine with him. Right now, the best of it was looking pretty darn good.

Thankfully, he hadn't completely lost his mind. When he learned she was the horse trainer he was looking for, he remembered one vital piece of advice McGregor had shared with him. "I don't recommend telling her you're a MacDonald, at least not right away. Not if you want her help." Frank had refused to explain why, except to say there was some old family history.

Instead, Alex had opted to use his middle name, Connor, which was also his mother's maiden name. All through college, he'd been a charmer and a partygoer, and had learned how to tell folks whatever they needed to hear to get what he wanted. He wasn't above using a fib or a little white lie if it served his purpose, not that he liked it. For some reason, lying to Bree felt wrong, as though she deserved better from him.

Unfortunately, old habits were hard to break, and even with good intentions tap dancing on his shoulder, he had felt compelled to hide his true identity. At least until he knew what she had against the MacDonalds. It didn't seem fair she should have the chance to dismiss him before he had a chance to win her over with his charm. After all, his charming ways had gotten him through college, and he trusted they would get him through this.

Sooner or later she'd find out he was a MacDonald; he couldn't keep it a secret forever, not if they were going to work together. But that could wait. First, she had to agree to take the job and prove to him she could do it. There was still a chance this would turn out to be a wasted trip and he'd be heading back to Placerville before sunset.

Skeptical, he wondered if she were really as good as McGregor claimed. Doing the math, he figured she couldn't be much more than twenty-two years old. That seemed a little young to be calling herself a professional animal trainer. Even if he did overlook the dubious advertising claim of twelve years of experience, he wasn't convinced a woman this young could work magic with his horses.

In her riding boots, she stood nearly as tall as him, and he tapped in at six foot one. She was slim, with an athletic build, but not overly skinny. That was nice. On the whole, she looked as though she could hold her own in a game of beach volleyball. Funny how that image had sprung to mind—including sand, surf and a tight bikini—considering she didn't look or sound like a typical California girl. It was obvious she was Scottish, through and through. Along with her pale, freckled skin, mass of coppery curls, and moss-green eyes, she had the sweetest Scottish brogue he'd ever heard outside Inverness. But her last name didn't fit. Ellers was an English name, as far as he knew, which meant the Scottish blood must come from her mother's side of the family.

She soon came back out with two large tumblers filled with ice water and set one in front of him before taking the chair across from him.

"So why do you need a horse trainer?" she asked, getting right to business. She sat back in her chair, looking relaxed. He did the same.

"My dad and I have a small ranch near McGregor's place up in Placerville where we raise Clydesdales. We've got half a dozen horses that are used to pull wagons. Our biggest coach runs four to a hitch with two standbys for rotation. Two of my best Clydes have been misbehaving, and I can't keep running the business without them."

"Sounds like a good-sized operation. What are the wagons used for?"

"The big rig is a fully restored stage coach. It's mostly used to work rodeos and county fairs, that sort of thing. We also have a few smaller rigs—a nine-passenger surrey and a couple of smaller carriages for weddings and such. It's a pretty successful business, and it usually pays the bills, but I can't keep running it with just the four. I need my full team to keep it going."

Alex was making the enterprise sound better than it was. The business was knee-deep in debt after his dad had taken out a second mortgage to buy and restore the stage coach, and the project was eating up every spare cent of profit. He needed to get the operation back up to full capacity, or he risked losing it all. It was already bad enough that he had given up his expensive apartment and was back living at his dad's ranch; not a happy place to be. The operation was hard work, but he loved those Clydesdales. They were a noble breed of working horses.

He worried if he appeared desperate, she wouldn't agree to help. As it was, he really couldn't afford to pay her until the team was fully restored and making good money. Even then, it probably wouldn't be until well into the summer season when they had their biggest jobs working the county fairs.

"I'm glad to hear you don't want to overwork your horses. It sounds like they're your bread and butter," Bree said.

"Yeah, you could say that."

"What do you think happened to your horses?"

"I wish I knew. For a while, everything was going great, but recently, Malt and Barley have been acting unpredictable. They've been giving my carriage drivers a hard time, refusing to perform like they should. I can't risk having them misbehave around the public. These are big animals. Someone could get hurt, and then I'd lose my business."

It had only been in the last year, since his dad's health started deteriorating, that he had gotten involved in running the day-to-day operations. When he looked back through the books, it seemed the company had done well for several years, but recently, after the economy had taken a nosedive, so had their business. Still, he had managed to keep it together until his two best Clydesdales had started to act up. Malt and Barley were beautiful draught horses, and he wanted to keep things going, but there wasn't much use for them if they couldn't pull their weight, and that meant pulling a wagon full of paying customers.

"I'll have to meet them before I can agree to take on the job," she said.

"You mean the horses?"

"Of course." She gave him a duh-what-did-you-think kind of look. "I have to know if I can work with them."

That sounded rather suspicious. Maybe she was hedging her bets in case the job was more than she could handle. "You think you can tell just by seeing them?"

"I'll know in the first meeting whether or not I can help." She took a sip of water, looking quite pleased with herself.

"Really?" he asked, raising a skeptical brow. "How do I know you have what it takes? Shouldn't I see some references or something?" He had come here expecting to interview her, and yet for some reason, it felt as if she were in control.

"I can show you a reference." She stood up from the table. "Here, turn your chair around."

"Why's that?" he asked, rising from his seat.

"You need to be facing the stables."

He repositioned his chair then sat down again, facing toward the back yard and the stables beyond.

Bree walked to the edge of the patio and turned to face him, her back to the yard. As soon as he was settled in his seat, she put two fingers to her mouth and let out a high, shrill whistle. A second later, a border collie came running from behind the stables. Before the dog crossed the yard, Bree raised her left hand up at a forty-five-degree angle, like a signal to stop. The collie stopped in his tracks, his tail wagging. With her back still turned toward the dog, she lowered her hand to a straight-out position. The collie sat back on its hind legs. Without looking back to see if the dog had obeyed, she lowered her hand toward the ground, and the dog dropped to his front paws. Next, she raised her hand back to the straight-out position and waved it from side to side. The dog sat up and turned his head, looking left and right. Then, she brought her hand back up to the forty-five degree angle and waved it forward. The dog took off running toward her again. Just as he reached the cement slab of the patio, she turned around and opened her arms to greet him.

"Good doggie. That's my good Laddy." She ruffled his fur, giving him an affectionate hug. The dog's tail wagged a rapid beat.

Alex was darn impressed; although, he tried not to show it. "How do you know what the dog did? Maybe he just ran across the yard when you weren't looking."

She looked up from praising the dog, grinning from ear to ear. "If he had, you wouldn't be asking me that question."

Tricia Linden, author of timeless romance with a touch of magic.

In this lifetime, Tricia has lived in five states, on two islands, and on a farm, and is now living with her soulmate in Northern California. Her travels have taken her to Canada, Mexico, Australia, Hong Kong, Guam, England, Scotland, several countries in Europe, and several states in the US. Besides her love of reading and writing romance, she has a great fondness for Pink Flamingos. Over the years, she's gathered a rather large collection of the fun pink birds.

Website: https://tricia-linden.com/

Facebook: https://www.facebook.com/TriciaLindenAuthor/

Tweeter: @TriciaLinden69

Email: Tricia.Linden@ymail.com